A Bird in the Sand

By Gail Hulnick

Media Mysteries
Book Two

From Sirocco Press, an Imprint of

The WindWord Group Publishing & Media
#200, 100 Bull Street
Savannah, GA 31401

www.windwordgroup.com

ISBN: 0998399019
ISBN-13:978-0998399010

Library of Congress Control Number: 2018904085

Cover design by David Stone
Printed in the United States of America

Books may also be purchased or authors contacted by emailing
admin@windwordgroup.com

A Bird in the Sand

GAIL HULNICK

Sirocco Press

An Imprint of

The WindWord Group Publishing & Media

Also by Gail Hulnick

The Lion's Share of the Air Time: A Novel

Resorting to Murder

Resorting to Larceny

DEDICATION

For Laurie, my sister, my friend

CHAPTER 1

1494

The water was as rough as Gabor had ever seen it. He had seen many things now, in fourteen years alive. For the past two of those years, he had been all on his own, now that his mother and father had both departed this earth. He missed them—and he did not.

He lowered the canoe into the channel and walked along beside it, pushing it toward the deeper places. For a dozen steps he fought with the reeds, which were pulling at it, holding it back. Then the vessel broke free and floated as it was designed to do. He sprang into the stern, settled against the pile of leaves that served as a seat, and dipped his paddle into the darkness. The boat leaped forward and in seconds he was putting steady distance between his village and his canoe.

He felt joy in the power of his muscles, still a new experience since his body had changed from that of a child to that of a man. He had very little beard, but he was sure it was coming. Soon. His long black hair, tied back with a piece of hemp, was usually a bit damp from humidity or from sweat; he rarely stopped moving.

He tried to go as fast as he could, even though he was entirely sure that no one had followed him. At this time of night, all the Taino people slept. No one expected that anyone—especially not a fourteen-year-old orphan who still needed the protection of the grown men of this jungle village—would be so stupid as to set out alone.

Gabor would agree with them all, except that he had no choice. The golden birds had to be taken, and he was the one to do it. With no father, brother, or uncles to speak on his behalf whenever the people gathered and decisions were made, he felt he was invisible most of the time. But he was not inclined to be quiet or to take the last seat after everyone important had been recognized. He had offended many of the men and there was no future for him here.

Something barked or screamed, but Gabor could tell that it was far away. Even so, he paddled faster, and the canoe responded like a crocodile lunging for food. Anything capable of speed, that was his magnet and his totem. When he was very small, as far back as he could remember, he had tried to run as fast as some of the creatures he saw darting past so quickly that he was barely sure he had seen them. The bee hummingbird, in particular, had fascinated and compelled him. He ran along the jungle pathways and through the clearing beside the sleeping places, pushing his legs to a hurting point, kicking the heels of his feet up toward his backside, trying to touch. Now that he was grown, he still carried deep inside that small boy in love with speed.

There was only one thing he loved more than speed and that was Ixcel. As she had promised, she was waiting around the bend, just where the water changed from black to green. Nimble as a jungle cat, she leaped into the canoe and he started to pull harder, to put as much distance as possible behind them before the sun rose. Her hair, as black as his, hung around her tender face. He saw that she had worn her best dress, the one taken out only on special occasions, the one that was made to show the village boys and men that she was beautiful, right down to her tiny, slender feet. Her skin was wet with the rain.

*

Fog had pushed in, alongside the arrows of rain. She could see no farther than the fingers of her right hand, clutching the pendants in her lap. Her left hand gripped the edge of the canoe. The golden chains lay across her leg.

"Gabor, I am frightened," she whispered, resisting the urge to look behind her.

"Hush, Ixcel, we are on our way. No one heard or saw us go." He stood behind her now, using the long paddle to push them through the weeds, but even if he were right in front of her, the storm and the darkness would cloak his face.

This was a good thing, because Ixcel dreaded any look of fear or anger, any change. She was always looking for the smiles and eager glances that had been there since that moment months ago when he had first approached her during the celebration after the hunt.

That change, that 'dying of love', that shift to tension—it was the way of the world with men and girls, her mother had instructed her. A short time of smiles, excitement, and heat, then everyone settled down. Down to life, down to work, down to doing what one must to survive. Down to sharing what came along.

She did not believe her mother, though, and escaping that vision of her life was part of her reason for being in this boat on this night. She might have waited a little longer, but Gabor was not one to stop for what came along or might come. By the time that feature of his heart became clear, it was too late for her. She had chosen him, he had chosen her, and their guardians had done the customary exchanges. They were bound, for love, for life, for family. All in the village knew it.

So, when he began telling of his plan to take the Jeweler's treasured trio of birds across the island to the men from afar and buy their way to a new land, Ixcel knew that she would share his journey, no matter how frightened she might be.

She had not expected such a storm, though, and she

was quite sure that Gabor had not planned for it, either. Nor had the bearded men who awaited them, out of sight in one of the coves, ready to take them back to the ship that would carry them to their new life. Ready to take Gabor back, more precisely. Ixcel was certain that her presence would be a surprise.

But perhaps Gabor would be able to explain to them that she was essential to the plan, to the obtaining of the birds. Obtaining—that was the word she was using for the moment, but it didn't feel quite right. 'Capture' didn't seem to fit, for a piece of metal that couldn't move to escape. 'Theft' was too harsh and not right either. Everything belonged to everyone here, and she was sure there would be little surprise to some of the elders when the Jeweler discovered his pieces missing. Hadn't Gabor done his best to persuade them all to give to the bearded men the gold they sought, the delicately made sun-flyers crafted so many generations before? They had been handed down to the Jeweler by his grandfather who said they had been passed down by many grandfathers before. Everyone in the village said the neck pieces were ancient, older than anyone could imagine. Old, yes, but more could be made at any time, and the Jeweler and his apprentices made more every week. The ancient ones could be traded for other things they needed, things the bearded ones had. Why did none of these old men understand?

They had all ignored Gabor's words, as usual.

The night sky flashed once more with a spear of white light, gone so quickly it was almost impossible to see. Ixcel braced herself, like a runner taking a breath before bounding forward, then the clouds opened and the rain poured down on them again.

In minutes, her dress was soaked and her hair plastered to her neck and shoulders. The wind picked up and the canoe rocked from side to side, each wave pushing it closer to capsizing. Up to this moment, she had felt little real fear, even when Gabor had told her the bearded men had threatened their families, and every generation going forward, with exposure, tragedy, and pain for all, if they revealed the truth about this secret voyage across the endless sea.

So much of what Gabor had told her that the bearded captain said seemed unbelievable and too imaginative, like the tales a grandma told little ones to stoke the fire in their eyes: faraway lands, terrifying queens, mighty ships, cities built of crystal and silver. But in spite of herself she began to dream. They would escape their tiny village, where Ixcel's future held only relentless toil, one baby after another, and Gabor's future held only a slow life of farming. If he was lucky, he would have an easy death in his sleep at a great age, and if not, a bloody death, fighting the Arawak.

And so, they took the pendants. The golden birds that had raised the glitter in the bearded men's eyes when first they heard of them. The treasures of the Jeweler and his family, the ultimate expression of their skill and their art with *caona*, passed down through generations.

It had not been difficult to sneak into the old man's hut during the heat of the afternoon rest. Ixcel had swept all three pendants into her apron while pretending to admire the Jeweler's recent work, and Gabor had kept him in conversation while she slipped out between the palmetto fronds at the back. She had gone about her evening chores while hiding the precious pieces in her clothing. After darkness had settled in, she picked her way through the swamp behind the village to the meeting point she and Gabor had chosen.

"Gabor, hurry! The storm is rising."

"The Spanish ship is there." He pointed, and she could see it. Only one or two more bends of the river and some time in the open water, then they would be on board.

The wind blew harder, and the rain pounded down. Flash upon flash, boom after boom, louder and louder.

She felt terror now. As the moments went by, she wanted only an end to this feeling; as her stomach knotted then heaved, she wanted only to be back home, safe on her narrow pallet in her father's hut. No Gabor, true; no exciting new life, no voyage to a shining city across an ocean. But also, no black water, no lightning, no wind, no rumble of thunder and imminent danger. A good trade.

A wave hit the canoe. Ixcel shrieked and her grip loosened. One of the birds was swept from her hand but she held onto the other two, her hold so tight the chain cut into her palm.

Gabor turned to look at her and she smiled back, with what she hoped was reassurance. She would tell him later what had happened. Soon enough, she would have to face all and she needed the time until then to prepare her courage. It would be impossible to find the missing bird now, in the rain and wind of the storm. Would the captain let them on board if they did not have all three of the promised treasures?

CHAPTER 2

2014

The heart wants what it wants. It is time to take it. Reaching, shaking slightly, hesitating. A quick glance over each shoulder. If someone comes in, if you get caught, your life is over.

Not that getting caught is the prevailing thought. No, the shoulder check is just an automatic action, something instinctive, born of primal fear. Fear of discovery, fear of capture, fear of annihilation. That's all. The prevailing thought, actually, is of success. You're already at Step Two of the process and on the verge of Step Three: get in, get it, get out.

The bird shines like a beacon in its blue velvet-lined box. Clearly the work of a master, the golden head arching away from a sleek, slender body, each feather carefully noted and placed. The eyes are not an obvious choice— not jewels, not sapphire or ruby or even black pearl. The eyes are copper, turned greenish with the passing of hundreds of years.

Lifting it just for a moment, wavering with the unexpected heft of it. Looks delicate but feels substantial. And warm to the touch, somehow.

Two unexpected observations. Two too many. Surprises delight only children. Get on with it.

The solution to so many problems, right there in that oval box. But perhaps just the generator of a dozen more? Investigation, discovery, capture? An investigation that leads to disaster? No question, the pendant will be missed, but it is insured. How hard would anyone really try to get it back?

Maybe rejection, a dead end, one more worthless burden? Could it be sold anywhere? Was there cash somewhere at the end of this road, a windfall to provide the resources so desperately needed? Or would it be impossible to trade away?

There are no answers, but this moment is now and sometimes you have to make a move without knowing how every single thing will turn out. Somebody, somewhere, would want this sensational pendant and compensate generously for it. Pay the big bucks. The exact identity of that person will be revealed in due time, just as the location of the bird and the window of time that it would be unattended had been.

What is this, extortion? Kidnapping? Embezzling? Bird-napping? Theft over five thousand dollars? That was amusing. What do you call it when the item stolen is priceless, not only rare but irreplaceable? You do have to understand the stakes and the guilt you might have to shoulder.

Out of the bush and into the hand, so to speak. Into a pocket, actually. Hide it in plain sight. Walk out of the office calmly, turn the corner just past the craft services table, and slide away. Wipe the sweat off your forehead, remember to breathe, smile at anyone you pass, and make eye contact.

This is the dry run, the shakedown cruise. It can be done, and now it is time to go away and think about when it will be done. The beautiful thing is left in its box. For now. This time.

CHAPTER 3

Savannah

E laine the housekeeper explained to veteran TV news director Nevada Leacock that she wasn't expecting anything unusual when she unlocked the door to the Ardsley Park mansion that the movie star had rented for the three-month duration of the shoot. She was looking down at the keys in her hand, thinking about Bible study last night. The heavy front door swung open to the grand foyer, the demilune antique tables with their bowls of fresh flowers and the painting of the salt marsh reinforcing the message that this was a classic sample of Southern life, honed over two hundred eighty years of Savannah charm and organized to meet every whim of her client, the movie star, Mr. Tom Leacock.

A crazy parakeet came flying into her face, squawking and screeching like a wild thing, thrashing its wings in a frenzied effort to stay aloft and find an escape route. Elaine dropped to her knees to get out of its way.

"I was so scared, I couldn't move another muscle?" She stared off toward the cars driving by as if she were reliving the moment. She and Nevada sat on a bench near Chippewa Square—not the *Forrest Gump* bench, but close—and Tom's director, Jeremy Walsh, sat on the grass by their feet. Elaine couldn't stop talking about the many things she'd seen in her years of cleaning houses in

Savannah and how Mr. Tom's living room beat them all. Her long fingernails, beautifully painted in a shade of green close to that of the live oak trees, carved imaginary diagrams in the air as she described the scene inside the rented house.

When she stepped through the door, she said, the whole place was nothing but noise and motion, noise and commotion. The TV was on full-blast and the radio too. The windows to the veranda were wide open, and the March wind was blowing the white, gauzy curtains around like the skirt on that fifties movie star standing over a grate on a sidewalk. The two cats were leaping from the couch to the top of the baby grand piano and back again, yowling and hissing at each other. There would be terrible scratch marks on that beautiful wood. They didn't like each other, those cats.

The birdcage lay on the floor, its door open. No wonder the bird was half-hysterical, flying around. Mr. Tom kept that bird safe in that cage, away from those cats, like the best diamond ring at the jewelry store. Tucked in there, with that purple velvet perch, and the little dish always full of fresh water, and the matching drape cloth to go over the bars just so, with a hole in the top for the handle used to carry the thing around. Elaine had never seen anything that fancy at the local pet store. Some of her clients had some mighty fancy things in their homes, but that velvet bird cage cloth beat all.

Nevada had often seen other such expensive and elegant possessions in her father's mansions and hotel rooms, taking note of the precision he had lavished on them. None of that care had ever come her way, in her memory, but at least there was proof that he was capable of loving something.

Other than himself.

Over her forty-something years as his daughter, she'd managed to pull away and carve out a life for herself. She'd earned and kept a senior management job in a major-market newsroom in Canada. She'd met and married one of the most wonderful men in the world. She was a grown-up—and yet her father's lack of approval bothered her as if she were still twelve.

Nevada took a long gulp from her to-go cup as she listened to Elaine and tried to avoid making eye contact with Jeremy. His round eyeglasses were faintly steamy, and his brow a little damp; it looked like the early heat and humidity were getting to him already.

Elaine had taken her story to Jeremy first, and then when Tom hadn't showed up on set the next day, Jeremy had called Nevada. He was as surprised to find out that she was in Savannah as she was to find out that her father had listed her as his emergency contact for insurance and work purposes. Not his agent, not his manager—he'd listed his daughter as his closest contact. Even though she told the director that this was all a total surprise and that she hadn't seen her father since their lunch two days earlier, Jeremy asked to see her right away. Nevada had suggested a quiet table in the riverfront restaurant, but Jeremy was paranoid about anyone overhearing their conversation about his star, and so the three of them met at one of the historic Savannah squares, on Hull Street just a few blocks from the cemetery.

Fancy cage cover or not, Elaine went on to tell them, it was clear that the bird didn't want to stay there. It was gone, off into the hazy sky.

"If I'da been more like thirty', instead of sixty, I mighta chased it but it was gone, Miss Nevada. Just like my niece Miracle, when she got tired of her momma trying to tell her all the time? Just gone."

She stepped into the foyer, she said, and shut the door so that the cats wouldn't get out too. Shut it gently, of course, she told Miss Nevada. Elaine prided herself on the care she took with her clients' homes. If a thing's worth doing, it's worth doing well, as Pops would say.

Elaine was also very conscious of the meaning and

stature of those homes. This neighborhood, Ardsley Park, was one of Savannah's jewels, along with The Historic District and the riverfront.

Truth be told, though, Elaine's respect had less to do with the ancestry of the houses than her beliefs about the spirits that still inhabited them. Not beliefs, really; more a sixth sense, an awareness, as she poked around in the dusty corners of the closets on the third floor or the butler's pantry behind the dining room paneling. She was not completely alone. Sometimes she felt a brief, sudden presence flash by the poster at the foot of a bed she was making. Other times it was a sudden smell, just a whiff of roses or jasmine. Didn't bother Elaine, but gave a lot of people the creeps, big time.

The houses in the Historic District had even more 'visitors', and some of the women Elaine knew wouldn't work there. Some were a lot less jumpy though and just accepted the presence of others as a part of life. Life in Savannah, anyway.

For all the noise and commotion, the living room seemed spooky when she walked in, Elaine told them.

"Then when the phone rang, I jumped higher than a catfish on the longest day of the year. A bit strange, to hear and see one of those nowadays. Everyone be carrying their own phone. Even if they can't barely afford anything else, they got a phone.

"But Mr. Tom is in the senior age group, I guess, and lots of folks his age don't have much use for the smart phones. Even big movie stars like him.

"That phone rang three times and then a machine hidden somewhere picked up the call. 'You've reached Tom's phone. Please leave a message.' I heard a woman— it was you, Miss Nevada, right?—saying, 'Dad, I'm at the restaurant you said. I've been waiting half an hour, where are you?' It's getting embarrassing, you said, and that you know being on time isn't the most important talent in the world, but you had some appointments later and he needed to call you so's you'd know if he was going to show up."

After that, Elaine had been so spooked she had just left everything as she'd found it, rushed out to her car, and called the cleaning service that employed her. They were being paid by the movie production company, so it was a short path to the director, and that's how Jeremy Walsh had been brought into the picture.

After they heard Elaine's story, Nevada filled them in on her lengthy wait at the restaurant, ending with the phone call she'd made to Tom. When she'd turned off her phone, she noticed a waiter watching her, listening to her side of the conversation. Damn! Why couldn't her father get on board with the twenty-first century and start reading and sending texts so they could all have some privacy?

The table in the Olde Pink House was as close to the doorway as possible. Nevada hadn't wanted to take a chance on missing Tom when he arrived, and she really didn't want to watch him make a dramatic, even triumphant, entrance and procession through the room. He was almost impossible to tolerate when he was in public and fans recognized him; he was totally impossible when they didn't. She had just asked for another glass of water—her third—and despite his impeccable manners and subtle air of pity, she thought she could tell that the waiter was becoming suspicious that she never intended to order a meal, ever. She put on her best self-confident, someone-important face, willing everyone in the room to believe that she had a lunch companion due to show up and take the second chair, set in front of an eye-popping display of china, silver, linen, and glassware. She had heard from the waiter all about the specials, the Food Network stars who had visited and resoundingly approved, the history of this building on Abercorn Street, and the live music she shouldn't miss in the tavern in the cellar. On his fifth visit to her table, the waiter dawdled to make conversation with her about her thoughts on Savannah, her reason for visiting, her nationality, his understanding that Canada was somewhere north of Seattle, and his affection for the Seahawks. The next waiter, a young woman with a blonde braid who came to refill the water glass, stopped to tell her all about the 1771 construction of the building and the ghosts that had been seen in the hallways since General Habersham's day.

She was beginning to think that she might be forced to order a drink although she was doing her best to stay away from midday alcohol. Back in the day, at age twenty-two, she'd had to worry about getting too tipsy at the wrong time; now in her late forties, she had to worry about getting too drowsy.

Nevada checked her phone again for messages and looked at a few other things—the weather, the stock prices, the neighborhood map. Time was just frickin' standing still. How long was he going to make her wait?

"Nevada." The voice was unmistakable, not only because it was known to millions—anyone who had ever seen a Tom Leacock movie—but also because she'd heard it as far back as she could remember, and even, once upon a time, singing lullabies.

She knew she should stay annoyed, but she couldn't help feeling relieved that he'd shown up. He was well-groomed, as always; he'd spent years making sure he was 'ready for the close-up' and he wasn't about to change now. When Nevada was in her 1980s punk rebellion stage, he'd tried and failed to convince her that what certain people thought of you, and especially your appearance, was important, even primary. Some days she cared and made the effort to look good, and some days she did not, and that was that. For Tom, that was like saying "maybe I'll breathe today and maybe I won't." Not a matter of choice.

He looked as slender and fit as always, moving with only a trace of the stiffness of age. His silver hair was carefully combed, and his face was as clean-shaven as possible. He'd worn a leather bomber jacket that would flatter a man forty years younger—a bit heavy for the Savannah climate, but hey. Fashion hurts, she thought as she smiled and lifted her face to Tom's for an air kiss.

Always good to have some sort of private joke going on, if you had to spend an hour with The Movie Star.

"How have you been, Dad?" She passed the breadbasket to him, but he waved it away.

"What are you doing here?" He took a two-second read of the menu, then held it out to a passing waiter. "Green salad. Water."

"Owen is here for a medical conference. I'm on vacation." Nevada stared at Tom's eyes, ready for any moment when he might decide to actually see her. "You?"

"Filming started Monday," he said, with a tone that seemed as though he was assuming she would be as up-to-date on his current projects as one of his fans.

A statuesque woman in a nineteenth-century gown, with a skirt so big she could barely pass between the tables, stopped at a nearby group and sang a verse of "Georgia." Nevada joined in on the polite applause; Tom did not.

"Filming started Monday," he repeated and Nevada sighed.

"What's the movie, Dad?"

"Civil War drama. I'm a Confederate general. That's all I'm going to tell you."

Maybe in so many words, but Nevada could hear a lot of other things. *I might be in my seventies, but I'm still relevant. I get the hero parts, the leaders. You may think you're some hotshot journalist or news director, but to me you're still an untrustworthy blabbermouth little girl.*

"It's not the role of a lifetime. No awards potential. But the money's going to be very welcome."

This was a shocker. Nevada had rarely ever heard her father talk about money, and it was part of the public persona, that he was a wealthy, successful celebrity actor. Even his own daughter rarely saw beyond the façade.

"Your mother is bleeding me dry."

Nevada's mother, Judith, had divorced Tom ten years previously after forty years of a relationship that was a mystery to almost everyone but seemed to work for them. Pretty much the same as everyone's, except for the length-of-time detail. Worked right up until the surprise ending.

"This is none of my business." Nevada had smiled at him, trying to soften her words. Offensive and annoying as he was, he was still her father, and she tried to do what she had to, to keep a connection going with him, however slight, without letting him pull her down.

The singer was heading across the room. "Let's get out of here before she recognizes me." Tom rose and headed for the door, leaving Nevada to slap a fifty down on the table, quite sure that, unlike New York or L.A., it would be more than enough for a salad, a couple of appetizers, and a tip.

They emerged on the front steps of the restaurant to hear the sounds of a sole saxophone, drifting across the street from Reynolds Square. Nevada tipped her face up to the lovely sunshine. "Dad, why did you call me?"

"Talk to her for me, would you?"

Ah, now we get to it.

"I don't have the money she's asking for. I'm barely making ends meet." His still-handsome face arranged itself in a subtle approximation of misery, and she heard his message—'pity me'.

He had her. Was it his looks, a masculine version of her own? The whiplash she got every time she looked at him—or any famous person? Or maybe her essentially kind nature, and her desire to respond to anyone who asked for her help, however much she might try to cover it up with sarcasm and wit? He had her. Right up to the next line.

"Clio wants us to move in together, and finances are a disaster."

Clio? Who is Clio? There's a new one?

"I might even have to sell some of my collection, if

she doesn't let up," Tom said. Her father had a movie costume, poster, and memorabilia collection that had delighted Nevada and her pals at playtime when she was little. He'd never known they'd gone into his closets and snooped around.

When Nevada told Jeremy and Elaine about it, she got stuck on her reaction to the news that her father was dating again.

"It's time he slowed down. He's seventy-five years old, for God's sake," Nevada said, looking at both Jeremy and Elaine for agreement. Neither one nodded. Both shrugged.

She shook her head. "Anyway, that's all I know. We had lunch, he asked me to run interference with my mother, I said, no, I'm not getting in the middle, it's between you two, and he got huffy and left."

"Have you tried calling or texting him since?" Jeremy asked.

"Why would I?" Nevada replied. "It's only been two days."

Jeremy stood up and stuck a hand out toward Elaine. "Mrs. Hardy, thank you for meeting with me and for calling us about this. We really appreciate it."

The housekeeper shook his hand then got to her feet. "I'll be goin' then, Mr. Jeremy. Have a good one."

Jeremy watched her walk away through the square beneath the live oaks, dripping with Spanish moss.

"What's your best guess on who broke into Tom's place?" Nevada asked.

He didn't answer her right away, and she could see that he was deep in thought. She tried again. "Jeremy, do you have any ideas about what might be going on?"

He sighed. "I don't. But I do know that I don't have time for this. I'm worried that something, or someone, is about to screw up a two-hundred-million-dollar movie." He straightened his shoulders and made eye contact that was like a concrete block being dropped on her face. "I refuse to go under just because your loose cannon of a father can't be controlled."

CHAPTER 4

"We've been in town for a while, and everyone says we need to see the fountain," Nevada said. "And I have to talk to you about my father and about Jeremy Walsh. Let's go this way."

She tugged at Owen's hand and pulled him toward the broad sidewalk that ran through Forsyth Park toward the silvery cascade pouring over the stone statues. The breeze in the trees was gentle, and the air had warmed up nicely in the late winter sun. The stately historic buildings surrounding the park, housing the Savannah College of Art and Design, seemed to gleam in the mid-morning hour.

She thought she was walking pretty fast, but she could tell that her husband was slowing his pace to match hers. He'd told her that the only time he strolled was when he was on rounds, seeing his hospital patients. Otherwise, he charged around like a bullet train.

But even when he was going top speed, he always seemed so calm, so unstressed. Nevada, by contrast, was waving her arms around, venting. She glanced at the two old men and the dog walkers passing by. "These people probably think I'm a nut case."

"They probably think you're just rehearsing something," Owen consoled her. "Lots of SCAD performing arts students live nearby."

He bent down to pet a poodle that had come to greet them as they stood looking at the famous fountain. Torrents of flowing water poured down over marble cliffs that had been sculpted and placed there before the Civil War. It was as beautiful as any fountain she'd ever seen, but with an additional point to note. The water was green, dyed in anticipation of the imminent St. Patrick's Day celebrations.

"Trip, your father is unlikely to change, you know. What did Major Tom want, anyway?"

"General Tom, this time, he says. He is playing General Dillard Franklin of the Confederate Army. The movie's called *Too Beautiful to Burn*." Nevada smiled at the woman at the end of the poodle's leash. Purple hair. On the woman, not the dog, although it was just as mesmerizing on the woman as it would have been on the dog. Very cute. Really. She had had no expectation that Savannah would be so cosmopolitan or so unexpected. Green water and purple hair.

She spotted an amazing example of antebellum architecture across Drayton Street and followed her nose toward it. The house was ringed by the same elaborate black ironwork that surrounded the fountain. Its black and ivory-toned façade had been meticulously maintained, and the columns on either side of the wraparound veranda rose, in perfect proportion and symmetry, to a peaked roof. Owen caught up with her just as she was reading the plaque on the brick wall that identified it as a historic gem.

"You know, he really didn't say. It was strange." What was actually strange was that Nevada had impulsively decided not to share with Owen her father's demand that she get involved in his financial dealings with her mother. "He had his assistant call me and make the appointment for lunch, then he showed up late and left really fast. Was grumpy the whole time."

"Not much new or strange about that." Owen's phone chimed with a text coming in, and he pulled it from his pants pocket.

She laughed. "Yeah, true. But that usually all comes after I've invited him somewhere and he's done his dutiful dad appearance." She scanned the rest of the historic houses on the block, letting her eyes revel in the visual poetry. "He did a lot of complaining about my mother."

That stopped Owen in his scrolling through the text messages on his phone. "Are he and Judith even in touch?"

"I didn't think so, but they don't discuss each other much with me."

"Let's go back to the hotel and figure out where to go for dinner and whether we have to get involved in this in any way." He grinned as he put an arm around her and she took a moment to appreciate, once again, a man like Owen. A sense of priorities—and no appetite for drama.

The manager met them at the door of their hotel, a two-hundred-year-old building refurbished in stylish shades of charcoal and lemon. When they'd checked in earlier in the week, he'd been gracious, friendly, and the epitome of Southern hospitality. His name was DeShawn, he'd told them, and it would be his privilege to help them enjoy their stay in old Savannah.

This afternoon there was no smile. "Mr. and Mrs. Heintzmann, I'm so sorry. There is a problem, and y'all will need to meet with the police."

"It's Ms. Leacock," Nevada said. Why was there so much intensity in the South about identifying female marital status?

"Yes, ma'am." The young man was as jumpy as a long-tailed cat on a front porch full of rocking chairs, one of the best sayings Nevada had heard since she arrived in the South. "Sorry, ma'am. I have to ask you to check whether anything's been taken."

Owen was concentrating. "So, what was it now? A break-in?" He stared deeply into DeShawn's eyes, using a technique that inevitably calmed the most fearful of his patients. Even people with cancer could be made to focus and control the panic.

"Yes, sir, a break-in." DeShawn guided them both to

take a seat on a wooden bench adorned with black iron filigree. "Not to the hotel, you know, but to your room."

"Our room." Nevada resisted his effort to get her sit down, out of the way of the tourist traffic flow through the lobby. The other hotel guests must not be spooked, of course. The tourist is a timid, valuable bird that will fly off at any hint of disturbance.

"Yes, ma'am. Sometime this morning, just after maid service and just before the fire alarm went off. I went up to your floor because guests on either side of your room had called about loud noises and the maids reported hearing shouting. They wouldn't go inside on their own, and when nobody answered my knock, I used my master key card."

Owen smiled at him, and DeShawn didn't need much more encouragement to continue with his story. He had pushed open the heavy door, bracing himself for a confrontation. But the room was empty. Television on full blast, windows open, A/C turned on full, radio on the night table going loud on a hip-hop station—but no people. Someone had been there a while ago though. The room had been thoroughly tossed.

"I knew you'd be in for a shock when you got back— that's why I waited to meet you. I think you ought to sit down."

"It's been a busy day for you, DeShawn. Us too." Owen dropped into the designated seat and rubbed a sleeve across his forehead. Despite the air conditioning, he was suffering from the unusual heat and he wouldn't miss an opportunity to add a little physical comfort to his day. Being bossed around was not one of his issues, and he was happy to comply if it led in some way to well-being.

Nevada was beginning to regret their decision to avoid the convention hotels and stay in something quaint and historic. But she caught herself before her thoughts led her down the road to Cranky-town, as her nanny, Philomena, used to say, years ago. Minor property crimes happen every day, and if you dwell on them, you'll spend your life hiding. She pushed herself to go curious, rather than scared.

"What did they take?"

"Most of our stuff is bolted down," DeShawn observed.

"Smart move," Owen contributed.

"We need you to do an inventory on yours."

Owen leaped up, stretching like the graceful big cat of a man he was. "Let's go see, shall we, Trip? The sooner we get it over, the sooner I can get dinner, and I'm starving. Let's go to that old restaurant where they have ghosts."

"That narrows the field to about three dozen," Nevada joked as they walked past the courtyard with the strings of light bulbs ready to turn the space magical for the evening diners.

Everything in the room—colors, furniture, linens, artwork—had been done in a subtle mix of historic and contemporary that had entranced Nevada the moment she'd seen it. Now their clothes were scattered over the sofas, dresser drawers were empty and ransacked, and even the vases had been overturned and emptied. A police officer stood beside the bay window, making notes.

"Any valuables left in here, ma'am?"

"Not a thing, officer. We put everything important in the safe."

"Any idea who'd be wanting to go through your things?"

"Other than a thief?" Owen asked.

If the police officer thought that was a bit chippy, he didn't show it. "Anything missing, that you can see right now?"

Nevada walked through the room, opening the closet door, the dresser, and glancing into the bathroom. She shook her head.

The officer slapped his notebook closed. "Let us know if anything turns up missing. We have your contact information; we'll be in touch."

He let himself out, and Nevada flopped into the gray armchair beside the balcony door. "Can this day get any more exciting?"

Owen smiled at her. "Livin' in the fast lane, Nevada. That's what we get for leaving Canada."

"Lots of opportunity to get mugged or harassed there, too, these days."

"Anywhere," Owen agreed. "So, do we let them scare us, or do we carry on?"

No answer needed. Keep calm and carry on.

CHAPTER 5

And that was the end of it, so far, Nevada explained to Jeremy. In answer to the director's text that morning, she had walked over from the hotel to meet him at the ice cream parlor on Broughton Street.

"So, what have we got here, and do we need to call in reinforcements?" Jeremy reviewed. "We've got break-ins at Tom's rented house in Ardsley Park and at your Historic District hotel. We've got Tom showing up really late for lunch and then going missing ever since. He hasn't shown up on set or been in touch with anybody from the crew. He hasn't been back to his rented house and he doesn't know it was ransacked. Or maybe he does, but he hasn't discussed it with anybody that I know. He also doesn't know yet that his sword is missing."

"His sword?" This was getting weirder and weirder.

"There's been a lot of pilfering on set, even in the few days since we got started. We've got some detectives nosing around, and we've asked everyone around base camp to be alert, but it can be a tough thing to control, especially with so many extras around. Your father brought along a sword that he said was vintage Civil War and wants to use it in his scenes. I haven't had time yet to get someone to check out the authenticity, and in the meantime the damn thing's gone missing. Along with Yvonne's favorite bag, Ian's leather jacket, and a picnic basket from Craft Services. Or maybe it was Props, I forget."

Jeremy sighed like a much older man. "Anyway, we've got some problems on this shoot, absolutely. Excuse me," he said as he responded to the insistent buzzing of a call coming in on a cell phone set to vibrate. "I have to take this," he said. "Nevada, can you hold on a minute?"

"Sure."

He stepped out of the lineup for the ice cream parlor and walked down the block. When he finished talking, he beckoned to her to join him.

"Tom showed up," Jeremy announced. "He told Traci, my first AD, that he'd needed a little break and didn't think he was on the call sheet. Apologized all over the place—that's a new one for me. Not having an actor go AWOL, but getting an apology after."

"Did he say where he took this little break?" Nevada resisted any urge to pass judgment or make a comment.

"Not to Traci, anyway. Maybe I'll hear more about it later."

Nevada waited for thirty seconds or so. "Jeremy? Is there more?"

"Yeah. So. Nevada, here's the thing. I can't have Tom Leacock roaming off on his own around Savannah while I try to get this film made. We're only here two weeks, and then we go north to Beaufort then Charleston."

Nevada stared into his eyes, trying to get a read on this situation. "We both know what the next line is, Jeremy."

"Why am I telling you all this? Is that it?"

"Yeah."

"I'd like to offer you a short-term contract to come and work for us, facilitating for your father, on set," he began.

Facilitating for Tom? Nevada thought. What on earth could that mean?

"I know you have about a dozen objections—let me start with the obvious ones. Yeah, he might complain, but we'll have a good cover story, a good reason for you to be there. Yes, it's an incredible intrusion on your time and your goodwill, but it's your father. I'd do it for my father, if he were still alive."

Ouch.

Jeremy's eye contact was intense. "And yes, you have other things to do, you have a life, but it's only three months. Maybe less—if you get on board, then we could look at making some changes to the schedule that might have his scenes wrapped up earlier."

Nevada squinted at him in the bright sunshine but decided to keep her thoughts to herself. For now.

"Yes, there are other people we could ask, and we might have to." Jeremy answered her next unspoken question. "But every one of them would come with some kind of baggage, and every one of them would require handling. You seem like a grown-up." He stared at her and she had the feeling that he was stopping everything around them while he turned a bright light on the moment. "Is this even a possibility? I know you're here on vacation and your husband's on a conference trip. Is there any way you could arrange for a short leave of absence? On what is very short notice, I realize."

Nevada tried to read her own reaction, get that instant, 'gut feel' for what she wanted to do. But it wasn't clear. Things usually weren't, when it came to her dad. It was even murkier because of her mixed feelings about work these days too. She'd told Owen that she really needed this vacation, but she was starting to realize that it wasn't helping. All of the weariness she felt about her job as a news director and her life in Vancouver wasn't lifting, even in the sunshine of the South, and when she thought about the prospect of returning to her office in a few weeks she could barely move.

Jeremy started to walk back toward the ice cream place, passing in front of the vintage theater, its marquee promoting an upcoming screening of *Casablanca*. A few more minutes in line, and then he guided her into the shop. A smiling young woman in a cheery uniform stood behind a row of tubs of ice cream. "What kind do you like?" Jeremy asked.

"I'll take butter pecan. I've been hearing about this place ever since I got to Savannah."

"I've been hearing about it since location scouts started using Savannah thirty years ago. A butter pecan and a pistachio, please."

"No problem," was the reply from behind the counter. Smiling face, Southern accent, diner hat with the name "Millie" handwritten and decorated in glitter.

Nevada explored the ice cream with her tongue. Yuh-huh. It was as good as they claimed. Better. She didn't feel like much of a grown-up.

She knew she should take some time to think over Jeremy's idea, try it on and compare it to her other options. But she didn't need to.

"Alright, I'll do it."

Jeremy's surprise was easy to figure out, as he inhaled a bit of ice cream and sputtered. "Just like that? You don't want a few hours to think it over? Crucify me as a sexist, but talk it over with Owen?"

Nevada had to smile. She liked this guy. Two or three months of being in his orbit would be an extra bit of compensation.

"Three months max?"

Jeremy nodded, maybe afraid to say anything and spoil the deal.

"I get paid?"

"Twice. Once as Tom's unofficial overseer and once for your official job."

"Which would be what?"

Jeremy savored the last of his ice cream cone, taking his time. "How about this?" he said when he was finished. "Script consultant, responsible for fact-checking dialogue for authenticity, helping with killing off the anachronisms before they're born and give the critics the distraction they're looking for. And maybe providing the director with an unbiased, non-career-building answer once in a while."

Nevada felt a sense of lightening up, which was odd, given that she was about to take on a full-time job with movie filming hours and daily exposure to a father who was more work than a bridezilla with a small budget.

"This is good," she said. "Alright, Jeremy, you got it. I'll watch out for him and help you get your movie done. I want to do it, and when I run it by Owen, that will be good enough for him. We'll make it work."

She could almost smell Jeremy's sense of relief. The stakes were high for him. They were high for Tom, too, but he probably didn't get that.

"Thank you. I'll make it as easy for you as I can," he said.

That didn't sound like any sort of guarantee, but Nevada wasn't really expecting any. She'd known her father a long time and she thought she knew what she was signing on for. This was a big deal for her, but to her father, the ups and downs in anybody else's life were about as significant as the weather to somebody living in a bunker. She doubted he'd appreciate the impact of what she was doing—in fact, she probably wouldn't tell him. But she knew and she was going to do it anyway. It just felt like the right thing to do.

CHAPTER 6

Key West

The Coastal Florida Historical Museum in Key West was scheduled to open at ten a.m. but, as usual, very few people were there when the guard unlocked the heavy wooden doors and the cashier took her place behind the ticket window. Too many other distractions in this beach town at the farthest tip of the southern states: the Ernest Hemingway museum, the candy-colored houses, the sun-soaked restaurants beside the sand, the nightlife on Duval Street—all of it alongside one of the most beautiful strips of sand in the U.S.

Lillian Howe waited patiently on the sidewalk out front. She imagined the guard opening the doors between the exhibits and the cashier unlocking her equipment in the moments before opening—the sudden glare as the bright white overhead lights snapped on and the sidelights angled upward toward the shelves of nautical artifacts in various shapes, colors, weights, and sizes, illustrating Florida's history.

Before her visit to the museum, Lillian had gone for her daily walk. These days it was taking her a little longer to cover her two miles, although she certainly wasn't as stiff as she had been in the days when she was sleeping in her car, back in Vancouver. These days she was stronger, happier, and more put together. Her silver hair was pampered regularly in a salon, and her nails were done in a bright blue that drew smiles and comments from women young enough to be her grown granddaughters.

This morning Key West shimmered in the tropical heat, the pink, turquoise, and lemon-yellow houses like so many candies in a row. Heat was a relative term, of course. It was hot if you were standing on a Chicago sidewalk, shivering in the raincoat you'd thought you could get away with now that it was March. It was not hot if you were used to summers in the South. Lillian had picked her way carefully along the beach sidewalk, looking out toward the sea as she loved to do, but checking the topography ahead every few steps. Falling was a much more likely event than getting mugged or encountering an alligator, and she knew how to put her worries where they ought to be. Her youngest daughter, Delores, lectured her six or seven times a month about getting a cane and watching her step, which was why Lillian had chosen about six years ago to move diagonally across the continent from Vancouver to this outpost at the end of the road.

That hadn't quite worked out for her because Delores and her family had arrived on Lillian's doorstep just a few weeks after she'd moved south. Said they were just stopping in on their way to Orlando, Florida, "one of the top three tourist destinations in the U.S.". But Lillian knew the truth; to get anywhere near her little apartment at the top of the fourplex near Duval Street, they had to fly into Miami, not Orlando, drive 160 miles through Key Largo, Islamorada, and Fiesta Key, Lillian's particular favorite, cross the Seven Mile Bridge and cruise past the clusters of crab shacks, tackle stores, and marinas that crowd US 1. Delores was there to spy on her, if that wasn't too paranoid a way to put it.

But it turned out that after a day of "checking on Mom" and two more days of the fourteen-year-old complaining "there's nothing to do!", the sixteen-year-old looking for boys, and the husband asking "are the green fees this high at *every* course?", Delores was ready to surrender and Lillian had her peace. They got in their rental car and headed north. Lillian still got the biweekly emails about nutrition and buying a cane, but emails were much easier to ignore.

She was damned if she'd admit it, but some days she did consider a cane. Her trick knee was throbbing today, and she hadn't slept well. But as usual, she ignored all unhelpful messages and got dressed, got out, and got on with it, as her mother used to say.

Some people might say that these days there was not much to get on with, but Lillian would disagree. True, there weren't children to be raised anymore or offices to get to or houses to clean. Not a husband to look after or a car to maintain. But there was this beach to be walked, with bits of litter to be grabbed and stowed in the next garbage can. There was that four-year-old to be smiled at, this bird to be admired, that museum to be explored.

Standing at the ticket window, she did the math and realized that the cost of an annual pass for the museum equaled the entry fee for only two visits. Oh, these places do demand more from the tourists passing through and the locals unwilling to plan ahead. She decided to invest, pulling five twenties out of her purse.

The Coastal Florida Historic Museum had been built about ten years ago after a design competition had stirred up a commotion of bidding and proposing. The selection committee had chosen this soaring example of a concrete, glass, teak, and bamboo dance. Yes, a dance. Architecture as art, as movement, and as music.

Today Lillian walked into the lobby, sat on a bench, and stared upward at the high notes of the ceiling. The admission fee was high even at the seniors' rate, but a few months ago she had decided to start spending a few more of the dollars that she was safeguarding from Keith Papineau's bequest. Six years ago, in 2008 in Vancouver when her path had crossed his in the last few months of his life, the TV journalist had decided to leave her such a surprising and substantial gift that her financial problems were solved. It was a turn of events in her life that still shocked her, whenever she gave a few moments to thinking about it; contemplating the past was not one of her regular habits. But it was the year that she met Nevada Leacock, Chelan Montgomery, and Keith's son, Kevin, and all three of them had become significant people in these later years of her life. The golden years, some people called them, and it was a good name. She'd rather not think of herself as old. 'Golden' was better. Or how about 'advanced'?

On her previous visit she had stopped to look around the main floor before seeing the visiting exhibits, located upstairs, but today she headed directly for "The Conquistador's Bounty", on display courtesy of the Prado in Madrid. She'd read about this exhibition in the newspaper. She couldn't say why she felt so drawn to it but she did. She was eager to see it, even if it meant her old knees had to put up with a little aggravation. She wasn't ready yet to hunt for an elevator everywhere she went.

The artifacts and museum cards were laid out like a spiral shellfish, with the modern-day photographs and events at the outer edges. Lillian followed the story of the conqueror's haul of gold, precious stones, and jewelry through the modern years back through the nineteenth century, the eighteenth, and into the early periods that were pieced together, like dinosaur displays, from a few bones and shards of facts, and much speculation.

At the center of the spiral, in a place of honor, inside a bullet- and theft-proof glass cabinet, was a gold pendant in the soaring shape of a bird in flight, so graceful, so detailed that it looked as though it could draw breath at any moment.

The lighting around the Spanish Bird, as it was called, was a rosy glow, chosen to imitate the effect of a coastal sunrise over the Caribbean Sea. Dozens of tiny concealed lights directed all of the attention in the exhibit toward this treasure, believed to have been handcrafted in Cuba in ancient times and now on loan to the museum in Florida while the powers-that-be in Spain continued to try to figure out how to get it back into the hands of the descendants of the one who made it. Or so they said.

Lillian could see that the unknown person who had created the delicate pendant had poured into it all of the soul, dedication, and yearning of a true artist. Somehow it spoke to her, told her what it was like to be that artist, that person, in a voice that carried through hundreds of years. She sank onto the padded bench in front of the display, thankful for the chance to rest her legs and knees.

She felt a few seconds of triumph, that she had made it in here early enough that it was well before the tourists and locals eager to document every moment and sight in their personal day on their smartphones. She'd asked the museum guard about it once, and he'd told her they'd given up on trying to police any rule that prohibited taking pictures. People wouldn't surrender their cameras and phones at the door, as they once had agreed to do years before when cell phones were not as common and not as stuffed with private data. It was tough enough to get people to patronize the arts nowadays, without requiring them to hand over a phone or submit to scolding for using it. So those who wanted a more dignified, serene museum experience timed their visits, as Lillian did, and gritted their teeth when the selfie crowd appeared.

Lillian stood, reading the information card. Circa 900 A.D., created by an Island or perhaps a Central American or Mayan artisan. Its early provenance unknown. Made from 24-karat gold, transformed into an elegant, graceful shore bird.

Lillian had chosen Key West as her new home for three reasons: the tropical weather, the Ernest Hemingway connection, and the American Caribbean flair. But this side benefit of art treasures was unexpected and entrancing. She stood staring at the words about the Spanish Bird. It was one of three, identified through oral tradition and journals kept by long-ago adventurers and explorers. The second pendant, the card detailed, was held in a private collection dating back to the U.S. Civil War era, and the third was said to have been lost in a Spanish shipwreck. The belief was that each of the three hung from a different, exquisite chain, but as no one had ever seen all three of them gathered together, no one really knew.

Now that's a museum sight that would be the chance of a lifetime.

The exhibit also included an ancient letter, written on yellowed parchment, long-faded ink conveying the thoughts and messages of an adventurer to his king and queen. It told of a voyage to the New World, soon to be concluded, and reported that the ship was bringing "natives and gold" back to Spain. Two in particular were described, a young man and a young woman, a couple, noteworthy for their youth and because they were not "brought by force" as were others.

Lillian had the feeling that the letter writer disapproved in some way, although she wasn't sure whether it had to do with the willing young couple or the unwilling others.

The young couple brought with them two indescribably beautiful pieces of jewelry, identical necklaces, each with an exquisite carving of a bird hanging from a gold chain. The exhibit information went on to explain that the one in this exhibit had been kept in Spain all these centuries in castles and palaces and then in the Prado in Madrid. The second was reportedly somewhere in the possession of a wealthy American family that had passed it down through generations that went back to the Civil War.

There were also rumors of a third pendant, the museum exhibit card stated— rumors, but no facts. All were thought to have been made by the same artist at the same time, and quite probably made in a time long before—perhaps even centuries before—the necklaces were taken on the ship from the New World back toward Spain. What happened to the third pendant and where was it today? It all remained a mystery.

Lillian took one last look at the exhibit, then made her way out into the blazing sunshine. She was supposed to meet her grandson Donovan at a bank in Miami, and it wouldn't do to show up late, if she expected him to be on time. It would take about four hours, but it was one of the most sensational drives Lillian had ever seen and she jumped at any excuse she could to do it. The Seven Mile Bridge, the blue water, the tiny fishing towns—she loved it all. Florida was home now.

CHAPTER 7

Jeremy gave Nevada a couple of days to get ready to go to work and she took advantage of the first of them by visiting the local outdoor clothes and equipment store, trying to find the right coat to buy for the early mornings and middle-of-the-nights that would be part of her life for the next three months. She had no idea what to prepare for, in Savannah's climate. Might be up to eighty degrees in the afternoon, yes, but what about the pre-dawn?

Her phone call to Matthew Dixon, her boss back at LV-TV, hadn't gone well. He thought three months was far too long for a leave of absence, and her efforts to lighten the mood by suggesting he take advantage of the opportunity to load up the newscast with more sailboat and dog show stories had been met with a lengthy silence. In the end, he agreed to three months ("and not a second more!") but he was grumpy about it. It didn't bother her, though, and she took that as one more sign that she didn't really know what she thought anymore about this career she'd worked so long to put together.

Nevada was enjoying the slightly off-balance tilt that this extended stay in Savannah was bringing into her life. She liked being the 'stranger in a strange land', although she hadn't mentioned that to anyone here. She doubted that anybody anywhere liked hearing their town referred to as 'strange'. Except maybe in Austin, where they urged people to 'keep it weird'. Which was different from 'strange'.

Savannah could be described in many ways, depending on the parts of town you visited and the length of time you spent. Historic. Snobbish. Haunted. Poised on the brink of an economic boom. Stuffy. If you weren't born there, in certain circles, you were invisible. If they couldn't trace you back to 1790, in certain circles, you didn't exist. Why that should matter, Nevada couldn't figure, but it mattered to a lot of the people she'd met at Owen's hospital-related fund-raising thing last week and it just wafted through the town like a puff of smoke, curling around the live oak trees and the pines.

She'd met people like that in Vancouver; old-time Savannahians weren't the only ones in the world who believed that being born into a particular family was the only lottery they'd ever have to win, that's for sure. Nevada had never been impressed by what some people would call pedigree, as if they were talking about dogs or horses. She was proud of her refusal to be easily impressed—or intimidated, as some of the "people from the right families" intended.

Thankfully, she'd also met quite a few people in Savannah so far who would rather ask you what you liked to drink than who your grandmother was.

That was another topic, one that Owen had some strong opinions on. Too many people in Savannah doing too much drinking for the good of their own health and their medical futures, he'd concluded.

It was a beautiful city, a party city, and also a religious city. She'd noticed a church on almost every second street corner, and while she certainly recognized the names of denominations that were familiar all over the world, she was also captivated by the unusual names. Her favorite so far was "Determined Church".

Her cell phone rang.

"Nevada? I'm here."

"Here, where? Here here?" Nevada looked all around herself and past the others who stood in front of and behind her in the checkout line.

"Here in Georgia!"

Her mother. That voice was one of the two Nevada had heard since her first moments of life. Her mother was a character, just like her former husband. She had asked everyone to start calling her Judith, after four decades as 'Judy'. She was once a beauty, but the 'once' was also about forty years ago. Her own forgetfulness put it at last week, though, and she went through life acting as if she still looked like the sort of woman who could get anything she wanted, just with a smile. She often tried . . . and failed. It was embarrassing.

"You know I get around, kiddo," Judith continued, using an endearment that drove Nevada absolutely crazy. "It's chilly in L.A., and I decided it was time to visit the South again."

"The weather has been lovely," Nevada said to Judith, desperate to find something to talk about and to buy a little time while she figured out how to manage this situation. She had only a few days to herself before having to show up for work on the movie set, and she hadn't planned to have to spend even a small part of it doing anything she didn't want to before she had to inhale deeply and go to work seeing Tom every day. Judith suddenly showing up in Savannah was a surprise. Not a happy one.

"Mom, it's great to hear from you. We'll have to get together soon," Nevada said as she tried to deflect anything more specific. "I'm in a store right now and the clerk is here. Gotta go!"

She just couldn't spend these precious few days dealing with her mother. She had a million things to do— find a place to live for three months, get her mail sent south, and make sure she and Owen had everything all good between them.

That last one covered many things. Tonight, it meant helping him with a bit of the socializing that was a part of his job. Staying onside with important fundraisers and

Board members was all part of the medical life, she'd learned, and she actually enjoyed his work-related invitations that were directed at both of them. She'd met some fascinating people that way. Tonight would be no exception.

She got back to the hotel with just enough time to throw her shopping bags into a corner, change to a pair of pants and a top, and put on shoes that weren't flat and made of rubber. When she stepped out to the sidewalk, Owen was there waiting for her in the car.

She was feeling happy about getting out. She wasn't a particularly nervous woman, and she wasn't about to let somebody else's larceny force her out of a place she'd decided to be in. But the hotel break-in had left her a little unimpressed with being there, in that room, when Owen wasn't there with her.

They were on their way out to dinner at the home of a couple who were major supporters of the hospital where he was working now. Nevada had been expecting that her decision to stay on in Savannah would mean that she'd have to do without Owen's company, until she got back to Vancouver. But he was a man of many surprises, as she'd told him appreciatively when he informed her that his brief appearance as the keynote speaker at the medical conference and his lengthy professional association with the cancer research community in Georgia would lead him easily to a stint filling in at the hospital for a specialist heading overseas on an extended vacation. Just look at where you want to go and start moving in that direction, that was Owen's method.

Just twenty minutes away from Savannah, another world existed. It was a glimpse of what the whole area must have been, a hundred and fifty or two hundred years ago. She saw long alleys of live oaks, curving downward like mothers dipping their heads to check on sleeping children, with Spanish moss hanging from their branches like strands of long hair escaping from a bun. The salt marshes stretched out toward the horizon, cut by rivers and estuaries, with herons, egrets, and ospreys standing like sentinels on the shore. The smaller residential and commercial lots gave way to more space around each building, and gated communities began to appear with as much regularity as the gas stations and strip malls closer to the heart of the city.

Owen listened carefully to the instructions announced by their robotic GPS assistant and, without a single wrong turn, drove across a small bridge, then pulled up to a security booth. He leaned over to give their names and destination; once the guard had confirmed their identities with his computer, he pushed a button somewhere and the wrought-iron gate between a pair of Savannah brick posts majestically and slowly swept open.

The drive to Frank and Linda Leonard's house in The Pines went on for another ten minutes before they arrived in front of a palatial three-story home that wouldn't have looked out of place on The Crescent in the Shaughnessy neighborhood of Nevada's hometown of Vancouver. The façade was brick with black shutters and railings. A four-tiered fountain graced the front of the grounds; to the rear, Nevada could just see the edges of a dock that led down through the marsh to a boathouse. Lots of room to roam around in, too; she guess-timated the property was about two acres. All in all, quite a bit larger and more expensive than every other house they'd passed as they drove through the neighborhood.

The vice chairman of the hospital board and his wife put on a nice spread for dinner, and Nevada was fighting with herself to stay alert, now that everyone had settled into the living room after dessert. Must have been that second glass of wine. She leaned back into the Eames chair that commanded the right side of the gas fireplace and stared through the picture window at the live oaks towering over a lawn that was outlined in royal palms and dwarf palmettos. Frank and Linda had retired to Georgia after a lifetime in the movie industry. They'd tried Sarasota, Florida and then Palm Springs, California. In Georgia, they'd fallen in love with the pines, the moonlight, and the exquisite manners of the people they'd met on their exploratory visits the previous year. They were clearly newcomers who reveled in their adopted home. Sheet music from Johnny Mercer's "Moon River" adorned the baby grand piano in the giant living room of this vaguely colonial version of a mansion on an acre near Romerly Marsh, and Nevada saw four copies of "the book", as locals called *Midnight in the Garden of Good and Evil,* scattered around the living room.

"Did you see the movie?" she asked Linda.

The tiny woman beamed in what she thought was mutual appreciation. "Of course. John Cusack is a genius."

"He didn't write it," Frank observed as he set their Arnie Palmers on the antique table in front of them. He had to bend a long way to do it. He was probably a full foot taller than his wife. "Or direct it. John Berendt wrote it." He motioned to the drinks he'd mixed for Owen and Nevada. "Are you sure you don't want something a little stronger?"

Owen and Nevada each shook their heads 'no'.

Frank settled into the sofa across from the fireplace and surveyed the view of the lagoon that dominated his living room window. "We've seen Florida, we've seen southern California, and this is the best of all, in our opinion." Nevada wondered whether Linda had the same opinion or only half of one allotted to them both. "We feel like we're stealing every time we buy something here, especially after New York and L.A. It's an absolute shock, what things cost here."

"Are you going to take in the parade next week?" Linda asked, sipping a martini.

"I hadn't thought—" Nevada just started when Linda cut her off.

"Oh, you have to! It's the biggest event in Savannah,

some people say—depends how you measure 'biggest', I guess, but who knew there were so many Irish people here? Their ancestors came here, as immigrants, apparently. It's the third biggest parade, after Dublin and Boston, they say, and it defines the start of the season— people come back from wherever they've been, the yellow pollen season is over, or close to it, and the weather gets better."

"Yellow pollen?" Nevada sipped her drink.

"You haven't noticed?"

"I did see what looked like dust on a few of the benches in the squares."

"I guess you just haven't been here long enough yet. Once you know what I'm talking about, you'll see it everywhere."

"But if she doesn't have allergies, she won't really notice it, Linda," Frank contributed. "It's from the pine trees, and it coats things for a week or two every spring. No big deal."

The doorbell rang, and when Linda returned from answering it, she had Jeremy Walsh, of all people, in tow.

"A last-minute arrival," Linda announced, as Jeremy grinned at Nevada and stuck his hand out to Owen.

"Jeremy Walsh, orphan in Savannah, and former personal assistant to Mr. Frank here, as the locals would call him." He dropped onto the sofa and took the beer that Frank brought him. "What did I miss?"

"We were bringing Nevada and Owen up to speed on Savannah weather and other things."

"I'm hoping the weather changes a bit," Jeremy said. We do much better when it's cloudy and a bit cooler. Especially with those woolen uniforms."

"What's the movie?" Linda asked.

"It's called *Too Beautiful to Burn*," Jeremy said. "Working title. Maybe. It's about Savannah in 1864 and why Sherman didn't torch it like he did Atlanta. Why there are still buildings here that go back to the 1730s."

"Sounds intriguing." Nevada gazed out at Frank and Linda's view over the lagoon, watching a heron balance on one leg while it waited for fish.

"Preproduction's been going well, and the script is a good one. Say, would you be interested in a set visit?" He looked at Nevada with a hint of a smile and the air of somebody bowing and extending a hand to invite somebody to dance.

"Why, yes—yes I would." Nevada almost felt like bowing back. They'd just ironed out the details of their arrangement over the phone an hour earlier, including a mutual commitment to keep it private. No one investing big bucks in a movie production would be happy to hear that one of the stars needed full-time adult supervision, and everyone reading the gossip sites online would be thrilled to know the dirt. Neither Nevada nor Jeremy wanted to let on to anyone that they'd met previously and were now employer and employee. Jeremy hadn't mentioned that he was on his way to The Pines for dinner, but why would he?

Nevada sighed and fiddled with the straw in her drink. Why did she have the feeling that this was going to become much more complicated than it had seemed when Jeremy first suggested it? She'd already gone from agreeing to keep an eye on her father while he was in Savannah all the way to committing to a daily attendance on set to prevent any one of a dozen ways he might screw up the day's filming. It was like the boiling a frog metaphor—they get him in the pot, turn up the temperature a degree at a time, and the frog doesn't notice the heat has got him until it's too late to jump out.

"We're at the plantation on Skidaway Road day after tomorrow, then out to Tybee Island later in the week," Jeremy said. "I'll get your name on the list."

CHAPTER 8

Four a.m. is a brutal time to start the day, any day, in any job. The extras shivered in their costumes. Even in Savannah, even with the gentle breezes of Coastal Georgia, the early morning brought a chill. Nevada stared down the three-hundred-year-old alleyway of live oaks, the Spanish moss dripping from them like silvery gray veils from the arms of a dancer, and cradled her extra-large coffee cup between stiff fingers. It was a thrill, being allowed onto this historic plantation movie location, but it didn't come without a discomfort price.

Many of the people on set were still hiding out in their trailers or their cars, while craft services unpacked and heated dozens of muffins, bagels, and cups of coffee. The costume designer had her racks of period gowns lined up for the interior scenes coming up later this morning, and in makeup, where Nevada had stopped by earlier to say hello to Chelsea, an old friend from Canada, they were setting out dozens of sets of mutton chop sideburns and moustaches. Thousands of feet of cable would be snaking across the grass and pathways, turning night into day, so that they could get the shots they needed in the hours the current owners had decided they could spare. People were usually flattered, eager to be cooperative, and pleased with the extra cash if they were asked to put their homes into a movie, but not in this case. Nevada had heard in various bits of set chatter that they had very little time to get the sequence.

This exterior shot was to be a simple one, when eventually viewed as part of a two-hour movie telling the story of a family destroyed due to greed and arrogance during the Civil War. Or, as they called it here, the War of Northern Aggression. Establishing shot of the live oaks, then the white columns of the mansion. Fingers crossed that no military helicopters from nearby Hunter Army Airfield appeared during any of the times when the cameras would be rolling. That would definitely not be a fortunate coincidence for a movie set in 1864.

In November, 1864, to be exact. Nevada was there to fact-check every date, every weather report, and every non-war event that might have had an impact at the time. Not that anyone in today's audience would have any idea whether or not the details were accurate and not that anyone would argue with an assertion that it was "creative" non-fiction and therefore subject to freedom with the facts. But Nevada had decided to take her job as script consultant on this film as seriously as she'd ever taken anything. She intended to cover every point as carefully as she always had during her reporting days and as she had demanded from her staff during her news director days, even if no one noticed or cared.

In the scene this morning, the hero of the movie was to arrive on horseback to meet his beloved at a hidden spot a short walk from the house. He was to dismount, carry his saddlebag to a gully behind the mansion, beneath a spectacular tree, and wait for one of the daughters of the house. It was a forbidden connection and a dangerous rendezvous as Sherman was storming through Georgia on his March to the Sea, having captured Atlanta a few months earlier and set fire to it only days before. The young woman, already dressed formally for the day ahead, was to rush to the soldier, embrace him, and hand him precious cargo—a long, golden chain from which dangled an ancient gold pendant in the shape of a bird. For a moment, he would drape it round her neck, kissing her passionately, then fold it into a velvet cloth and slide it into the saddlebag. As the sun rose over the salt marsh, he was to mount, lean down to caress her face one last time, then ride off.

Nevada watched from a concealed spot some sixty feet away, partly to stay out of the actors' sightlines and partly to keep her presence on set the secret that she and the director had agreed on. If her father saw her right now, they were all doomed.

After countless light meter readings and camera tests, the scene was ready. Jeremy took his spot on his chair behind the playback machine; everyone in video village went quiet. The actors inhaled and reached that moment of readiness. It was like the silence before the first motion of a conductor's baton or the downward sweep of the flag at the start of a Formula One car race. The director called "action", and the male lead took two long strides toward his co-star, Yvonne Lee, playing the southern belle. She thrust the soft gray velvet bundle toward him—and the director called "cut".

"Perfect. Next set up." Jeremy and two ADs had their heads bent over the shooting script. The props intern approached with a question—"Time to bring in the jewelry, boss?" Jeremy nodded and the young man hustled away, returning minutes later with a group of people hovering around a box. Nevada recognized the insurance man and Sandra, the props supervisor, in the crowd. The box was the home and the travelling vehicle for the spectacular pendant that was the MacGuffin of the movie—the family heirloom that set the whole chain of events in motion, priceless and treasured for more than hundreds of years, pursued against a backdrop of the final events of the Civil War. Eventually, this object was to reunite them all, but that didn't happen in this movie; that was sketched out in Movie Three of what the producers hoped would be a trilogy, if it took off with the public.

The cameras moved into position, Jeremy set up his

shot and lights were adjusted, Sandra opened the box, and Yvonne reached for the necklace. There was a group gasp among the crew on set this morning—a long moment of silence and then a mumble of confusion. There was supposed to be a bejeweled, ancient masterpiece of a bird lying nestled in the silk lining of the box.

There wasn't.

Jeremy was irritated. "Traci, where's the bird thing?"

"I'm not sure, Jeremy," the assistant director said. "Props was taking care of it. Sandra?"

"Props, maybe, but me, mainly." The comment came from the fat man in the seersucker suit, bow tie, and straw hat. Nevada had seen him hanging around and deduced that he was the insurance company rep. Now there was a job they'd have to pay her a million dollars a year to do.

Jeremy nodded grimly. "Yes, Mr. O'Keefe, we get it. No insurance man watching its every move, no insurance." He rose from his canvas chair and towered over Sandra. "So where is it?"

"We handed it over to Mr. O'Keefe at the end of the day's filming yesterday," Sandra said.

"Mr. O'Keefe?"

Doyle O'Keefe tilted his chin up and his head back. "We locked it up in the location safe last night and brought it out this morning."

"The box or the bird pendant itself?" Jeremy asked.

The insurance man was beginning to look as though he might be sick. "The box."

Jeremy glanced around at the crew, the actors, and the extras whose curiosity was growing in the suspended moments like the intensity of a pack of caged tigers pacing an enclosure while they awaited the arrival of some sort of lunch. "Did anyone check the pendant in the box before it was put away and locked up?"

From her unobtrusive spot on the edges of the scene behind several dozen of the extras, Nevada saw her father come storming over toward the director. Tom Leacock had made the equivalent of a dozen people's livings as a motion picture actor for more than fifty years, and he'd played every type of role devised for 'alpha male' that there was. He knew how to enter a scene.

Tom had been watching events unfold and holding his tongue immobile for what must have been an eternity for someone used to being the center of attention. He exploded, spraying around a lot more than a morning's worth of frustration. "I told you to use a prop! Why in the name of Saint Francis did you bring the real thing here? A piece of paste looks just as good! That's what cinematography *is!*"

"And I told you, Tom," Jeremy replied calmly, looking like a man who had already checked out of the conversation he was in. "Authenticity. Realism. Actor motivation."

"Publicity value," Doyle muttered.

Jeremy turned on him. "Yes, publicity value, Mr. O'Keefe. Something someone in insurance probably wouldn't get. But a hefty part of the value of this pendant, of any historical piece, of this movie, of all of our careers, has to do with reputation, and yes, with publicity. This pendant is one of only three ever made."

"I don't know anything about the other two, and I don't really care," Doyle said. "My concern is this one, the one that's the property of a private collector whose family has passed it down through generations, on loan for this movie."

"One was lost at sea in a storm in the fifteenth century," Jeremy continued calmly. "There's another one that was on display in Madrid for hundreds of years and is currently on loan to a museum in Florida. Then we've got this one, this third one. All this has been in the media, and the pre-release chatter on this movie—as a result—is more than enough to let us set a budget big enough to get this sucker done. And big enough to pay your company for an insurance bond and for security, I might add. Security that has failed." Jeremy pulled back and headed off toward his trailer. "Let me know what your company's investigation plans are, Mr. O'Keefe. I'm going to go call the police."

Nevada shrank back into the shadows behind a live oak tree as Jeremy stalked past her in the direction of the convoy of white movie trucks that lined the plantation avenue. Tom followed shortly after, but Yvonne and Ian, the two leads, dawdled and hung back to chat with the crew. Nevada knew she couldn't keep her presence on set a secret for long. She anticipated big drama and a battle with her father if Tom found out that Jeremy had asked her to be there during his key scenes, to help watch him and get him to his mark on time. Her cover story, level one, was just a visit to see old friends from the movie business, while she happened to be in Savannah completely coincidentally. Eventually, they would have to reveal to Tom and all the others that she was actually working there, helping as a "script consultant". Cover story, level two.

This wasn't entirely new territory. When she was much younger, in her early twenties and struggling to find her first career jobs, she had worked as Tom's assistant. She quit when she realized that her mother, Judith, had encouraged her and inserted her into the job so that she could pump her daughter for information about Tom's comings and goings during a shoot. Ultimately, Nevada found her way into the right school, the right job, and the right circle with the right mentor, and now she was News Director at LV-TV in Vancouver, Canada. A news director on an extended break ... and now a babysitter for a seventy-five-year-old father with money and behavior problems.

Remind me again—how did I get here? And why am I such a sucker when it comes to my father?

So, there she was, trying to keep a low profile on her first day of her two new jobs, one official and one so unofficial that she was pretty sure Jeremy Walsh would deny all knowledge of her and her mission, if confronted. As it was turning out, it wasn't hard to stay off the radar since everyone was completely blindsided and stunned by the theft of the priceless heirloom that had been loaned to the production.

When Tom saw her, though, any thoughts about the bird pendant were replaced by his surprise at her presence there. His professional actor's facial expression was absolutely uncontrolled for a moment—although Nevada was never sure with him. It might have been faked disbelief. He hurried over, his pretend Confederate Army sword swinging awkwardly from his hip. The temperature had climbed to seventy-five degrees and even though it was barely noon, that scratchy woolen uniform had to be uncomfortable. Nevada could see a red flush above his stiff collar—rash, heat, or irritation?

"Nevada, you aren't supposed to be here!"

So much for a warm, paternal greeting.

"Your director invited me," she said, looking around and scoping out the locations of the restroom facilities and the craft services tables. "I met him at a dinner party and he invited me."

"When he heard you are my daughter," Tom added to her sentence.

Nevada sighed, resisting the urge to say 'whatever', like a teenager. "You look great, Dad. Tell me about the story."

Two late-middle-aged women in fleece vests, flat shoes, and sensible hair approached, eight-by-ten glossies and pens in hand. Tom scrawled his autograph; one hand held out a phone to him and he graciously lined himself up alongside them, then held the device high above them as they all three grinned skyward at the lens for a selfie. So, he *was* in the twenty-first-century then. As the two fans drifted off, looking for Yvonne Lee, he got into storyteller mode.

"A Union Colonel visits a plantation just before

Sherman's army is expected to come through and meets a Confederate widow with a houseful of art treasures. He promises to help her protect them, especially a beautiful golden bird pendant . . ."

Why did almost everything sound like a story pitch?

"Tell me again how you met Jeremy Walsh and how you got an invitation? Did he get you to sign the non-disclosure? We can't have this leaking out."

"Dear God, spare me." Nevada tried to smile. "Dad, don't worry. Let's just relax and enjoy being in the same part of the world, okay? Usually, we're five or six thousand miles apart—this is a great opportunity to hang out, get caught up . . . and someone else is covering the expenses, right? We could have dinner a few times, maybe explore some of the historic sites on your day off, maybe." She wheeled around to head in the opposite direction from him and ran right into Jeremy's chest.

"Nevada! I want you to meet Roger Ridley, our screenwriter." Roger was a tall, well-built young man with a trucker hat, a hoodie, a major gold watch, and a cell phone currently getting one hundred percent of his attention. "Roger, Nevada is our script consultant slash fact-checker." And then Jeremy was gone.

"Script consultant? Fact-checker? What the hell?" Roger was now paying attention.

Nevada stuck out her hand. "Nice to meet you, Roger."

Anybody could tell that the screenwriter was offended by the implication that his own fact-checking had not been thorough and on point. He was not offended enough to take it up with his agent, though, Nevada was willing to bet, especially once he had determined that he was not going to be required to share credit in any way and once he was reassured that no actual re-writing was going on. But right now, he was as huffy as a prima donna whose understudy was being allowed to breathe down her neck.

On many movies, the screenwriter wasn't allowed

access at all because the director was convinced the writer wasn't capable of seeing him or herself as just one more moving part in an elaborate machine. Roger was privileged to be there, Nevada thought, and she wondered whether he got that.

Roger shook her hand as limply as was possible. "Good to meet you, Nevada. I think you'll find there won't be much for you to do here. But I'm sure if you think there is, you'll be contacting me about it first." He fished in his cargo shorts pocket. "Here's my card, my contact info's there. Shoot me an email or a text if there's anything you think might need changing. But as I said, I doubt there's anything."

Was he telling her she reported to him? Nevada had to allow herself a private laugh. He looked all of about twenty-four years old.

"Script consultant?!" Tom had followed her and overheard them. "I thought you said you were just here for a set visit today."

"I'll be doing a little freelance work for Jeremy," Nevada confessed. "Fact-checking."

"Don't need no fact-checking." Roger looked ready to boil over, but then he got hold of himself. Nevada watched a curtain fall over his eyes, as if he'd closed away some part of himself. "What I mean is, the facts have been checked. I have all the assistance I need—not to mention an MA in history from MidSouthern State and an MFA in creative writing from Iowa."

"This isn't important," Tom pronounced. "It's like being a producer on a list of credits, means nothing." Tom seemed to be sensing a drama building; probably because it didn't involve him directly, he decided to stifle it.

"Then why is she here?" Roger demanded.

"Yes, Nevada, why are you here?" Her father moved just enough to stand shoulder to shoulder with the young writer, and both glared at Nevada. She steadily held the eye contact, flicking back and forth, first the tall, then the short, the old man, then the young man. It was just an act of bogus self-confidence, though; she felt unwelcome, to put it mildly, and sad that her own father had sided against her. Roger must have felt something of that because he blinked first and relented.

"I will talk to you about my story, if you're interested," he said, fiddling with his large gold watch and staring at its face with as much intensity as he'd directed at Nevada moments earlier.

"I'd like her to see the treatment you sent me at the very beginning, Roger." Jeremy had returned, smooth and quiet as a really good server in a top-end restaurant. "She's signed the NDA. Email the treatment to her, please. And you'll get your full copy of the shooting script tonight," Jeremy said as he herded Tom and Roger away.

She knew that Roger wasn't pleased at all. She wondered, too, whether he thought there might be something else to it. Who was this woman, really, and why had she been brought in here? She could imagine a lot of them being jumpy; everyone was on edge since the bird pendant prop had disappeared. It felt like almost everyone was under suspicion. The whole place had eyes.

Nevada watched as the filming went on and marveled, as she always had on all the sets she'd visited since she was a kid, at the money spent. Television stations like the one where she worked back in Vancouver were expensive to run, yes, but they were bare bones compared to the typical movie production.

She sipped her latté—thank God you could get a decent cup of coffee in Savannah—and thought over the possible budget numbers for this film. It was top-of-mind for her because her own finances were in very rough shape. Her salary as news director at LV-TV was healthy enough, but her appetite for nice cars, hotels, and adventure travel had her out-go regularly outstripping her in-come in a take-no-prisoners way. Owen, on the other hand, always seemed to be on top of his finances, despite a loan for medical school that would probably stay with him for another fifteen years. He liked to keep their money separate and didn't think that damaged their marital togetherness. Nevada agreed; she was quite sure that it was one of the secrets to their success.

That night she dove into the treatment. Just two pages, what a blessing. She'd seen screenplay summaries that ran as long as thirty or forty pages, the creation of writers who weren't really sure what their story was, in her opinion. For the two cents that her opinion was worth, perhaps. Her job involved writing fifteen-second news reports, so of course she was biased on the subject of length. She sprawled across a striped armchair and started to read.

CHAPTER 9

Nevada had taken care that her father didn't see her again during the shoot at the plantation on her first day. The next day, when Tom spotted her leaning against the Tybee Pier sign and watching the movie trucks move into position, she patted herself on the back again for her decision to stay under the radar. He didn't look pleased, even though he'd now had a night to sleep on the idea.

"Good morning, Dad!"

Cheeriness was never a bad strategy.

He stopped in front of her, arms crossed across his chest and eyes at full angry glare. "I have three things to say to you, Nevada, and then I'll thank you to stay out of my way."

Apparently, sometimes cheeriness didn't work.

"One, I don't believe for a second that you're here to work on the script. Two, stay out of my way. And three, if this has anything to do with your mother and her demands . . . her unreasonable demands—"

"Oh, Dad, give me a break. Nothing has anything to do with Mom. It doesn't have much to do with you, either. It has to do with the director and what he wants, that's all."

Tom glared at her one more time, narrowing his eyes and projecting every bit of aggression he could summon up. Then he swept off toward his trailer and Nevada relaxed, as much as she could. She felt a little shaky, though, and when Jeremy stepped up to stand beside her and watch Tom go, she appreciated the shoulder-to-shoulder support.

"Don't let him bug you," Jeremy said. "He's playing a soldier and a commander in this one, and he's just trying to stay in character."

She smiled. "That's what they tell you in acting school, but the truth is for a lot of them . . . for him, at least . . . he's just choosing parts that let him play himself, over and over again."

Jeremy shrugged. "If he's that absorbed in himself, it keeps him from bugging the rest of us too much."

Okay, that made her laugh. Maybe this job wouldn't be so bad after all. "You know, I often wonder why I care about his opinion at all any more. God knows I'm old enough, it shouldn't matter."

"I think we're wired at birth—or in the first three years of life, anyway—like little ducklings, imprinting. Have you seen those ones in Memphis at the famous hotel? They're imprinted on their trainer, and they follow him from their home on the top floor into an elevator and down to the lobby where they swim around in the fountain all day then follow him back to the elevator to go home to go to bed. Crazy."

"So, I'm a duckling and Dad is a hotel employee wearing a uniform?"

"Yeah, whatever. Listen, I have one more task to add to this job description."

Nevada thought watching her father while doing research on a screenplay was a full work week as it was. She waited.

"I want you to move in with Tom to the house we rented for him in The Pines," Jeremy said.

"Move in with him? Jeremy, I haven't lived under the same roof as my father since 1983. This is not one of those families where everyone lives in each other's pants or manages each other's apron strings or whatever mixed-up metaphor you want to use."

He laughed. "I get that, Nevada, but I'm concerned about him. His girlfriend isn't here, he has no friends here, and he's not making friends with any of the new people he's meeting here. He's just going around being grumpy and then disappearing on me. I can't have that happening. It's only three months, but every single minute counts and the budget has absolutely no wiggle room. There's some mixed metaphors for you."

Nevada stared out toward the ocean. She and Owen hadn't really settled anywhere here yet; the hotel break-in hadn't done much toward making them feel at home, and the near future was very uncertain. Now that Owen was working at the hospital and she was on the movie they had to find somewhere to live for a few months. They would both have some rearranging to do with the details of their Vancouver lives and they needed more than a hotel room here.

"What did you have in mind?" she asked Jeremy.

"I talked to your father this morning. He doesn't want to stay in the Ardsley Park house, and I don't blame him. There are some very nice places available for longer-term rental over in The Pines, and I thought if we could organize one that's big enough that you and Owen would have your space and Tom would have his, the two of you could ride in to set together, and I'd have just a little more of a handle on his whereabouts and his ability to deliver, you know what I mean?"

Nevada certainly did know what he meant, and she mulled it over all morning as she watched the actors playing Union soldiers do take after take on the beach. At the break she called Owen, and he surprised her with a positive response.

"Well, we have to make a decision, Trip, and I was impressed with The Pines when we were over there for dinner," Owen said. "It would be a nice place to live for a few months . . . and that's really all it is, right? Just a tiny tick in the great sweep of time!" She could hear his smile over the phone and she was convinced.

She didn't expect that Tom would be, though. Hadn't he told her, not just hours ago, that he wanted her to stay out of his way?

Apparently, Jeremy had said something persuasive to him, and he sought her out at lunch.

"So I hear we're going to be roomies."

And, apparently, he took her agreement as a foregone conclusion. "Well, Jeremy approached me about it and offered me an incredible house on a lagoon with a view. The only catch is that I have to share it with you," she said, trying to set a tone of joking and taking it all lightly, right from the beginning.

"Actually, I'll be sharing with Owen," her father said. *Back atcha.* "We'll be watching a lot of basketball and golf, and you can bring us beers."

Nevada looked him in the eyes. "Really, Dad? You're cool with this?"

"I heard from my agent this morning. They've added it as a rider to their side of the contract. A condition of my continuing in this role, just because I was gone for a few days. Conrad says that, legally, they can do that."

He didn't sound pleased, and she decided to leave it be. "We'll have a great time, Dad. And yes, I will bring you beers."

"I've been edgy ever since that break-in at my first place, in Ardsley Park," he said. "That's why I took off for a few days. I can't hack it, if this new move turns out to be just as stressful."

"It will be fine, Dad."

"You will stay out of my way and treat me with the respect I deserve," he commanded. "Plus, if Clio decides to visit, you will welcome her. And if Judy pokes around at all, you won't tell her anything about me. Not even where I am! Do not tell Judy we are sharing a house or that you see me at all!"

Going to be interesting, Nevada thought. "Of course, Dad."

Tom looked down at his boots and, for just a moment, she thought he looked like a much older version of himself. "You don't think it's possible they're suspecting me of having anything to do with this jewelry theft, do you?"

"They're suspecting everybody, Dad. It'll be that way until they have a better answer. Don't stew about it—you have to focus on your role and on the movie. That's what Jeremy would say."

He met her gaze and then squared his shoulders. "Alright, then. You're right," he said in the deep voice he used for action climax scenes.

Nevada watched him walk away. No 'thank you' . . . but 'you're right' . . . now, that was a new experience, from him. She'd take it.

CHAPTER 10

The birds fluttered between the palm, the pine, the live oak, and the crepe myrtle trees, their shades of brown, black, white, blue, and yellow occasionally brightened with a flash of red from the wing of a passing cardinal. Their songs just made Nevada smile—when you stopped the noisy chatter in your own head long enough to truly hear them.

She put her feet up on the wrought iron railing and gulped her sweet tea. The temperature had been climbing since dawn, and everyone said this heat wave would be a record-breaker. The neighbors' cats were seeking out the shady spots even if it meant moving much more than they liked. She couldn't quite see the sizzle of heat on the air above the lagoon, but she could imagine it.

She'd been going to the movie set every day for a week now. The production company had rented several lovely homes in The Pines, as recommended for the execs who flew in periodically to check on things, and Jeremy had pulled a few strings to put Tom, her, and Owen into one of them.

What a situation! Rooming with her dad, after all this time. Owen was in favor of the plan at first but now that he'd had a chance to see more of the old guy's act, up close, he was annoyed most of the time. But Owen was away so much of the day that he hadn't had much time to register any real protest. This new challenge at the Savannah hospital was keeping him incredibly busy, and now he'd agreed to take on an additional teaching load. Nevada couldn't fault his work ethic and she knew he was happy with the new responsibilities at work.

Of course, it was easier for Owen since he was so seldom home. But for Nevada it meant more Tom than she wanted. Much more. No question, this stately house with its view of the golden salt marsh, and wildlife that people drove for miles to see, was far lovelier than anything that she and Owen could have afforded on their own.

The plan was that the filming would take only three months, but they'd doubled that to make sure no one would be evicted if they ran over-time. There were no short-term rentals in this community either, so it was 'take a six-month lease or go away'. Just one of many rules intended to make it a very secure place to be, definitely a priority for movie people all the time, and this crew on this shoot in particular.

Ever since the bird pendant had disappeared, everyone had been on edge. It seemed like everyone felt accused and under surveillance. Many people also had a "gut feeling" about who might have taken it. Chelsea in Makeup thought one of the extras, a local with an eye for an opportunity, had seen it and grabbed it. Sandra in Props thought it was an international antiquities ring that had been tracking the piece for years. Clearly, she was a wannabe screenwriter.

Nevada's curiosity had led her to the internet—as it did every ten minutes these days. The pendant that they were all so upset about, it seemed, was worth the concern. Crafted from molten gold and made by an artist in Cuba was the theory, although it might have been the Cayman Islands or Dominica. Taken from the islands by Spaniards in the late fifteenth century and then dispersed . . . one still held in Spain but often loaned to museums around the world, one brought back to America, and one a complete mystery.

The doorbell rang and interrupted her online journey. Her computer and her desk were at the back of this dramatically renovated house on Lone Heron Lane, overlooking the lagoon and about a mile of green lawn. The sun lit up the water and made it sparkle. As she got up to go to the front door, she saw a fish jump and then an osprey dive. On the grass, an anhinga sat, holding out its wings to dry. The cardinals looked like they were playing tag, their brilliant red feathers and black head markings gleaming like intricate native beadwork. Nevada was getting used to seeing the constant bird action here—used to it, but still amazed.

She walked to the front door and opened it to a stranger, a woman wearing something flowing and turquoise. Nevada had a long-time habit of stopping to take note of the one word that blasted into her mind when she first met a person. With this one, it was "color." Clothes, hair, shoes, jewelry. Color.

"Yes?" Nevada had never before been suspicious of people she didn't know, and she wasn't about to start now. Journalists have to talk to strangers all the time. Owen had questioned her about that, especially now that she was in the South, thought to be a riskier place with a more painful past than they were used to in Canada. Nevada believed that there was just as much risk and danger no matter where you might be. They shoot people in Calgary, they use knives in Toronto, and they do 'drive-bys' and 'home invasions' in Vancouver. If it's your time, it's your time, and it wouldn't matter if you'd spent the last however-many years hiding and being careful. If it wasn't your time, you could dodge danger with a smile on your face. That's what Nevada felt, although she rarely spelled it out, in so many words. In her world, reporters and senior managers were expected to be down-to-earth, serious, even more than a little cynical, given the facts and bad news they covered every day.

"Are you Mrs. Heintzmann?" The deeply tanned

woman was dressed in a flowered gauzy top and leather pants, with multiple turquoise bangles, massive hoop earrings, and hair an eggplant shade. She might have been fifty and she might have been ninety.

"No, I'm Nevada Leacock. But I'm married to Owen Heintzmann." Nevada hadn't been in the South very long, but she'd already picked up on the drive to distinguish between the married women and the available ones. Maybe it was pride of ownership for the wives, or maybe it was a shortcut for the predatory bachelors? On that she wasn't clear.

She had noticed this several times and found herself returning to it in her thoughts. Maybe that said more about her than about the culture here? Said more about the observer than the subject?

"This is for you. The delivery man left it at my place by mistake."

"Well, that's the first time *that's* ever happened." A quick look at the woman's face showed that this was exactly her sort of humor. Nevada glared at the unsolicited "free gift" package from some financial planning company, then shook her head. The woman at the door stood there longer than Nevada expected and then stuck out her hand.

"Cassidy Sullivan. Married once upon a time to Bobby Sullivan. Always liked the sound of Sullivan more than Smith, the name I was born into, plus it was a sunovabitch to change it back when we broke up. Why don't men ever change their names? 'Cuz they know what a pain in the ass it can be, that's why. Nice to meet a woman with a liking for her own childhood name. Some days I do wish I'd hung onto my own."

"You don't see that too much here in the South, I've noticed," Nevada said.

"No, you don't," Cassidy agreed. "Fact is, most of the married ones not only want to use the husband's name, they want that MRS slapped on everything too."

"As if it were some sort of prize they've earned?"

"Well, isn't it?" she said ironically. "And likely to be the only one?"

The two women grinned at each other in their mutual amusement. Nevada couldn't nail it down, but she was feeling a sort of vague familiarity about this woman. Maybe it was just her sense of humor and that they were simpatico. *Or should that be 'simpatica'? We say 'bimbo' not 'bimba', don't we? Sympatico is probably right.* Nevada was off on a vocabulary tangent, an occupational hazard ever since she'd started writing as a teenager. She realized that Cassidy was staring at her in an odd way and forced herself to re-focus.

Some people just pop up in your life, unexpectedly, randomly, and repeatedly, Nevada remarked to Owen later in the week. They both had Saturday off and, partway through a drive toward the outlet mall, they saw a sign for an estate sale and decided to stop by. Soon they were looking over the collections of a lifetime laid out on tables throughout the house. Nevada had never been much for going to garage sales or tag sales, but in Savannah it seemed to be as regular an activity as going to the baseball game or hearing some live music outdoors on one of the squares. Owen was in search of an antique clock to add to his collection, and when he suggested he skip the office on this Saturday afternoon, she had jumped at the chance to spend a little time together. The sight of Cassidy Sullivan, with her purple hair and turquoise bracelets, standing by a table full of cookbooks, was a surprise—and yet it wasn't.

"Why cookbooks?" Nevada asked.

Cassidy was startled to see her. "Hey. Well. Small world, yeah? It's not really cookbooks I want. I came by to look at the jewelry but there's too much of a crowd over there, so I'm just browsing here while I wait."

"Not an aggressive tag sale shopper then," Nevada observed as they both looked over a forty-year-old copy of a barbecue book.

"No, I believe the right item finds its way to the right

buyer."

"How very fatalistic of you." Nevada looked around the kitchen at the piles of battered cookie sheets and murky mugs.

"Karma." It wasn't clear whether Cassidy was agreeing with her or not.

"Do you collect any particular type of jewelry?"

"Pendants, necklaces, chokers—and I like bangles, as you can see." She gestured with her right arm, which displayed a ladder of metal circles stretching from her wrist to her elbow. "I also have quite a collection of buttons, a lot of Civil War stuff."

Nevada grinned. "And are you in it for the personal ornamentation and indulgence, or do you think your genius at spotting undiscovered masterpieces will bring you unexpected fortune, like my husband does?"

Cassidy grinned back. "Oh, the second one, absolutely. Just last weekend I found a garnet ring from the 1920s. That must be worth at least five dollars."

"Are you sure that's all? Maybe you should have someone else have a look at it." Owen said, coming up behind Nevada, some sort of miniature motor in his right hand.

"This is my husband, Owen. The doctor, asking for a second opinion."

"Hello, Owen, I'm Cassidy."

She seemed friendly but had a sort of detachment to her, Owen said that evening as they drove toward the restaurant and discussed the day. He agreed with Nevada that it was noteworthy, the way she'd popped up on her radar twice in such a short time. Random, yes, but still noteworthy. Nevada had enjoyed chatting with her but not so much that she'd decided to reach out. She wanted to wait for a while and see whether there would be a third meeting by chance. But she was still debating with herself about it; it wasn't often that she ran across another woman whose company she enjoyed, who seemed like a tranquil breeze—soft-spoken, understated, serene.

Very unlike the in-your-face-sandstorm that was Judith when she arrived at Eighteen Hundred to meet them for dinner.

"My God, what a ghastly place!" she announced after she air-kissed her daughter, gave Owen a hug, and dropped into a chair facing the pianist.

Nevada was instantly on the defensive. "Why, what's wrong with it? It's advertised at the airport as one of the oldest and most interesting buildings in the city." Then she had to spend a few moments silently berating herself for letting her mother still have the power to judge her and rattle her.

"Thank you, son-in-law," she beamed as Owen passed her a menu. "I have to say, I don't really get why people are so excited about all this history. Savannah Historic District. Savannah and Lafayette. Savannah and General Sherman. Savannah 250 years old, blah blah blah."

"That's because you're from L.A. You're from the youngest child side of the country." Owen spoke but didn't lift his eyes from the menu.

"And this place too!" Judith looked around the dark room. "Haunted, they say. Ghosts in the rooms upstairs. Ghosts where the stable used to be, or the kitchen, or something. You know, when I was parking the rental car, I saw a hearse go by, creeping by at about ten miles an hour, and there was a loudspeaker tour guide, pointing out a cemetery!"

"Mom, can't you just relax, be a visitor, get into whatever it is they want to serve you up? History is the thing here." Nevada reached for the basket full of warm biscuits. *Carbs as defense.* "One of the things. Cuisine is another."

"No, I can't. I am who I am." *No smile to take the sting out, show a little empathy or awareness of the irony.* "And California has nothing to do with it!"

"Say, Judith, if you saw the tour hearses, did you

happen to notice those bicycles going by? With a dozen people or so, peddling sideways and going forwards? I think they call them slo rides."

"Yes, I did. Looked like they were having fun. I saw one bunch who called out to me that they were celebrating one of them getting married."

"It's very popular for bachelorette parties, I'm told," Owen said. "I've never been invited, though."

Judith smiled. "Neither have I."

"We could try it, together, if you think it looks like fun. Nevada, what do you think?"

He was trying hard to get along with his mother-in-law, and it was working. *Why is my mother so easily charmed by others and not by me?*

And why did she judge her mother so rigorously? It was a two-way street, Nevada had to admit to herself, and she took another bite of biscuit to cover her smile. It was, but it had to have been built and opened by somebody, and Judith had been there first.

"Come on, Judith, you have to admit Savannah has a special something," Owen said. "It's got an air of calm and depth and dignity, no matter what is going on."

"Maybe because of the heat," Judith contributed. "Nobody wants to move too fast."

"So you don't like it." Nevada didn't put in the question mark.

"The only reason I'm spending more than half an hour here is to keep an eye on your father and try to figure out what he's up to."

"Mom, you've been divorced ten years. It's none of your business now."

"His cash flow will always be my business."

The server arrived at their table and was briefly confused by Owen's energetic shaking of his head. "Wrong, wrong, wrong."

Judith held out her open menu to the server. "I'll have this, this, and this. I'll think about dessert later." She continued talking while he went around the table for Nevada's and Owen's orders. "I got him his start, and he would have made a lot of mistakes if it weren't for me. I coached him on all his major parts, I chose his clothes, I did more for his image than his publicist did, and I navigated Hollywood for him. I gave up my career for him."

"You were a cashier at a drugstore, Mom."

"I was about to become an actress!" Judith's glare at her daughter could have scalded milk.

Owen decided to try to lower the emotional temperature at the table. "Judith, it takes some time to figure out how to be independent again, I know. But it's been a long time since the divorce. Why don't you find someone new and do all those things for him? Or her, for that matter? Find a new challenge, a new project . . . you say you're that good at it, go do it again. Or start up a new career for yourself, if you feel that you have talent that was wasted. "

"It's too late for me. I gave him my best years—why should I start over?"

"Why not?" Owen observed. "People do it every day."

"It's a lot of work, Owen, too much work. I'm not young any more. And why should I? It's time for me to cash in my chips, not start taking another big risk."

"But Dad has to take big risks, all the time. Annoying as he is, he works really hard—at least he tries to. He's got his agent hustling for him as much as he did thirty years ago. He has to make numerous career decisions, numerous choices about parts, constantly. Why doesn't he get to cash in his chips?"

"I've already told you how it was in the early days, how he owes me for everything he's got. Why aren't you listening to me?"

"Ten years ago, when you divorced, you got everything, Mom! He gave you the house, the summer house, the cars, the boat, the motorcycles, his tools, the furniture, and even his personal souvenirs!"

"Yes, well, he owed me then and he owes me now." Nevada had heard her mother touch on this topic many times over the past decade, but she'd never heard her be so direct and so bitter. *In vino veritas?* Maybe Judith had arrived at dinner one or two drinks already in? Maybe she'd decided that she was done with tact and diplomacy? Or maybe she was going to insist it was time for everyone to take sides?

Nevada had gone through all the biscuits and was eagerly awaiting the fried green tomatoes she'd ordered. "He's been paying you all along, Mom, even after you took all the stuff, and not just for a few years, until you got back on your feet."

"I deserve to live just as well as he does."

"Forever?"

"Yes."

"Even though you don't have the skills or the talent or the reputation or whatever he has that lets him make what he makes?"

"Yes."

"Even though the way he lives may not have anything to do with his real income or assets? What if he has nothing saved, for the day when he can't work anymore?" Nevada made eye contact with Owen. "That's highly likely, now that I think of it."

"Too bad for him." Judith had polished off her glass and was looking around the restaurant, trying to signal the waiter for another. "I'm having trouble getting by as it is, and he isn't sending me enough to cover my needs. I've told him we're going to have to have another visit to the judge."

"You won't get far with that one, Judith." Owen seemed mesmerized by this side of Judith that Nevada had told him about but he'd never before seen. "I've had friends and family go through this process, and it's standard that the agreement you signed is a final deal. You can't come along and re-open it every time you think you need more money or realize you messed up in managing what you've got."

Judith stared at him. "That's not what my attorney is telling me."

"Your attorney can't bill you for anything if you don't tell him to try taking action on something."

Judith did not like the way this conversation was going. "Well, Tom owes me, Nevada, in a way you just can't comprehend."

Owen wasn't done. "Think of it like a business, Judith. People negotiate the end of partnerships all time. He bought you out, in a way. You got stuff and money, now your business dealings are done."

"I don't accept that the financial marriage is over, Owen."

"But you signed a piece of paper. You said you were finished."

"I take it back."

Owen looked at Nevada in disbelief, and she almost laughed. As she'd often said, it was like talking to a child sometimes. Same thing with Tom.

"Mom, you sound like you're six years old. Come on."

"Well, anyway, I need some help from him. Or somebody. I'm in over my head and I need some help."

"What do you mean, in over your head?"

Judith sat up straighter and tried to look taller and older. "I'm not discussing that with you, young lady. It will be between your father and me. And just your father and me. Not you, and not that bimbo, Clio."

The waiter had finally arrived with her third cocktail, and she sipped at it.

Nevada saw her opening. "I think that's wise. Keep it between the two of you."

"I will say, though, that if he disappoints me—

again—you and Owen could be my next stop. Then, I'll tell you all about it."

Well, there's something to look forward to. Nevada made eye contact with Owen, and they both silently groaned.

CHAPTER 11

Nevada leaned against a battlement next to a cannon and stared out at the salt marsh surrounding Cockspur Island and this fort. The script pages scheduled for the shoot today came from a point about halfway through the story, when soldiers were discovering the disappearance of one of their officers.

Fort Pulaski was built in 1829 to secure the river lines of attack that might be used against Savannah, and it was named for Count Casimir Pulaski, a Pole who had died a hero during the American Revolution in 1779, some eighty-five years before the conflict in their story's spotlight.

She'd been up late last night, cramming facts so that she'd be ready for any challenge from Roger. The fort fell to the Federals in just thirty hours in April of 1862, after Union soldiers hauled thirty-six weapons, including ten rifled cannon with a range of more than a mile, across the sand and marsh of Tybee Island, at night and in silence, using them to bombard the solid brick walls.

She stared at the pitted brick. It was hard to imagine firepower that could cause damage to walls ranging from seven-and-a-half to fifteen-feet thick around the gunpowder magazine. Harder yet to imagine thirty hours hearing the sound of cannon fire. Nevada shook her head at the madness of it all—how and why had people ever decided that warfare was the way to resolve disagreement? Of course, she knew it was a lengthy, slow process; the story of the human race is one protracted story of combat. She would really rather not think about war or strife at all, but she was a firm believer in the adage that those who ignore history are doomed to repeat it. The problem was that there seemed to be an infinite number of variations in the ways that people could do battle. They didn't ignore history, they didn't repeat it, but they kept on inventing new methods for avoiding peace.

"So, your father is Tom Leacock." Sandra from Props leaned up against a wall alongside Nevada, ready to pass the time in conversation. There's a lot of time to be passed, waiting for setups on a movie shoot. She poured another half cup of coffee down her throat. "What's that like?"

Nevada had sculpted and polished many answers to that question over the years. It was complicated. When she was twelve years old, her dad had written her the only letter he'd ever sent her, a long one describing his feelings about not being nominated for any acting awards that year. She had replied, eagerly, but he'd never written again.

When she was sixteen, he'd called her on the phone to berate her for what he called 'slutty behavior' after a buddy had reported to Tom that he'd seen his daughter in a disco. The letter and the phone call were the only two communications she had from him after she reached puberty. Her mother told her he was one of those men who just didn't know how to talk to young people. Maybe. All she knew for sure was that for most of her life he'd been very remote. Remote, and for that reason, glamorous—like Antarctica, maybe.

Judith's rationalizations of Tom's treatment were kindly and comforting when Nevada was little, but as the teenage years went by and things got worse, her mother stopped trying to explain him or justify his behavior. Eventually, she became his biggest critic, and Nevada could pretty much predict the way any conversation about him would go. She wished she could get to a conversational place with her mother where the topics ranged only from the weather to recent books read or movies seen. But even when they did, her mother wanted to talk about how much nicer the weather was in Hawaii and how Tom could afford to go there and she couldn't; about the latest book on the 'men are pigs' theme; and about the plot of Tom's latest movie and how he was making a fool of himself by continuing to try to play the action hero or the leading man.

Nevada gave Sandra a smile. " 'All the world's a stage, right?' And to a man like Tom, everything is a story. Being his daughter means I have a part to play."

The story in this latest movie was about a Confederate officer who tries to protect a family's treasured heirloom, a golden bird pendant necklace, a symbol of the grace and beauty of the old South. At least, that was the story as Tom saw it, and as he described it to Nevada. In fact, when she read the treatment, she'd seen it quite differently. It was the story of a Civil War–era heroine who was forced to endure incredible suffering until she decided to buy survival for her family by turning over the necklace to the Yankees. Once she had her own copy of the shooting script and had time to go over it, line by line, however, Nevada redefined it in her mind as an allegory for the insanity of war and the inability of people to recognize true value.

Jeremy saw the story as something else. An officer in a conquering army had earned the 'right' to burn and destroy but chooses to preserve the South's treasures by stealing them instead.

"What do you think, Sandra? What's this story about?" she asked.

"Easy," Sandra said. "It's a story of forbidden love between a Northern man and a Southern woman, with an ancient necklace that keeps the story moving."

"It's about the tragic loss of a priceless work of art that is mishandled and allowed to be lost amidst a tide of people concerned with nothing but their own fortunes," a voice announced behind them. They turned to see Doyle O'Keefe, the insurance company official, glowering at them. "A story from yesterday and, it turns out, a story for today. I intend to find out where it is very quickly, though. It won't be lost for long."

"Isn't that the cops' job?" Sandra asked.

Doyle sneered. "I'm not going to wait around for results."

"Have you had much success in the past, Doyle? Recovering lost or stolen valuables?" Nevada asked.

"If I were a baseball player, I'd be batting a thousand," he bragged. "People usually leave a trail of some kind, and I've got the gift of sniffing it out and picking it up. Whoever took it can't have gone far, and I'll get it back in no time."

"Well, we'll all be celebrating when you do," Jeremy commented as he joined their group. "I can shoot around it for a while, but eventually we're going to have to have it—or some kind of replacement—back here on set."

"CGI?" Nevada asked.

"No computer-generated stuff would hold up to the kind of close-ups I had in mind for this beauty," Jeremy said. "But I'm confident that Doyle here, or the cops, will find it and bring it back."

CHAPTER 12

Donovan Howe sat in the Miami banker's office and signed his name to the papers, then Lillian leaned forward and added her name as guarantor to her grandson's loan. This was a lifetime dream, he'd told her.

Her grandson had been born with flippers rather than feet, practically. She remembered him as a jolly baby almost from the first day, sleeping, eating, and smiling in a regular rhythm that was a joy for everyone around him. Officially, he had learned to swim at three, although his mother swore that it was much earlier and that when she'd had him in a pool at ten months old and let go for a second, just to see, he floated and moved his arms and legs as if he already knew how. He grew up wanting to be near the beach every chance he got, and when it was time to choose a career and a life, he chose boats. He spent a lot of time alone, partly because of his job and partly because his looks didn't leave women wanting to beat a path or swim ten lengths to his door. He seemed very comfortable with that, though, a reaction Lillian understood very easily as she also prized her solitude and her independence.

Donovan had come to visit her in Florida and had stayed on, taking casual jobs in Miami, then catching on with every crew he could talk his way onto, every boat he could work his way aboard. He had captained a small fishing boat in Vancouver, but it was a lot better here he said, with the constant sunshine, the warm air, and the world built around the sea. He loved the colorful houses, the Cuban food and music, the sound of the surf, and the sparkling water almost as much as she did.

After they finished doing the deal to get him the boat, they decided to stop at a small sidewalk café to celebrate before driving back. Lillian threw her head back to bask in the sunshine; just as she did so, she saw a very handsome man turn to watch her. Tall, silver-haired, and wearing jeans that somehow looked like a Sunday suit, he was eating alone. She was starting to feel awkward about the concentration he was sending in her direction when he stood up and walked over to their table.

"Donovan? Donovan Howe?" He stuck out his hand, and Donovan rose to greet him.

"Mr. Brecklin! Hey."

"Small world," the man commented. "How is it I bump into you all the way over here on the other side of the continent? And please, call me Adam."

"Adam," Donovan said. "And this is my grandmother, Lillian Howe."

"Mrs. Howe," Adam Brecklin said, reaching toward her to shake hands.

"Ms.," Lillian said, stifling a weird impulse to curtsy.

Donovan looked back and forth between them, then turned to glance toward Adam's table. "Are you eating alone? Would you care to join us?"

Adam hesitated. "Well, I've already eaten . . ."

Lillian had a sense that he was undecided, and almost before she realized she was going to speak, she said, "What about dessert? Have you had your dessert, Mr. Brecklin?"

He smiled and the light went all the way up to his eyes. "What do I have to do to get you to call me Adam?"

Donovan jumped up and moved his chair to the left, then fetched one for Adam from a nearby table.

As they shared slices of key lime pie, she heard the story of how Adam had hired Donovan to crew on his boat *Viva Vancouver* a couple of summers back.

"Are you a fisherman, too, Adam?" Lillian asked.

He smiled in a sort of phony attempt to be mysterious. "Of a sort, of a sort."

Lillian took a bite of her pie and savored it, staring off over his head. Might as well try to enjoy the food, since the conversation wasn't going too well. Why was he playing games?

He picked up on the chill in the air immediately. "Did I say something wrong, Lillian? Is it best if I be a fisherman?"

His grin was so disarming that yes, she was disarmed.

"Alright, Adam," she laughed. "Alright. No, it's not 'best if you be a fisherman'. It's just that I couldn't understand why you didn't answer a direct question with a direct answer. I hate playing games."

"I'll keep that in mind," he said, forking up his pie with enthusiasm. "I'll be back up north again in July, Donovan. How about you join up with us again?"

"No, I don't think B.C. is on my radar again that soon, Adam. What about down here, though? You have anything going on down here?"

Adam looked at him thoughtfully. "I just might, I just might. Do you have a card?"

Donovan fished in his jeans and came up with a rumpled piece of white cardstock. Adam tucked it into the front pocket of his linen shirt.

"Well, we'd better be going, Donovan," Lillian said.

"Are you driving straight back, Grandma?"

"No, I've got a booking in South Beach to stay over one night."

"Driving back where?" Adam asked.

She smiled at him. "I live in Key West."

"I love Key West! Go there all the time, fishing's great."

"We have a few other features," Lillian said.

"Oh, I know." Adam had quietly signaled for the server during that brief moment of conversation, and the bill had appeared in a leather folder on a plate by his elbow. "I visit the Hemingway Museum and the Coastal Florida Museum there all the time."

"So do I!" Lillian couldn't help herself; his exclamation marks seem to invite some back. "Have you seen the jeweled bird pendant?"

"I have. One of the two birds in the bush . . ."

"And the third in the sand," Lillian finished.

"And is it worth the two in the bush?" Donovan asked.

"It definitely would be, if someone could find and retrieve it," Adam answered.

"I think it's fascinating, don't you?" Lillian asked Adam. He didn't reply and seemed distracted and, in a moment, she knew why. He reached into his front pants pocket, then pulled out a cell phone and stared at the screen.

"I'm sorry, I have to take this," he said, rising and walking off to a far corner of the restaurant.

Lillian watched him for a few minutes, then made a decision. "Well," she said briskly. "I think I'm ready to go, Donovan."

Donovan looked a bit confused. "We're leaving?"

"Yes, I think Mr. Brecklin will understand," Lillian said as she got to her feet, picked up her purse, and waved in Adam's direction.

"Oh, I get it now, Grandma. You're letting him know who's boss." Donovan grinned at her.

"Sshhh, I'm doing no such thing." She grinned back. "And please leave him the cash to cover our part of the bill."

Lillian said goodbye to Donovan as he climbed into his Jeep to head home. She picked her way through the traffic, the slow speed giving her plenty of time to take in the views of the high-rise luxury condo buildings and the boats on the Intracoastal Waterway. She was almost distracted by the sight of some of the super-yachts docked at marinas spotted throughout the area like sprinkles on a donut. Almost, but not quite; she was a very careful driver, and she'd already seen a few things in her lifetime. She wasn't about to be so impressed by some new sight that she lost her concentration on the road. She wasn't one of those white-knuckle, little-old-lady drivers, but she wasn't a flighty teenager with the attention span of a gnat either. She was going to get herself safely through Miami Beach and tucked into a nice parking spot and a cozy room near the shore.

South Beach was a neighborhood that was all about glamor and 'livin' large' for many people, but it also had room for many other types, including the 'oldsters' like herself.

Lillian was still working on a name for her demographic group. She got the echo of 'youngsters' in 'oldsters', and that wasn't too bad. She hated 'seniors'; it seemed like every commercial enterprise east of St. Paul and west of Minneapolis wanted to declare the senior age benchmark to be declining rapidly, as they tried to capture more market share by offering pancake dinners to 'seniors' over forty or discount transit fares to 'seniors' over thirty-five. She also hated 'older'—than what? Or whom? She was lukewarm on 'woman of a certain age', and 'mature woman' sounded like someone who hadn't had any fun since the 1950s. She couldn't figure it out; what did the Europeans do?

The art deco buildings on Ocean Drive looked like colorful parrots perched on a community branch. Three, four, five stories, just a low line facing the beach in the midst of towering high-rises that bookended the neighborhood. Holding the line since the 1920s, these hotels with names like *The Colony*, *The Winter Haven*, *The Carlyle* were obviously the colors of cotton candy, on first look, but when she inspected them more carefully, Lillian could see that they were also ... what was the word? Delicate, that was it! Delicate in a way that so many of the copies and 'retro' versions done in the 1990s and 2000s were not.

After she parked the car near her hotel, she walked over to Española Way, as she often did when she came to South Beach. It was a magical walk of patio restaurants, twinkling lights, happy people on foot, and no cars. The ocean was close by, and between the buildings, she could see the sunshine glistening on the waves. Later tonight it would be a view of a full moon, beaming down a silvery path on top of the water.

Many things about Miami reminded her of her hometown of Vancouver, oddly enough. Yes, it was a lot warmer and drier than the northwest coast, and there were no mountains. But both had the glimpses of the ocean, so fierce and open with a horizon miles away—watery wilderness right beside concrete and glass construction, covering the living and working activities of millions of people. Both had such a variety of people, with many nations, many languages represented—and both had some people living in unimaginable luxury and comfort, while others scraped the streets for what they needed to survive.

Lillian did not often think of those days in Vancouver when she was one of the ones at the low end; she didn't believe in dwelling on the past. But she tried to hold onto them, too, not thinking of them but just letting the memories be there, like an old chair in a corner of a room or a scent of lavender that came from a candle on a bookshelf. She knew she could remove them at any time, but she chose to leave them there as reminders of where she'd been.

It didn't hurt to think of those days of living in her car, but it scared her now, in a way that it hadn't at the time. Why was that? Maybe at the time she was just making it from day to day, from hour to hour, and she didn't have the strength to pull back the focus and see the entire picture. Maybe it frightened her to realize how close she'd come to falling off some sort of cliff, into a void.

Anyway, that hadn't happened. The unexpected bequest from the Vancouver television reporter whose death she had witnessed gave her the stability she needed. Her friendship with his two friends from the newsroom, Nevada and Chelan, had grown in the months after those events and she was grateful for it, but neither those connections nor her ties to family were enough to hold her on the West Coast. She was restless and eager to experience more geography before her allotted years were up, and so she set out for the opposite coast, for a new place and a new program of things to learn, thanks to her windfall.

The next day, Lillian checked out of the hotel, ready to enjoy every minute of her drive back to Key West. Just near Marathon, her phone rang. She pulled into a crab shack parking lot and took the call.

"Lillian, hello. This is Adam Brecklin, from the restaurant yesterday. I hope you don't mind me calling . . . I asked Donovan for your number. I know it was horribly impolite of me to take another phone call while I was sitting there with you, and I promise it won't happen again."

She could hear the smile in his voice, a quality she'd always appreciated. As the conversation went along, she found herself forgiving his lack of courtesy yesterday and remembering his abundance of charm. He told her that he was going to offer Donovan a contract to do some work for him, using his newly purchased boat, in the Miami area and around Key West too. He was particularly excited about the diving expedition he was planning to look at a Spanish shipwreck and wanted Donovan on board as soon as possible. By the end of the call, when Adam asked if he could look her up for a coffee or lunch the next time he got to Key West, she had decided that everyone deserved a second chance.

A second chance, but not a guarantee of success. Lillian was at the age now where caution outdid attraction most of the time. He seemed so nice and the whole situation seemed promising, but . . .

CHAPTER 13

S aint Patrick's Day dawned sunny and warm, perfect weather for the parade. Nevada had been hearing about the events on this day since she arrived in Savannah. It was said to be one of the oldest March 17 celebrations in the U.S., first celebrated in 1813 or 1824, depending on the source you consulted. It was also one of the liveliest and largest in the world, on a par with Dublin and Boston, although New York also had plenty to say about its zest for celebrating Irish antecedents, and she'd also run across similar claims from Tokyo, of all places.

Lots of local people insisted the Savannah event was the second largest in the U.S., although she had yet to see that verified anywhere. Doyle O'Keefe would say you could put that lack of confirmation down to a media conspiracy. It was Nevada's experience that there weren't nearly as many media conspiracies as those who felt misused by the media would like to think. Mostly, she had seen a lot more incompetence, mismanagement, and general screwing up than strategizing, power-grabbing, and attempts at puppet-mastery.

But all of her professional experience had been in Canadian media and, even though she'd only been here a short while, she saw the differences vividly and repeatedly. She wasn't used to being such a fish out of water and being unable to jump to her conclusions as quickly and comfortably as she was back home.

But maybe that was a good thing.

The days leading up to the parade weekend had been very wild downtown, she'd heard, although they'd been working so hard filming that she hadn't had a chance to take a look for herself. Traci said she'd heard that the color green was saturating the town—the clothes, the water in the fountains. Even the horses pulling the tourist carriages were in on the party, with their manes and tails dyed green. It was, she heard at first, just a big drunk, and she'd left those hard-partying days far behind decades ago. She felt sorry for those in their forties, fifties, and sixties who were still imbibing and behaving more like those nearer their beginnings than their ends.

But as the days went by, she started to see the St. Patrick's Day spirit looking more like a community event, although there were still plenty of references to the partying. As the Friday of the parade approached, the hotels downtown filled up; one article she read said that the population roaming through the Historic District would swell to about half a million people.

She was surprised when Jeremy called a day off for everyone but, as she went around town trying to do a few errands, she realized that almost everyone in town took that approach. Door after door had a *Closed for St. Patrick's Day* sign, and she began to see that he'd probably made a very smart boss move, letting the crew and extras have the day to themselves.

The parade was scheduled to start at ten a.m., but Owen said one of his patients told him that if you wanted to see it in person, arriving around eight or even earlier wasn't a bad idea. It would be on TV, apparently, but Nevada wanted to see the event for real. In her days as a TV reporter and news director, she'd watched many, many occasions in miniature, on a small screen or in a room full of monitors, and if she didn't have to do it for work, she'd rather not. In person was always better.

Bleachers had been set up along the route, and Nevada almost decided to cough up the cash to take a seat at the ones in front of the Cathedral on Abercorn. But Owen had convinced her that there was too much time spent sitting, in life, and that everyone would be a lot healthier if they stayed vertical more of the time, so she decided to save some money and burn some calories by choosing this spot on Bay Street. Sitting is the new smoking, Owen said.

So, they were packed shoulder to shoulder with families, teenagers, friend groups, and countless merrymakers of every description. Green was the one common theme.

"Nevada!"

She heard her name coming from two different directions and two voices, one male, one female. Well, great. And what were the odds? Of all the gin joints in all the world.

"Mom, hi. And Dad," she said, sending a silent pretend-threat in Owen's direction. He was rolling his eyes and clutching his throat in pretend-agony. Had they seen him? Did it matter?

Even with the crowds, Judith managed to stride up to them. She was a walking advertisement for that phrase 'own the room'. Wearing a green skirt and matching jacket that vaguely said 'Chanel', she leaned forward to give Nevada a hug, then nodded curtly at Tom.

Tom barely seemed to notice her, or even recognize her. That was a surprise. Nevada was under the impression that her mother's demands for more money were one of Tom's most absorbing concerns at the moment.

"Happy St. Patrick's Day," Judith said. "I think I hear them coming down the block. Wow, it's bright." She stepped in front of Nevada and started to fumble in her bag, coming up with a pair of sunglasses. Apparently, she planned to watch the parade from this spot. "And hot. Nevada, did you have to pick the warmest place on the route? Somebody at the hotel told me yesterday that there are places everybody knows about that will be in the shade.

That's where we should be, not here. Did you know it's such a big parade, it's going to take four hours to pass by?"

"Mom, it's springtime in Georgia. It's too warm for a suit that would be terrific for New York in February," Nevada said in as mild a tone as she could manage.

"You don't wear anything but black in New York, Nevada. You know that," Judith said as she fished deeper into her bag. Who could guess what she was looking for, but Nevada said a silent prayer that it wasn't spray sunscreen or insect repellent.

Tom was working his cell phone, sending texts and scrolling through messages. "Nevada, I need to talk to you about something."

"Oh, Tommy, it can wait until after the parade." Judith spoke over her shoulder without turning her head.

Nevada wondered how many divorced years it would take until Judith stopped speaking of Tom as if she still thought she owned him. She turned to look at the green crowd heading their way.

The only time Nevada remembered four hours going by any slower was when she was stranded in the Minneapolis airport decades ago, before some bright light got the idea to put in a club lounge and a massive mall where you could shop till your credit card company made you stop. It wasn't that the parade itself was slow or boring. True, it was unusual for a parade; there weren't that many floats, high school marching bands, or horseback riding clubs. But it was charming, in its way, and unique. What it mostly had was walking people, in groups, many of them following a clan sign. O'Haras. O'Riordans. O'Roarkes. Macdaniels, Maclarens, Macleans. Donegans, Lonnigans, Flannigans. Connors, Matthews, Finlays. It was also multigenerational, with elderly seventy-somethings leaning on baby strollers, pushing little ones barely a year old sitting forward, so straight and alert. Business men and women in suits and good shoes, with their green salute in a tie or a blouse. Teenagers with hair dyed green, maybe for this occasion alone, and maybe not.

There was a significant military presence too. Nevada watched line after line of marching soldiers pass by. Young women from the bystander crowd ran out to plant big kisses on the cheeks of the passing troops.

Tom seemed amused by the display. "What's that all about?"

"I read about it online, Dad. Long-standing tradition here. Women put on extra red lipstick, run out to give a kiss and flowers to the soldiers."

"Just the men soldiers?" Owen asked. Oh, he did like to stir the pot.

"How are you enjoying Savannah?" Judith asked. Funny how she took on that hostess tone no matter where she was, as if she owned it and she'd invited you to it.

"Love it, Mom. Very cool."

"We especially like the house we're renting," Owen contributed. "It's huge, the three of us are rattling around in it."

Thanks, honey.

"Three? Who else—oh, I see," Judith said after making eye contact with Tom. "Your father is staying there too?"

"We'll be four pretty soon, actually," Nevada said. "My friend Chelan Montgomery from Vancouver is coming down for a long weekend."

"Father staying, friends staying ... sounds very sociable, Nevada," Judith said.

Shoot, was she going to ask for an invitation?

"For myself, I prefer an upscale hotel," Judith said. "The linens, the maid service, the concierge. In case you were wondering."

Whew.

"Tom!" Jeremy Walsh, his rugged, outdoorsy face shaded only slightly by a Boston Red Sox ball cap, was calling to them from about six feet down the sidewalk. How did this man end up as a director, rather than a movie star? He certainly had the looks to be front of the camera. But perhaps not enough patience? Or need for attention?

Tom barely looked up from his phone. "Hi there, Jeremy. Sorry, I'm just in the middle of something. But here, join us. Everybody, meet Jeremy, my director. Aren't you staying somewhere near here?"

Jeremy nodded. "I was planning to stay at the house and get some notes done. Got an appointment at five to review the past week's footage. But this parade was going right past my window, so I decided to surface and take a look."

"Are you rethinking your decision to rent a house in the Historic District rather than get something farther out and little quieter?" Nevada asked.

Jeremy grinned. "Not really. I'm away—on set—sixteen hours most days anyway. And these old houses are all haunted, they say. I'm looking forward to an encounter with a spirit."

Nevada shot him a quick look. Was he serious? She'd assumed he had the same well-educated, sophisticated outlook on ghosts and goblins that she and Owen had. Fine for the tourists. Fine for entertainment and for generating adrenalin-on-the-cheap-and-quick in horror movies, but not anything serious people thought about.

Tom pocketed his phone and straightened his shoulders in a signal that he was ready to join them all, and take over. "Well, I'll tell you, there was something spooky going on in that first house I was in. The housekeeper gave me an earful about what she'd seen and heard there—drawers opening and closing, shadows in corners, smells of perfume . . . and burning toast, one day! I am happy to be where I am now."

So, maybe it wasn't quite a declaration that he was pleased to be in Nevada's company because of her, specifically, but at least he wasn't complaining about the new arrangement.

"Was that why you took off from that first place?" Owen had the binoculars up to his eyes, and he wasn't looking directly at Tom when he asked the question. But his tone of voice made it clear that he *was* asking the question. "I forget, did we ever hear where you were or why you went?"

"Took off when?" Judith perked up like a dog spotting a squirrel. "Right in the middle of a shoot? Where did you go, Tom?"

"Hey, look, here comes Uga!" Jeremy's attention was on the parade, and clearly he wanted everyone else's there too.

Worked for Judith. "Uga? Who is Uga?"

"University of Georgia Bulldogs' mascot. UGA. Best-known mascot in the college football world," Tom said, obviously happy to have the spotlight shifting from him. Not his usual response. Nevada didn't mind that her father had slid out from under the questions right now, but she intended to raise the subject again once they were back at their rented house at The Pines.

The buzz through the crowd around them, particularly among the children, showed that Uga was a crowd favorite. The bulldog trotted along down the middle of the street and almost looked as if he were nodding to acknowledge the cheers and applause.

"He's the ninth in a line of bulldogs that goes back to the mid-fifties, all raised by the same family," Owen said. "Lives a life of luxury in his own room in the house, rides the four hours from Savannah to the games in Athens in his own bright red, air-conditioned car, wears a jersey just like the ones they give the players—a bit smaller, of course. Uga was on the cover of *Sports Illustrated* in the nineties. His painting is over the fireplace mantelpiece in the living room at home."

Nevada whirled around to look at her husband. "How do you know all this? Oh, I get it," she said as she spotted his phone in his hand.

Owen grinned at her. "And he gets a suite at the hotel when he goes to the games. Let's get a dog, a mascot dog."

"And start going to every college football game?" she laughed. "Who are you, and what have you done with my husband?"

Her face fell the instant she saw Tom glaring at them, and then she noticed another laser beam of disapproval coming at them, this one from Judith. What? Was it Owen's question about Tom's whereabouts? Her neglecting to mention to her mother that her father had been gone for a few days?

"So have I told all of you the update on the bird pendant case?" Saved by Jeremy, once again.

"No, what's happening?" Tom asked, at the precise moment that Judith chimed in, "No, what bird pendant case?"

"We've had a theft from the movie set," Jeremy told Judith. "A family heirloom that goes back more than a thousand years. Worth about three million bucks . . . although nobody knows for sure, since it's never been on the market."

"What's happening?" Tom repeated. "Has it turned up?"

"No, but apparently the police are working all of the better-known fences and collector rings," Jeremy said. "But the latest is that another one has gone missing."

"Another one what?" Owen asked. "Another bird pendant?"

"Identical one," Jeremy said.

"Three of them were made by an artist somewhere in the Caribbean islands hundreds of years ago," Nevada said. "One was lost at sea, one is in a museum in Spain, and one, this one, has been owned for generations by a Michigan family that acquired it sometime during the Civil War." She stopped when she saw all of them staring at her. "What? I read it in a book. Several books. Part of the background for the movie."

"All correct," Jeremy said. "Except that the one that was in the museum in Spain was on loan to a museum in Florida, in Key West."

Key West. Nevada remembered that her friend Lillian, the lovely retired lady from Vancouver, lived in Key West now. Ever since they met during Nevada's TV station's coverage of its star investigative reporter's death, they had stayed in touch. Nevada liked to take Lillian out for a burger with triple sauce and listen to her stories about back-in-the-day in Vancouver and in Toronto. Lillian liked to give Nevada advice about men and marriage and ask her questions about the choices made in the news reports she saw on LV-TV. Then Lillian had decided to leave the wet weather and the family interference behind and head to the bright lights of Florida. She'd sent Nevada a few postcards from her new subtropical home, and it definitely looked like a place you'd want to visit.

"There you go," Judith said. "In a museum in Florida. Borrow that one for a few months."

"Good idea," Jeremy continued. "Except for the fact that that one has been stolen too."

That was a conversation-stopper. Nevada could see that he was enjoying building the suspense, keeping them all hanging on. A storyteller at heart.

"Yesterday, the museum security guard opened up at ten a.m., as usual, and found the alarm system disabled, the glass case shattered, and the pendant gone."

"And where's the third one?" Judith asked.

"At the bottom of the ocean, lost there since the fifteenth century or so," Jeremy answered. "That's one theory but really, it's a mystery. It's never been found."

"What about video?" Owen suddenly contributed. "If there was an alarm system, there must have been video surveillance at the Florida museum."

"There was," Jeremy said. "Camera lenses were covered. We had video surveillance set up in the props trailer where we were keeping our bird pendant too."

Nevada felt Tom stiffen beside her. "And was the camera covered up there?" she asked.

"No, the camera worked, and they got the video. Cops are looking at it now."

"What will you do now, for the shoot, if borrowing another necklace is not an option?" Judith asked. "Use the footage you've already got?"

"He goes back to what he should have done in the first place," Tom grumbled. "Get somebody to make a paste copy and use that for the movie. I've never heard so much hysteria about a prop, for god's sake!"

"Tommy, you're being rude," Judith put in, always ready to correct his behavior. It was an exchange, a skirmish, really, that Nevada had been watching since she was a child.

It might have been regular fare, but it appeared that today it was not a day that Tom Leacock could or would stomach it.

"Nevada, I have something to take care of—I'll be back in a little while," he said, then gave Owen the young-guy shoulder-to-shoulder hug.

"Something I can help you with, Dad?" Nevada asked.

"No, just a quick errand. Get in, get it, get out."

"Tom, you're spoiling the party. Don't you want to see the rest of the parade?" Judith didn't turn to look at him but tossed the question over her shoulder as she watched the Savannah Shamrocks Rugby Club march by. He snarled some incomprehensible word and stomped off through the crowd. Nevada wouldn't have sworn to it, but she thought she saw the edges of Judith's mouth twitch in a smile.

"Don't worry about him," she said to the director. "He's rather unpredictable."

"I've noticed," Jeremy said.

"He and Nevada have switched roles," Judith said. "She's the grown-up now, and he behaves like an irresponsible, moody teenage girl sometimes."

Sharp tongue, Mother, Nevada thought. Evidently Jeremy thought so too, as he gave her a rather fake smile and made an excuse to leave a few seconds later.

By the time Nevada and Owen reached the Diamond Causeway on the way home after a special-occasion lunch that included a few beers dyed Irish green, they were feeling the fatigue of a day that had started at five a.m. When her cell phone buzzed, she was inclined to ignore it, but her dozy glance at the screen showed Jeremy Walsh's name and she decided to pick up.

"Hey, Jeremy."

"Nevada. I hope I'm not interrupting anything?"

"I wouldn't have answered if you were."

Jeremy laughed. "True. So, here's the thing. I'm thrilled you're on set with us, keeping an eye on Tom, and giving him some stability at the house."

"You're welcome."

"I just wanted to ask you to watch him even a little more closely."

"Why? What do you mean?" She looked over at Owen, who raised an eyebrow at her. She rolled her eyes; this was starting to feel like it was over the line, even with the two salaries she was being paid. Hadn't this Savannah stay started out as a month of time off?

"He seemed skittish to me before, just unreliable, and I was trying to put in place a few extra supports, a little insurance, you know? But it's gone beyond that now, I think. At the parade this morning, he seemed outright hostile, very jumpy."

"Well, that's the effect my mother always has on him."

"Very funny, but—"

"Not meant to be a joke," Nevada replied.

Jeremy cleared his throat. "Alright. Well. Just keep him in your windshield, okay? What's he doing now?"

"Well, I don't actually know."

"He's not with you?"

"He is not," Nevada said. "He met us at the parade, said he had his own car. We offered him a ride, but he didn't want it."

She heard a sigh. "Okay, well, we might need to assign him a driver. Most of the big stars want one—I don't understand why he's been resisting the idea."

"He's actually been talking about getting a motorcycle."

"What?"

"Jeremy! Calm down. That *was* a joke."

Owen turned into their driveway then put up the garage door and drove in. No sign of Tom and no sign of Tom's rented car. Nevada opened her car door and got out, still talking. "Look, I'm sure he just stopped somewhere on his way back, and we'll see him shortly. He's made it all the way to seventy-five years old, and I think you're worrying just a bit too much."

"You try carrying the responsibility for a two-hundred-million-dollar movie, then we'll talk," Jeremy said.

"Point taken," Nevada conceded. "I'll text you when he gets in. Do you want to talk to him?"

"No, just want to know he's there. Thanks, Nevada."

"Hey, do you want to take a walk?" she asked Owen as she went into the kitchen and started to unload the dishwasher. She saw a piece of paper on the counter, and as she stopped to read it, she didn't hear his reply.

"Are you ignoring me?" He came up behind her and put his arms around her. "I said, do we have any leftovers of that pasta you made the other night?"

"What? Sorry, honey, I wasn't paying attention. Look at this," she said, pushing the note in his direction.

Nevada, I'm off for a while. Got a few matters that need my personal attention. I've let Jeremy know, and he's made arrangements. Not sure when I'll be back. Keep my stuff here—I'll pick it up later or send somebody to get it.

Wasn't he on the call sheet for tomorrow? Nevada

was sure he was. And if he'd let Jeremy know and arrangements had been made, why had Jeremy called her not ten minutes earlier, asking about Tom's whereabouts?

She'd known her father to pull many stunts over the years, but this had to be one of the strangest. Definitely the one that had had the most impact on her life. For decades now, she'd been nothing other than a bystander, an observer of her father's life, and he of hers. But within a few weeks, she'd found herself living in a house, doing a job, hanging out with people, immersing herself in studying a war, dodging decisions about returning to her regular life . . . and it was all directly linked to her father. Now she was here, and he was gone. What the hell?!

Should she stay or should she go?

GAIL HULNICK

CHAPTER 14

When Nevada invited her to take a break from this year's incessant rain in Vancouver, Chelan Montgomery was skeptical about the distance to Savannah. She wasn't even sure she could find it on a map! And what would she do with her time while Nevada was working? Most important, could she handle the heat while she was five months pregnant?

But come on, people had lots of babies in Georgia—and survived. Plus, it was only March, not July; the weather wasn't *that* hot. These were the reassurances offered by her husband, Drew. For a week or so, she watched the weather report from Savannah, the temperature climbing and the sun always shining. Then when Nevada repeated the invitation and that coincided with Drew's mother asking her what she might like as a pre-baby birthday gift, she spoke up for a plane ticket. It wasn't hard to decide—big house, too big for three people; historic city with a reputation for hospitality and charm; close friend wanting to pamper her for a few days—why would she say no?

Chelan was not a novice traveler, but she wouldn't call herself expert either. She was comfortable with the lining up at the airline counter, the marching through security, and the hierarchy of boarding. Follow orders; yes, sir; yes, ma'am. She had no fear of flying, but she knew that many of her fellow passengers did, and it was that fear that made the whole system work. She doubted that obedience and loyalty were the guiding motivators in

104

making all these people so compliant.

She rang her fingers through her red hair and gave it a shake. It was growing so fast since she got pregnant that she almost thought she could see it lengthening, inch by inch, while she watched herself in the mirror. One of these days, she'd just get the whole thing cut off . . . maybe as soon as the baby came. She'd heard enough stories about the sleep deprivation and nonstop activity of those early days that she doubted hair styling could be her top priority.

Drew had a client he needed to see in Toronto, so he'd flown with her this far and then seen her off at Pearson Airport. She had a feeling he'd cooked up the Toronto appointment, just to go along with her for part of the journey and make sure that she would be alright. Funny how a move that, pre-pregnancy, might have struck her as overprotective and sexist seemed endearing right now.

Chelan had no fear of flying, but her fear of authority kicked in whenever there were borders to be crossed, even though she was pushing thirty years of age and had crossed many borders in her lifetime. Going to the U.S. from Toronto, you followed instructions that took you up and down corridors and sometimes escalators, pulling your possessions along behind you in an effort to save a little money and time by not checking the luggage and letting someone else handle it. You met uniformed officers before entering the security line where you deposited your purse, your carry-on bag, your laptop computer, your jacket, and your shoes for inspection. Then you walked through a device that somehow (Chelan wasn't really clear on the science) confirmed that you weren't carrying any lethal weapons and weren't a danger to your fellow passengers or the flight crew. You proceeded to the U.S. border that runs through the airport, in theory, and you met another uniformed officer who examined your ticket and ID, stared into your eyes, looked back down at your photo, asked a few questions, then wrote some cryptic mark on your boarding pass.

This day, Chelan's honesty, but more significantly, her fear of being caught got her. Yes, she answered the question from the short, round officer, yes, she had food. "A banana and some dates", she was about to clarify, and hand the stuff over, if ordered to. But instead, he said, "Booth number two" and handed back her piece of official paper with a big X scrawled across it.

Booth Number Two, where was that? Chelan looked around the cavernous room, panicking. She didn't see any Booth Two, but she did see video cameras everywhere, tracking every traveler's every move. She wasn't doing anything wrong, but she just had this deep feeling that if she did, even for a moment, the videotape proof of her infraction would be instantly available to the authorities and would turn up on some yellow-rag TV show or online, to be looped and repeated endlessly. Never mind that even at important trials, key videotape was often lost due to human error, and never mind that millions upon trillions of feet of video were shot every day, she had no doubt that in her case, a photo of her making a mistake would never be lost. Paranoid much?

She couldn't find Booth Number Two anywhere, so she went back to ask. Impatiently, the border control officer indicated a direction behind him, where there was nothing but a set of double doors. Chelan knocked at the right one hesitantly and, when nothing happened, she gave it a push.

On the other side was a scene of chaos. Dozens of people, each with far too much luggage.

She found the place to pick up a number and sat down to wait her turn. Thirty minutes later, an officer called her name. How long would this take? She had another forty minutes until her plane was scheduled to take off. This man was even more unpleasant than the first, accusatory and yet bored at the same time. Why did she find them all so intimidating? If she had ever met any one of them at work or even in a public place, she wouldn't be daunted. She'd discussed this once with a group of women, and one of them had tried to sum up the core of it when she said, "They're in charge and they have guns."

Chelan had tried to argue the point. "They don't have real guns. Well, okay, they do have guns, but they're not going to *shoot* you."

"They might. Otherwise, why have guns?"

"So nobody shoots *them*." It was one of those logic traps that seem inescapable and yet made out of nothing but smoke somehow.

Chelan stood in front of the officer's desk. She was determined to stay placid and get out of here without any further problems, not like the supermodel who had called a flight attendant who tried to control her a "basic bitch" and ended up thrown off the plane and banned from the airline for life. She answered the questions politely and was told she could keep her banana. The dates required discussion with another officer, details shouted across the room from one desk to another. Permission was eventually granted, and Chelan was told it was a good thing she'd said 'yes' in answer to the food question, even for one banana and six dates; if caught, it would have meant a five hundred dollar fine.

Twenty minutes until flight time. The officer finally scribbled something on her customs receipt and handed it to her without making eye contact. He pointed toward a hallway leading out of the interview room, and Chelan rushed toward it. A sign reading "To Gates" was the cheeriest thing she'd seen in the past hour, and she hurried toward it. The next customs officer was even faster. He stepped from a door that opened into the hall and moved directly into her path.

"Stop. Where are you going?"

Chelan pointed to the sign, unable to speak. She held out her receipt toward him, but he ignored it, looking over his shoulder toward the room he'd just left and grinning at someone inside. Was he laughing at her? Just practicing being a border guard? Going to stop her, at this point? Seriously?

He stepped back, and she scuttled along the hall toward another set of double doors. She pushed through them and joined the river of passengers in the main corridor, heading toward any one of a dozen normal, regular airport places that seemed like paradise to her right now—a souvenir store, a spa, a bookstore, an information desk, a restaurant, a boarding lounge. It all looked so ordinary, while the hallway and rooms she'd just left seemed so sinister. Was it just because it was an unfamiliar experience? Would she be much less anxious if it were her second or tenth time? She hoped she'd never find out.

Chelan looked down at her curvy middle. *Hey, Baby Drew, I'm pretty sure we're not in Kansas anymore.*

By the time she landed in Atlanta, her nerves were settled, thanks to her earbuds, some Beyoncé, and a nice conversation with her seatmate after they landed. That conversation was her first tangible proof that she really was leaving the Great White North for the South. Instead of that accent that Canadians are convinced is no-accent-at-all, she was hearing the melodic drawl that made her think of moonlight, strings of lights around a deck, and a riverfront nighttime picnic. Well, hush mah mouth.

"You headin' home or goin' on a visit?" The man smiled at her with just the right tone of neutral courtesy as he stood up in the aisle and pulled his bag down from the overhead bin.

"Visiting friends in Savannah," she said, noticing his jacket, tie, and briefcase. "Are you here for work?"

"Yes, ma'am," he said, pulling her carry-on bag down too. "There you go."

Her bag was tiny, compared to some of the others she saw people hauling up the airplane aisle. Drew had insisted on unpacking half of what she intended to bring, saying that a pregnant lady shouldn't plan to drag so much luggage around—it was bad for the baby. She had invited him to come along, but he said no, somebody has to stay here and earn some money.

The Atlanta airport, she'd been told, was the largest and busiest in the world, and today it certainly seemed as though half the population of Georgia must be hurrying up and down these hallways. Correction: some hurrying, but a lot taking their own sweet time. And she'd never seen so many people being pushed in wheelchairs.

Chelan heard the loudspeaker crackle into action. "Pagin' Mistuh Walkah Mayah Junyuh." If she was feeling any doubt that she was in the South, it was gone now.

Finally, she got to the end of Terminal F and found her way down the escalator to the plane-train, which whisked her over to the B gates, where her connection to Savannah was already boarding. Ten minutes later, she was settled into 10A, looking out as the ground crew drove around the parked aircraft, loading and unloading bags. A huge man walked slowly up a ramp, his uniform much too tight and warm in the heat outside.

Inside and across the aisle from Chelan, what looked to be a much younger man sat, staring down at his cell phone. Certainly, he was a much fitter one, his biceps bulging under his black T-shirt. He looked like a football player—a Falcon, maybe, since the tarmac they were sitting on was in Atlanta. His hair was done in dreads, long enough to reach his waist, and coiled in a bun at the back of his head. He was intimidating and would be anywhere, but no doubt was particularly thought-provoking on a football field. After a few minutes, one of the flight attendants came and spoke to him, then Chelan watched as he stood up and followed her to a seat in First Class. She carried his bag.

She looked out the window again at the airline employee trudging around outside. What was it that put one in First Class and one in minimum-wage purgatory?

Had the guy in the dead-end job once shown promise on a high school football field? What had happened to him?

The flight from Atlanta to Savannah was to be very short, only about half an hour from wheels up to wheels down. Chelan watched the view the whole way, and in the busy airspace outside Atlanta she saw two other planes in midair going past. Whenever she watched an airplane from the ground, passing overhead, her main thought was of grace and power, but looking at one sideways, from inside another plane, the overwhelming shock was speed—how incredibly fast they move. As the minutes went by, she found herself gazing down at fluffy popcorn clouds, then at forests and estuaries as the aircraft began its initial descent. In the final few minutes before landing, she could see residential neighborhoods, the turquoise boxes of swimming pools, the broad, gray flats of parking lots, and the sweep of the Savannah River, with what looked like an immense cargo-loading facility dominating one end of the shore.

The pilot set the plane down with a little too much enthusiasm, and everyone braced themselves with a hand against the seatback in front and toes digging into the floor. Through the window, she could see a small airport with about half-a-dozen jets parked at the gates.

Once inside, her impression of a small airport was reinforced. But it was more than small—it was delightful. Cozy boarding lounges, people strolling rather than racing and jostling one another, an ice cream parlor and a bar in the wide hallway that led to the arrivals area, palm trees, park benches, a grand piano, a vaulted ceiling, and a massive antique clock—it almost felt as though she'd dozed off (and she had, quite a few times on the plane—she was a pregnant woman, after all) and awakened in 1935.

Nevada greeted her at the edge of the 'passengers only' area, just a few feet from a sign that stated "No weapons allowed beyond this point". They made eye contact and then hugged, Chelan feeling very happy that she'd decided to visit. She followed her friend out past a fountain featuring torrents of green water and along the lane of parked cars.

"How long a drive?" Chelan asked.

"About twelve miles," Nevada said. "I thought we'd cruise through the historic area downtown first, then go to my place."

The drive from the airport was nothing much, but once the Savannah College of Art and Design buildings came into view, the picture improved. Chelan was entranced with the historic architecture and the live oak trees, and by the time they reached the riverfront, with its cobblestone streets and riverboat queens, she was in love.

Nevada parked and guided her into a boutique hotel with a sidewalk café near the water. In the distance, Chelan could see a convention center and upscale chain hotel on the other side of the water. She thought she saw another entire building moving against the horizon and then realized she was looking at a massive cargo ship loaded with containers.

"Beautiful place, Nevada," Chelan said. "Thanks again for inviting me."

"Thank you for coming here," Nevada said. "I know it might seem like a long way . . ."

"I love to travel," Chelan said firmly. "How do you like it here? How's the weather?"

"Fabulous. Winter seems to consist of a few cloudy days and wearing a sweater once in a while. I'm told the summers are really hot and humid but, of course, I haven't seen that. And that the thunder and lightning storms can be pretty intense, but I like electrical storms, so I'm looking forward to that."

Chelan looked around. "Well, this is certainly a beautiful way to take a break from the Vancouver rain."

"Yeah, that's true, but there's a lot I miss about Vancouver too. The low cost of health care and the size of the social safety net, for two."

"What don't you miss?"

"The real estate prices. The winter weather."

"What's the story back there, Nevada? Did you quit your job in the newsroom?"

Nevada shook her head. "Leave of absence. It started out to be a trip to Savannah to be with Owen for his medical conference but it morphed into a freelance contract on a movie set. I have to admit that the time away has me thinking about future, though. I feel like some kind of change is in the wind."

"Have a baby."

"Hah. That would be a drastic solution." Nevada laughed. "Not sure it's technically possible, at this late date . . . wouldn't be easy, anyway, although I guess there have been some my age who haven't let that stop them."

Chelan gazed at the menu as though mesmerized. "Well, if you need somebody to talk to, I'm here. So—I think I have to start with dessert right now. Would you go for peach cobbler or key lime pie?"

"How about both?" Nevada asked with a laugh. "You're eating for two."

"I am!" Chelan exclaimed. "Thank you for the permission. And thank you again for inviting me."

"Well, I'm hoping you'll have a lovely getaway weekend, but I'm also hoping I'll get a chance to lean on you for some research help too."

Chelan smiled. "Absolutely. I'd love to. What's the project?"

"I'm sort of researching, sort of re-writing for this movie script about the Civil War, and I've got a detailed list of questions that needed answering. I thought we could divide them up and go searching—I'd like to have at least three, maybe four sources on everything. If we could find some primary source material, that would be awesome."

"Sounds intriguing. And fun. I'm in," Chelan said, then gave the server her dessert order.

Nevada stared out at the river traffic. "I have a couple of other searches I'm doing right now that you could help with. We've had a theft on the movie set, a valuable family heirloom that was loaned to the production company for this shoot. Nobody's making any progress on solving the thing, and I wonder whether we might turn up something online that could help."

"What sort of thing?"

"I don't know, exactly. Maybe something in the history of the bird pendant itself? Maybe something about similar crimes on other movie productions in the past?"

"It's a bird pendant? What kind of bird?"

"I didn't actually see it myself, only photos. It's sort of a generic-looking water bird, but the lines are very graceful, especially around the neck and head. Made of gold." Nevada shook her head at Chelan's offer of a mouthful of her dessert. "I don't know, how would you hunt for something like that? And if somebody were to be falsely accused of taking it, how would you go about clearing somebody's name?"

"Whoa, there's a curveball," Chelan said. "Who is accused of taking it?"

"Nobody, officially, yet," Nevada said. "But they're turning the spotlight in my father's direction."

"He's acting in this movie, isn't he?"

Nevada nodded. "He's had all the opportunity in the world, and lately I've been hearing that he might have had the motive. Money problems."

"Has he ever been involved in anything like that before?"

"Never. But—it's not looking good. He's taken off, which just sends the message that he's guilty, doesn't it?"

Chelan shrugged. "Maybe, maybe not. Depends why he went, where he's gone, what he's doing."

"I have no idea why or where. And it all looks very suspicious."

"I know, right? But there's an answer, and I'll help

you find it," Chelan said.

"I don't think I want to look," Nevada said.

Chelan stared at her for a few minutes. "I know. Sometimes a parent asks too much, and you have to say no. But I don't think that's this case."

"Why not? Because he is who he is?"

"Because you are who you are. You wouldn't be thinking and re-thinking it like this, Nevada, if it weren't biting you, if you were ready to just brush him off."

"It just feels like the right thing to do, you know?" Nevada didn't look happy about this conclusion, but she did look convinced.

"I know," Chelan said, smiling at the server who'd arrived with two plates full of treats and two forks. "Then let's go to work. I can get a lot done in a couple of days."

"You're sure you don't mind? I have to apologize, too, that I will have to be going to work at the movie set and you'll be on your own at the house quite a bit."

Chelan shook her head and smiled. "I don't need babysitting."

"Unlike my dad."

"Unlike your dad."

CHAPTER 15

You take your chances where you find them. That's good advice when you're speaking to a millionaire but it is especially true if your words are being heard by someone finding himself short of money.

Working the nine to five, punching the time clock, that's never been your thing. If all you want is security, get a blanket. But if you want wealth, livin' large, you have to take risks, keep your eyes open, accept that you are nothing like all the other guys.

Accept it, and make sure nobody forgets it.

The chances come along much more often, and faster, if you have them all believing you are rare, indispensable, one of a kind. If they so much as hint that they think you can be replaced, you quit. You don't care if that makes the cash flow a little irregular some times. It's worth it, to make sure nobody forgets you are unique.

They won't forget it if you are unpredictable. They won't forget it if you don't seem to care about the things everybody else cares about. And they won't forget it if you display wealth and control over things that no one else has. Or, if not 'no one else', very few people.

The cars that very few people have. The houses, clothing, jewelry, fine art, experiences. They all cost money but having them brings in more money.

You can get a bit mixed up about the direction of the flow, but generally you just want to keep it moving. Collect, trade, sell stuff, buy more stuff. Keep it moving.

Because when you stop moving, you're dead, you're done.

You've taken your chances and you've kept it moving. Time to prime the pump even more, get some of the old stuff back into circulation in order to raise the funds to get the new. Go to Plan B, now that Plan A is toast. Scrubbed. Ditched. Abandoned.

You hope there are no repercussions from that screw-up. They say there is video but that might be good, not bad. A good enough picture would show getting in and getting out. Not getting it. The shakedown cruise, not the actual expedition.

But if it's a bad picture it won't show that much. It will just show you.

And a picture's worth a thousand words.

CHAPTER 16

The highway to historic Fort McAllister led past the community of Richmond Hill, where the automobile tycoon, Henry Ford, built his winter residence in the 1920s, moving materials and parts from nineteenth-century plantation sites to create a haven from the blizzards of Detroit. The story goes that he set up housing, a school, a clinic, and a church, drawing people to live in the area with a financial fertilization that continued to bear fruit well into the twentieth century.

All along Highway 17 and then Ford Avenue, Nevada followed golfers, heading for the courses, and boaters heading for the water. She saw a few signs pointing the way to the set and slowed down as she got closer to the gatehouse at the edge of the parking lots.

A middle-aged man about the size of a refrigerator was sitting behind the window. He looked up from the Bible he'd been reading.

"Y'all here for the movie people?" he asked.

"I am," Nevada confirmed.

"Park just over there by the gift shop," the park attendant instructed. "We're closed to the public today while you folks are here, and there's lots of room up close."

Nevada wedged her rented car between two massive pickup trucks. *Who needs a truck this big? Are you carrying a moose back home with you?* She laughed at herself—wrong country, wrong animal. Alligator would be more likely.

The gift shop was in a small building that also served as the fee collection desk, the bookstore, and the museum. A stack of brochures about the Fort's history had been left out on the counter beside the cash register, and Nevada grabbed a handful. A couple of days earlier she'd tried to add to her knowledge about the place by looking online, even though she still had her doubts about the trustworthiness of sites where information could be added, randomly and without judgment, by just anyone. She'd found quite a bit of info about Georgia history but very little about this park in particular.

The brochure labeled it as 'the end of Sherman's March to the Sea'. Its location on the banks of the Ogeechee River put it in a prime spot to protect Savannah and the valuable cotton and rice plantations along the river's shores.

"Hey, Nevada." Chelsea Mack, a petite woman with tattoos ringing her wrists and stretching across her collar bone, walked by carrying a huge makeup kit already opened and ready for service. They had crossed paths back in Vancouver many years before, when Chelsea was just starting out on crews in Hollywood North. Nevada had always appreciated her easy way of passing along information.

"Hi, Chelce. Effin' early, isn't it."

"That it is," Chelsea said. "Hey, did you know that Jeremy's called a full-set meeting before we start rolling?"

"I did not know that. Thanks," Nevada said. "Where?"

"Just outside the back door of the building. The one that leads out to the Signal Tower and the Greenway."

"Sounds like you already know where everything is."

"There was a dispute about where our makeup trailer would go," Chelsea said. "Jeremy wanted us over on the Greenway. It's very central and handy for everybody. But apparently, it's the location of what were the primary sleeping quarters for the enlisted men during the Civil War, rows and rows of tents. Very important and historic, the state park boss man said, and wouldn't hear of any trucks or trailers pulling in there. So then we're all gathered around, looking at the map, trying to decide on the place where we would be allowed to set up."

"And?"

"In the parking lot, along with the rest of base camp," Chelsea said. "We're walking back and forth carrying our supplies, but it's not as bad for us as for some of the actors and actresses. Those dresses with the hoop skirts? Those woolen uniforms? Makes me glad I'm behind the camera."

"One more time," Nevada agreed.

She watched Chelsea bustle off toward the fort and turned her attention back to the brochure. The map showed the signal tower, the Greenway, and the officer huts just at the edge of the bridge that led to the parade ground. Replicas of guns designed to fire heated cannonballs were set up throughout the battery. Eventually, the fort's walls, mounds, and earthworks became essential in guarding south Savannah from 1861 to its fall in December of 1864.

Warships tested the fort's defenses for almost two years, with one, the ironclad U.S.S. *Montauk*, steaming up the river and anchoring 150 yards away from the fort, bombarding it for almost four hours, with the earthen walls absorbing the heavy fire. The fort eventually fell, however, when Sherman's army fought its way to the Georgia coast and overpowered the 230 Confederate soldiers there.

Savannah surrendered shortly afterward and General Sherman wired President Lincoln that he was presenting the captured city to the president as a Christmas gift.

It was not burned, the way great swathes of Atlanta were, and that was one of the reasons there was so much evidence of the early days of the city, right back to its founding in 1733. It was "The City Too Beautiful to Burn".

Nevada tucked a couple of brochures into her shooting script, then rolled it all up and put it under her arm. She could see a large group of people gathering in a clearing at the edge of the river near a wooden tower, as Chelsea had described. She hurried over just in time to see Jeremy making an announcement.

"Every movie shoot should have a break about a month after shooting starts, for everyone to regroup." It seemed that Jeremy had rounded up the entire cast and crew for a pep talk, but so far it wasn't sounding very peppy. "Unfortunately, we're not going to get that. The production company has put on a push for us to wrap it up on time, and even a little early, if we can manage that. With the long-range weather forecast turning left, that's going to be even more challenging."

"What does that mean, 'turning left'? Speak English, Walsh!" Ian Lamontagne, the actor playing the movie's main character, said it in a joking way, but there was still a bit of edge behind the words, Nevada thought.

"It's been a weird spring," Jeremy said. "Hotter than normal, and the season's changing earlier than usual. We're expecting more thunderstorm activity and, since our movie is supposed to be set in December, we don't really have the option of just trying to write in the weather. Thunderstorms are June and July, maybe May . . . except this year."

"Nobody's going to notice, boss," Ian said. "Your typical movie-goer won't even be clear on what city it is we're portraying, never mind the details about the weather."

Jeremy still seemed stressed. "Anyway, whether it's accurate for the movie or not, and whether anybody notices errors or not, thunderstorm activity makes for challenges in the filming. We'll work around it, but it is a new factor, that's for sure."

He cleared his throat. "Another one is that one of our lead actors, Tom, will be away for a while. We'll be shooting around him, but it will mean some changes to the schedule. I'll send the updates around as soon as I get them."

A buzz went up; this would have an impact on everybody. A different shooting schedule meant different scenes on different days, new plans needed for different costuming, makeup, props ... the list was extensive. Jeremy took the opportunity to make his getaway while it was all still sinking in for everyone and before the buzz grew to a roar.

Nevada intercepted him about a hundred yards away from the signal tower. "The note that Tom left for me on the kitchen counter said that you knew in advance about his absence and that arrangements had been made."

Jeremy did not look happy. "I had a note left on my car windshield. Said *you* knew in advance and that arrangements had been made." He stared at her. "So. I gather that we both got blindsided."

"Yeah, pretty much."

"I don't have a lot of sympathy for you, Nevada, I have to say. It was your job to keep an eye on him and to prevent something like this. We're paying you—and paying you pretty damn well—and he's gone anyway. It's just total crap."

Nevada had years of experience in keeping her cool and she was usually ready (and often called upon, in her job supervising and managing young reporters in the TV newsroom back home) to cut people some slack when they were trying to cope with stress. Even so, she felt pushed to her limit on this one. She didn't like his tone and she didn't like his language. "What was I supposed to do, rope him and tie him to a bed? He's a grown man, Jeremy. There's only so much anybody could do."

"Somehow I thought a daughter could do a little more."

Jeremy stalked off, leaving Nevada flinching from that last remark. Total crap, indeed.

She saw Doyle O'Keefe approaching.

Great, just great.

"Miss Nevada, I need a few moments of your time." The insurance investigator was dressed in a cream-colored, three-piece seersucker suit and a green bowtie. Didn't he feel the heat? Did the light color of the fabric really make any difference?

"Good morning, Doyle. Nice tie."

He looked down, as if to check it, although he couldn't really see it. "Thank you. I collect them—quite a few people do. It's a thing. "

Nevada wiped the light sheen of perspiration off her upper lip with the back of her hand as surreptitiously as she could. "What can I do for you, Doyle?"

"I'm speaking to everyone who was on set the day the golden bird pendant disappeared," he said. "If necessary, after that, I'll expand into the list of everyone who was on set any other day."

"That will be quite a list, I imagine," Nevada said, her mind not really focused on what he was saying. Jeremy's shot about the relationship with her father had hit some sort of nerve—was she really a failure as a daughter? Was this something she should be obsessing over at the advanced age of forty-nine? Why should Jeremy Walsh's opinion matter to her? Or anybody else's?

Normally, it didn't. She knew her own mind and had been shrugging off others' opinions and attempts to control her ever since she was a teenager. Except in this one category. She was vulnerable here.

Tom Leacock struck again.

With an effort, she pulled her attention back to Doyle.

"Where were you between the hours of six p.m. March tenth and six a.m. March eleventh?" he asked.

"Excuse me? *Excuse me?*" She focused on his bushy eyebrows, trying to find his eyes somewhere under them.

"We know that the heirloom disappeared sometime

during the evening of March tenth or overnight. It was used in the scene shot that day, in the parlor of the main house of the plantation. It was carefully put away in the safe, brought out the next morning, and when the case was opened, it was found to be missing." Doyle cleared his throat and looked down at the computer tablet he was using to take notes. "You came in for work on your first day that morning. What were you doing the afternoon and evening before?"

"I'm not answering that!" This would be appalling if it weren't outright funny. Where did this clown get off, playing pretend-cop and trying to interrogate her?

Something, some instinct, or some reaction to the offended look on his face warned her to calm down. A bit.

"Unless I'm under investigation in some formal way, I don't think I need to cooperate with being spoken to in that manner or asked those sorts of questions. I understand that you have to ask everyone, but—"

"Oh, no, ma'am, I'm not asking everyone these questions," Doyle said.

"Pardon me?"

"I said, I'm speaking to everyone, but the questions are different for you." Doyle looked up from his screen and made aggressive eye contact. "Your father has gone missing from the set and from his job. For the second time in less than two weeks. He was sharing quarters with you. This puts you on a different list from some of the other people on this crew, and it results in different questions."

"You think I had something to do with my father taking off?"

"I don't know anything about that, Miss Nevada. I just know he's gone, the golden bird pendant is gone, and you're one of the people closest to him." The insurance investigator tapped out a staccato series of characters on his keyboard. "What's the current state of your father's finances, ma'am?"

"I don't know anything about that!"

"Are you sure you don't?" he asked mildly. "Sometimes people don't know what they know, until they think about it."

Somewhere off in the distance, she heard a helicopter and, even farther off, a siren. People over there were going places, helping other people, using the best of modern technology, aviation, and vehicle mechanics to do their thing. It all felt so normal. But here in this old fort, standing on a piece of ground where soldiers once marched or fled from cannon fire a hundred fifty years ago, everything seemed weird and surreal.

"Are you suspecting me of something, Doyle?" she asked.

"I'm just asking you to think about everything that's happened in the past two weeks and about your conversations with your father," he replied. "*Should* I be suspecting you of something?" He seemed to be debating with himself about something, then deciding to plunge in, one hundred percent. "Should I be suspecting Mr. Tom of something? Should I be thinking of the two of you as a team?"

Maybe in some families, Nevada thought. Not in mine.

"I heard there was a camera near the safe where the necklace was kept," Nevada said. "Any info on what the pictures are showing?"

"We're going through that video now," Doyle said. "Any ideas on what we might find there? I probably don't need to tell you, Miss Nevada, that if you help us out and there *is* anything that implicates your father . . . or you . . . things will be a lot smoother if you've given us a heads-up on what we might discover."

"Smoother for who?" Nevada asked. She took a step back from him. "I think we're done here."

CHAPTER 17

The drive from the Fort McAllister set back to The Pines seemed to take much longer than the drive there at 4:00 that morning. Nevada leaned her forearms against the wheel and tried to stay focused on the road. It was only about twenty miles from Richmond Hill to Skidaway Island, but today it seemed like about a thousand. Nevada tried not to speed as she went past Pin Point but she was so eager to get to the main gate and on her way to the last few turns before home that she couldn't help it. Interesting how it was feeling like 'home' already. Maybe just in contrast to the off-balance, on-guard feeling she had on the *Burn* set.

It had been a miserable day, like walking through mud. Jeremy did return, eventually, to a tone of professional courtesy, but she could tell that he continued to blame her for Tom's no-show. He told her he'd offered to put a limo and driver at Tom's disposal and been turned down. He thought that was because Tom and Nevada were riding to work together every day. Nevada said she'd offered, but her father said he'd rather drive himself. The direct quote was "I didn't go to all the trouble of sourcing one of my favorite Corvettes just to have to park it and be driven like a child."

Or like the senior citizen you are, Nevada had thought.

How was she supposed to do the things Jeremy expected her to do and supervise her father that closely?

Maybe if she'd ever been a mother she'd have some clue, but as it was she just reverted to an irritated sense of powerlessness and indignation. Tom was a grown man—she could certainly try to keep him on track and away from substances or people who might derail him, but she couldn't tie him down in the back of a Town Car and keep him in her sight 24/7.

Nevada tried to stay positive. It was possible that when she pulled into the driveway of their rented Colonial on Tidewater Square, she would see his red C3 'Vette parked in front of the steps to the front door.

No such luck. She pushed the remote-control button on the visor of her leased BMW and watched the garage door open. Maybe he had parked it in here?

No luck.

Nevada wandered through the kitchen, opened the refrigerator door, and poured herself a lemonade. She hoped that Chelan had managed to keep herself busy and found everything she needed. Beyond the kitchen, through to the lagoon at the end of their yard, Nevada could see a lone heron stalking along the water's edge. About thirty feet out, a fish jumped, slapping its side against the water, then taking one more jump, then another, like a skipping stone. Maybe it was taunting its landlocked predator? Maybe just jumping to escape the warm water?

It was inspiring. Maybe she should do some jumping of her own, or at least some bike riding. The exercise would help her mood. She took a minute to change into shorts; it was a lot warmer now than it had been at four a.m. She took a look into the guest bedroom, where Chelan was asleep on the bed. Apparently, pregnant women needed a *lot* of naps. The bikes were parked by the back patio, and as Nevada kicked off the stand and rolled hers out, she felt her spirits lift.

The streets past the golf courses were quiet; most of the lawn and garden care people had finished their day's work, and the homeward-bound office workers coming from Savannah were not yet arriving. Nevada relaxed into the pedaling and got her speed up to twelve miles per hour.

An elderly golfer drove by in his golf cart, leaning over the wheel, intent on having his right-of-way on the trail. He looked like he thought he was driving a racecar or a Brink's truck, Nevada thought, as she passed a lagoon. Uh-oh, here comes a family with kids on scooters, babies in strollers, and grownups in running clothes. A collision about to happen.

And then it didn't. The old man slowed down and smiled at everybody, the kids stopped shouting and smiled back. Maybe there was hope for the generations to all get along, after all. Nevada winced at her own eagerness to find the good news here, somewhere, anywhere.

The Filling Station was open for business, with ice cream and hot dogs on offer to hungry sailors heading out or arriving back from a few hours on the water. The small building reminded Nevada of the tiny coffee shop trailers that she'd seen set up in parking lots all over the towns and cities near Seattle. They were obviously easily towed in and easily removed, if the customers just didn't show up.

This one was about six feet by six feet with light blue stucco siding and a tar-and-paper roof. A blackboard outside the front (and only) door had the day's offerings printed on it. Two round iron tables with matching chairs were set up along the dock just a few feet from the door, and both were occupied, one by two young mothers taking care of toddlers and babies sleeping in strollers, and one by an older couple holding hands.

The area around the little restaurant was fairly tidy, but there were a few dropped paper napkins and one half-eaten cone, melting in the sun. A couple of cardinals and a squirrel hopped and skittered nearby; farther away, a crow sat on the dock railing, apparently keeping an eye on that abandoned ice cream cone, ready to claim it.

The Filling Station was usually pretty quiet at this

time of day, and Nevada was surprised to find she had to wait a while, behind two young preteens who were taking their time in choosing between butter pecan and vanilla. The word, or phrase, actually, that popped into Nevada's head when she first saw them was 'best friends'. Two kids, two words.

"The vanilla is the best!" The young boy was a bit small for his age, usually leading to a label as not one of the 'cool kids'—but then, aren't all people, especially kids, labeled at some time or other? He had a happy face, dark-rimmed glasses riding low on his nose, and blond hair heading off in all directions but the well-combed one.

"I know, Austen, but this pecan is enough to make me just swoon," the girl said as she licked the ice cream and then slurped it.

Nevada grinned at them both. "Looks good."

"Yes, ma'am. You should have one," Austen said.

"I believe I will," Nevada replied. "Chocolate for me," she told the teenager staffing the ice cream buckets.

"Chocolate is challenging," Austen informed her. "The ice cream melts fast and chocolate stains are hard to get out. Vanilla, not so bad."

"Good point," Nevada agreed. "But you will be amazed at how fast I make this disappear." The young mothers had departed, and their table was now vacant. Nevada moved toward an empty chair, and the two young ones followed her.

"Are you new?" Austen asked her.

"How did you know?"

"You talk different from us."

"Usually a good clue." Nevada worked on devouring the ice cream. "I'm from Canada."

Their eyes popped a little at that, but they were too polite to make a big deal of it. "Where in Canada?" the young girl asked.

"Vancouver. On the west coast."

Austen nodded. "We saw that on TV. The Olympics

a couple years back. You got an ocean and big mountains."

"Not quite as big as the Rockies a little farther east," Nevada said.

"I've been there! My daddy took our family on a camping trip there one time."

"It's beautiful country." Nevada waved toward the marina and the river beyond. "This is beautiful too."

Austen nodded with enthusiasm. "Yes, ma'am, it is. It's home."

It was so cute, the way he said it. So sure and so proud. Nevada wondered whether she would respond the same way to the mention of any one place. Vancouver? No, not really. It was the location of her career, but it wasn't home.

"I'm Nevada Leacock, by the way."

The boy stuck out a hand. "Austen Patterson. And this is Lyla Jean Bishop."

The young girl nodded her head, her mouth full of ice cream.

"What do you like about it so far?" Austen asked. "What's 'beautiful'?"

"Well, I'd have to say the birds."

This was the right answer. Austen's face lit up and Lyla Jean leaned forward in her chair.

"We saw a pileated woodpecker this morning!"

"Where?"

"Up in one of the pines along the main road. We rode our bikes out to the aquarium."

"Skidaway Island has an aquarium?"

"It does."

"And an ice cream store. What else do you need?" Nevada finished her cone off with a smile. "Are they rare, the pileated woodpeckers?"

"Not really, but they're very big. People often mix them up with the red-headed woodpecker, which is much smaller and has a completely red head. The pileated woodpecker has a red crest on the top of its head." Austen was a natural-born speech-maker.

"It's a wildlife goldmine here," Nevada said.

Lyla Jean and Austen exchanged a look.

"Okay, that's a weird combination, wild animals and goldmines. I apologize." She laughed and they laughed back. "What else do we have here, besides birds and fish?"

"Deer, squirrels, foxes, turtles. Alligators. Raccoons. Owls."

"We love birds," Lyla Jean said. "We watch them all day long. When we can, when we're not at school, anyway. We ride our bikes to the marsh to see the egrets and the cormorants. The lagoons are the best place for the blue herons."

"Are there a lot of migrating birds?" Nevada asked. "In the fall in Vancouver, I used to watch the ducks and geese forming lines in a V-shape to fly south for the warmer weather. Do they come through or stop here?"

"Some. The mallard ducks. The snow goose. Not the Canada goose now, though," Austen replied. "They live here year-round."

"Do you have a favorite?"

"I like the osprey," Austen said. "Their nests are spectacular."

"The painted bunting is the same," Lyla Jean said. "Their colors are gorgeous."

"And the warblers, maybe," Austen added. "For their songs."

"And the way they jump around."

The three of them stared out toward the open water and watched a shrimp boat far off on the horizon. The conversation dwindled but nobody seemed to care, and Nevada noticed that she was missing the usual sense of trying hard that she had when she was with children.

"Do you take photos?" Nevada asked. "Or just watch them?"

"Sometimes," Austen said. "I put them up online, and I swap some with the people in this club I belong to.

Would you like to see them sometime?"

"I'd love to," Nevada said. "What else should I pay attention to, on Skidaway Island?"

Lyla Jean didn't hesitate. "The sunrises! I go out to watch them two or three mornings a week."

"Where do you like to go?"

"The path along Romerly Marsh. I was out there this morning, and I've never seen one so glorious. I watch them from my front yard, too."

"Isn't one sunrise pretty much like any other?" Nevada winked after she saw the startled look that Lyla Jean gave her. "After all, the result is pretty much the same."

A white egret flew over the harbor, its image reflected in the water, so crisp, so clear. "Not at all. They're different, every place you are," Lyla Jean informed her with authority.

"Lyla Jean is an expert on sunrises and sunsets," Austen said.

Nevada grinned at him. "And you? Are you an expert on birds?"

"I'm getting there," he said. "There's a lot more to know about birds, and it will take a while to get to the expert level. But I'm working on it."

Nevada was enjoying this more than almost any other conversation she'd had since she arrived here.

"I'm dying for a second ice cream cone. Does anybody else want one?"

Austen and Lyla Jean looked at one another, then shrugged. "Yeah, thanks!" Austen said.

"Another vanilla? And a butter pecan?"

"I'll have chocolate, ma'am, if I may," Lyla Jean said.

"Me too!"

"We'll make it three then," Nevada said as she stood up to go inside.

Austen jumped to his feet and in front of her to open the door. Less than three minutes later, she was back with a cone in each hand. She passed them over and went back for hers.

"So, tell me what you're doing, to become a bird expert," she said as she leaned back in her chair and focused on sweeping her tongue over the ice cream. So, so good.

"I ask questions," Austen said. "Like, why do they hop around to some places and fly to others?"

"Some are close by and some are far away?"

Austen shook his head. "Too easy."

Lyla Jean wanted to be included. "He's very interested in bird calls, too, and bird songs. He's making a study of them. He can recognize about a dozen of them by hearing them, without even seeing them."

"Oh, maybe one or two," Austen said, but the correction had no sting, and he looked very flattered by what she'd said. Starts early, doesn't it, Nevada thought. Maybe all any of us wants, from the beginning, is just to be heard. And seen.

"And why do they pick up some seeds for themselves but pick up other ones and put them in their mate's mouth?" he continued. "And how do they know they're with another one of their own species when they don't really know what they look like, like we do? They don't look in mirrors."

"Tame birds do," Lyla Jean said as she surfaced from her ice cream cone for a second or two.

"That's an exception," Austen said. "Not natural behavior. And why do they travel most everywhere in pairs, anyway? Humans don't. Alligators don't. Wolves don't—they'd rather be in a pack, or alone."

Nevada could hear the buzzing of a cell phone from somewhere nearby. She knew it wasn't hers; she'd left it at home. "Austen, is that your phone?"

"Yeah, it's my mamma. I'll get it in a minute. Now, here's another good question. Why do we say 'birdbrain' as an insult? Birds are pretty smart, it seems to me. Especially for their size and what must be the size of their brain. How do they know how to fly from their breeding grounds all the way across continents to their winter places? How come they don't get lost? Why do they all get together in a big flock, when it's time to start the journey? How do they fly in a flock like that, without bumping into one other?"

"I've heard that birds have a collective consciousness," Nevada said, wondering if she was stepping out of the zone with that one.

Austen looked sharply at her. "I've read that."

Apparently not.

"It makes sense," he said. "Answers a lot of questions."

"You better look at your phone, Austen," Lyla Jean said.

He sighed. "You're right, I better." But he made no move to pull it out of his pocket. "What if we had a collective consciousness, like birds? We could all read each other's minds."

"It would save a lot of explaining," Lyla Jean said. "And wondering what other people meant by what they said."

"Especially adults," Nevada said.

They looked at each other and then at her. She had to spell it out. "I'm joking, you guys."

"Maybe, but it's true," Austen said.

"It is," Nevada agreed. "But kids can be confusing too."

Austen nodded.

"Although I do think that kids deliberately try to make adults feel baffled," Nevada said as they both began snickering. "Am I right?"

"Yeah, pretty much," Austen said. "Kinda like the way we mutter on purpose so that grownups can't understand what we're saying."

"No way, are you still doing that same thing to your

poor parents? I used to do that to my dad and mom all the time, when I was growing up," Nevada said.

They laughed and dug a little deeper into the last of their chocolate ice cream cones. Bonding over dairy, Nevada thought.

"That reminds me. My dad," she said. "I'm kinda looking for him. Not really, but he's around somewhere, and if you happen to see him I wouldn't mind hearing about it."

"Sure," Austen said, pulling his phone from the pocket on his cargo shorts. His thumb hovered over the screen. "What's your number?"

Lyla Jean pulled out her phone, too, and waited.

Nevada gave them her digits. "Thank you both."

"Yes, ma'am," Austen said as he typed in her contact information.

"My dad is in his seventies, but he looks a lot younger. You might recognize him—he used to be on TV."

Neither Austen nor Lyla Jean responded to that. Maybe because they were talking about an older man, not a bird. "Tom Leacock is his name, and if you happen to bump into him, tell him his daughter wants him to call."

There, she thought, as she pedaled away from the harbor and toward her house. Now she could tell Jeremy she'd started to make an effort to track Tom down. Hah.

She couldn't get past resenting that he'd asked her. She knew she was being quite juvenile, but again, what did he expect her to do? It wasn't in her nature to be one of those controlling types of women—ironic that she'd ended up in a leadership position at a TV station. But she had other characteristics that made it a good fit. And lots of people were in careers or jobs that wouldn't, on first look, seem to be the right choice.

She would do what she could to help find Tom, and she had a few ideas about ways she could put out the word to him that he should reach out to her. But she had to draw a line. Indeed, she'd already drawn it. She wasn't going to get hysterical and pour her whole attention into finding him. She wasn't going to talk to the police multiple times in the day or think about hiring a private detective. She had done enough for now, spent enough time thinking about him, she told herself; she felt sure he was alright.

He was probably just off taking some private time, maybe just blowing off some steam after the unpleasant effects of seeing Judith. Maybe he'd even flown Clio in and they were taking off on a getaway weekend to Jekyll Island.

Right about now, Chelan would probably be waking up from her nap. Nevada was looking forward to hearing more about the latest behind-the-scenes gossip at LV-TV.

When she got back, she parked the bicycle near the door. Maybe Owen would be down for getting some exercise when he got home. She walked in quietly and stopped to listen at the foot of the stairs—no sound of Chelan from the guest bedroom. Nevada roamed through the big house, heading for the bathroom and a shower. She noticed her phone on the counter and stopped to take a look at her emails.

Tom/Dad. Subject Line: My Plans

What the hell?

Nevada clicked to open the email.

There was no text, just a link attached. When she opened it, she saw a video. A click on the arrow and Tom's familiar face appeared on the screen. His distinctive sea-green eyes looked tired, and the lines between them a little more pronounced than they were on screen, with the added help of makeup and good lighting. His mouth was moving, but there was no sound.

She fumbled around, found the audio button, and turned it up.

It was a video that Tom had recorded on his own phone and sent to her. He was speaking directly to camera.

"I have to admit it, I am a bit of a hypochondriac," he said.

No 'hello Nevada', no 'I'm sorry if you've been worrying about where I am'.

"Since the very earliest days with your mother, I knew, deep in my heart, that I was worried—no, more than worried: deathly afraid—of death. That's what it was all about, this fretting about every twinge in my chest, every ache in my head. I had to agonize over every symptom or sign because to do less would be to thumb my nose at death," he said.

So dramatic. Every thing he does, even a selfie video, it's like a scene, diving right in, getting into character, delivering lines.

"And everyone knew what would happen then. What Death does, when he feels he is disrespected. He would make sure that that would actually be the end."

Tom cleared his throat and wiped his forehead with the back of the hand not holding the camera.

"So I paid close attention to every message my body sent, showed my proper respect to Death. I took every opportunity to 'obsess over imminent disaster', as your mother put it. Judy eventually stopped commenting or taking part. I would tell her about some physical thing that was going wrong with me, and she would show how much she didn't care. When we were very young, I thought it was a sign that she was losing interest, that she was falling out of love with me. Later on, I realized that she never really did love me, and she had grown tired of faking it. She told me that I was always crying wolf, that it was all just self-indulgence."

And this isn't self-indulgence? Dad, for somebody who spends most of his life looking in mirrors, you really don't see yourself, do you? Self-indulgence and self-pity, big time.

"I don't know why she'd call self-indulgence such a crime. It's an actor's second skin. It's just as important as my face and my body, and that's what paid the bills, put the food she ate on the table, paid her rent. While everybody else pats themselves on the back for being so realistic, so down-to-earth, an actor has to stay open, has to protect his ability to dream and to feel. While the rest of the world was learning to deal and "facing facts", I had to stay open, let people project their dreams on me, relate to me. My stock-in-trade is my ability to feel—and to show that feeling on my face!"

Wow, he is getting really worked up. It doesn't even seem like he's talking to me—it's like he's talking to somebody else. But who?

"Nevada, I have to take off for a while. It doesn't matter where I'm going . . . and I will come back, just not as quickly as last time. I didn't take it, you know, but they're starting to think I did, and there are a few things going on that make it look very bad, for me. I'm in a bit of a squeeze, financially, and your mother's entrance has made it worse."

Tom pulled the camera phone closer to his face, probably in some sort of instinctive zoom to a close-up, but all he did was make his nose look enormous and the rest of him kind of pathetic.

"The thing is, there might be some proof that I was near the Props area the night the pendant was stolen. I didn't take it, I swear. I wouldn't know what to do with it if I had it. But I was there, and I did see it and I thought about taking it. And the very next morning it was gone.

"I have no idea who did take it, but I do know I can't hang around and let them pile up circumstantial evidence around me. I'm going to work a few connections that I have, to try to find some answers, and to do that I have to hide out for a while. Jeremy is going to make a lot of fuss and get all stressed about it—that's what directors do. But really, you've seen the shooting script, you know they can work around me for a while. It's not like I'm the leading man."

Another surprise. Never would have expected him to say those words out loud.

Tom went quiet for a few minutes, almost seeming to forget that he still had a camera going. But maybe he was just letting his words sink in or was pausing for dramatic effect. His eyes were downcast, eyelids lowered, then suddenly he looked up full-force through the screen, making eye contact with his daughter.

"Nevada, I didn't steal that pendant. But I do need money, and it's a matter of life and death. I have to do something—and I can't wait around for you or Owen or anybody else to help me out here. When I took off to go to Atlanta in early March, I thought I had a solution, but it fell apart, so . . ."

Ah, so that's what was going on. Dad, Dad . . . why won't you just talk to me? Let me help, let Owen help, let Jeremy help.

"None of you has the maturity or the smarts to solve this. I'm sorry to say it, Nevada, but I'm better on my own. If I let you take an inch, you'll take a mile, and before you know it, I'll have you sticking your nose into my business. I'm not ready for the nursing home quite yet, and nobody's going to baby me or force me in there."

Paranoid, much?

"When I get back, I'll have this all sorted out. Tell Jeremy I'm in St. Barts or St. Croix or Ibiza or somewhere, had to take a break."

The video ended, and Nevada didn't move.

"Hey, Nevada, how was your bike ride?" Chelan asked as she walked into the kitchen. She spotted Nevada's expression. "What's wrong?"

"My father."

"Is he back?"

"In a way." Nevada opened the refrigerator door and pulled out two beers. "Oops, I forgot for a second that you can't have any. Well, I'll have yours for you."

"Hah, sure," Chelan said with a laugh. "Sounds like you need it."

"Or like I'm picking up Savannah ways by osmosis or absorption or something," Nevada said as she popped one of the caps. "I thought I'd seen some partying, but I've never seen as much drinking as I do around here. Morning Bloody Marys, pinot grigio or champagne at lunch, wine in the afternoons, cocktails all the time."

"You're just a sheltered wee Canadian," Chelan said.

"Yeah, maybe that's it."

"Or maybe it's just the particular groups you've been introduced to here and there," Chelan went on. "I'm betting Savannah is pretty much like any other place. You've got your young party animals, you've got your serious, straight types, you've got happy ones, you've got depressed ones, the same as anywhere else." She pulled the milk carton out and poured herself a glassful. "I've got two hours until you need to drive me to the airport to get back home. Tell me, what's going on with your dad this time?"

CHAPTER 18

When Nevada arrived on set on Tybee Island the next morning, she had to stand in a long line at the security checkpoint. She'd been concerned about getting there on time, and she'd had to slow down going through Thunderbolt, where a stalled vehicle made the traffic bunch together like a crumpled piece of paper. By the time she got to set, she was royally annoyed about the delay and tense about being late. But she needn't have stressed over it. The lineup took twenty minutes to get through. Each person's identification was being carefully checked and crosschecked by the police.

She'd had no further communication from Tom, and although she wasn't hopeful, she did scan the lineup and the trailer area, looking for him.

Roger's was the first familiar face Nevada saw after they let her in. Seconds after she approached him to say hello, Doyle O'Keefe joined them.

"Have we got a nice case here of 'closing the barn door after the horse has escaped'?" Nevada settled her wallet back into her bag and straightened out her jacket after the pat-down.

Roger smirked, but Doyle didn't see the humor or the point. "The horses are just out in the meadow for some exercise, and we'll be getting every one of them back in where they belong before supper time," Doyle said. "By the way, Miss Nevada, when's a good time for us to talk some, today?"

"About what?" Nevada asked as she looked over his shoulder toward the beach, where all the activity was taking place. She could see the cameras being rolled out near the sand, track being set up, and several extras in costume standing in a huddle, listening to assistant director Traci give them their instructions.

"As you know, I'm interviewing all of the cast and crew about their whereabouts when the pendant went missing, what they might know about it, their thoughts on where it might be," Doyle said.

"At home with my husband, nothing, and no idea," Nevada replied. "There you go."

Roger smirked again, and Doyle looked quite disappointed.

Nevada relented. "Look, I know you're just doing your job, but you're going in the wrong direction here."

"How about Mr. Leacock?" Doyle continued as if she hadn't spoken. "Where was he at the time the pendant went missing?"

"I'm not his babysitter," Nevada said. "And why do you keep on saying it 'went missing'? Isn't it more accurate to say it was stolen? On your watch?"

Doyle glared at her. "I thought I heard that you *are* his babysitter," he muttered.

Nevada could see Jeremy coming toward them from the seaward end of the pier. He was dictating notes into his phone as he walked; ". . . to the guy in Key West . . ." Nevada heard him say into the phone before he put it into his pocket and joined them.

"Good morning, y'all," he said. "How was that, Doyle? Am I saying it right?"

Doyle tried to break a smile. "Yes, of course."

"What's up today?" Jeremy asked.

"I'm trying to continue with my interviews about the missing pendant," Doyle said.

"Your company isn't calling it 'stolen' just yet?" Jeremy didn't wait for the reply. "Well, whether 'missing' or 'stolen', doesn't matter to me. The point is I have to get another one for the film. Next scene we need it for shoots on Thursday."

"Will you have some sort of copy made?" Nevada asked.

"I'm going to have to, though I hate like hell to use a fake," Jeremy said.

"Any leads coming from the theft of the other one, the one in Florida?" Nevada asked. "Was it the only item stolen from the museum?"

"There's a good question!" Roger said to Doyle. "That's what you need, Mr. Doyle, you need to take some question-making lessons from Miss Nevada."

This was bordering on toxic. Nevada wondered what it was that was making them both so defensive and offensive—just the very fact that she was there and had been given a job to do?

"At the risk of being too helpful, I want to say that I do have a very good contact in Key West, and I could make a call, try to find out what the latest is, whether there's any chance it might turn up soon," Nevada said. She wasn't at all sure that Lillian Howe could be of any assistance at all—but then she didn't know that she couldn't.

"That's good of you, Nevada. I have a few contacts in Miami and Key West too," Jeremy said. "We'll figure something out."

A garbled voice burbled out from the walkie-talkie he had on his belt, and he pulled it out. "Gotta go, kids. But, Nevada, really, what you could do that would be more helpful would be to get a handle on what it is your father is up to. Speaking of going missing."

Both Roger and Doyle looked intrigued by this latest input.

"He's not missing," Nevada said. "He's taking a few days off. He isn't on the schedule—"

"Yes, he is, actually. There have been some revisions.

Yvonne's costume wasn't ready, and we've had to shoot around that. Now we'll have to shoot around Tom's little getaway." Jeremy shook his head. "Beam me up, Scotty. Get me off this horse, or whatever. I wouldn't mind a little getaway myself." His walkie-talkie crackled once more. "Now I really gotta go. Look, Nevada, if you're talking to him, tell him I'm getting pissed off and he should come to work."

"Isn't there a contract or something?" Doyle wondered aloud.

"He has 'personal days', and he's just taking some of them," Nevada insisted. "He isn't in breach." She looked down at her cell phone screen, then started scrolling through her contact list, looking for Lillian Howe.

It felt better to do something constructive, rather than continue to stand here, taking abuse on her father's behalf. Everyone was used to multi-tasking being as normal as breathing. At first, she'd found it hard to get used to the constant use of phones, people staring at the electronic plastic piece of brain in their palm, thumbs working like miniature pile drivers. She often saw people who never bothered to put them away, just holding them or perhaps sliding them into a pocket, ever-ready. She'd read somewhere that the average person who used a smartphone checked their email or their texts about 150 times a day.

At first, she thought it was insane, but now she often found herself doing exactly the same thing, particularly when she was bored or having to wait in a line for something. In other words, at any time when, in the past, she would have spent the time thinking.

A good thing or a bad thing?

"He may not be in breach of contract yet," Jeremy was saying. "But he's getting close to the line."

"And I'm not in touch with him, Jeremy," Nevada continued.

"Fine, but if that happens to change, just give him my

message," Jeremy said. "I might not need him until after the Beaufort scenes, but I will definitely need him for Charleston."

"In the meantime, I'll call my friend in Key West and see what she might have heard about this other 'bird in the bush'," Nevada said.

"And which one is the one in the hand?" Roger was a word player.

"I'd say the one that went into the water during the storm in 1490-something," Jeremy said. "Two of them are out there, somewhere, stolen or missing or whatever. Two in the bush. And one in the sand at the bottom of the ocean somewhere."

"I'd say that's three in the bush," Nevada said. "Nobody's got any one of them."

"The one that went into the water is probably worth the most of them all, too, if anybody could prove it had been there more than five hundred years," Roger said.

"Well, gang, it's been a slice," Jeremy said. "I have to get to work now."

"So do I," declared Doyle. "I apologize in advance, Jeremy, if I disrupt some of your work because of my interviews, but I know you're as eager as I am to find out who is behind the loss of this golden bird pendant."

"You won't be disrupting any of my work, Doyle," Jeremy said. "I won't allow it. Once you have actual suspects, rather than innocent people you're just going to bully and accuse, without any proof of anything, then contact my assistant and let him know you need to schedule some conversations."

Nevada almost cheered, it was so much like the hero's victory speech in a movie. She grinned at Jeremy, totally forgiving him for being such a jerk about Tom, and headed off in the direction away from the movie circus. She was starting to feel much better. Now that Tom wasn't there, it occurred to her, she wouldn't have to hang around watching his every move, hoping he wasn't planning to make a break for it. He'd already done that.

The breeze off the Atlantic was gentle and sweet this morning, and she breathed deeply for a few seconds. A glorious place. Everyone said the summer months could be unspeakably hot and humid in Savannah but, with this sandy oasis just a few miles away, so what?

Her phone buzzed with the half hourly push of emails into her inbox, and she pulled it out to take a look. There was a text from Owen, too, reporting that he and Chelan had had a nice brunch and then he'd driven her to the airport just in time to get her flight back. It seemed such a short visit but Chelan had insisted, over and over, that she felt it was worth it.

Nevada opened her email program and the first one that popped up was from Chelan. She had already blasted into action.

Hey, Nevada. I've been online to research some of those battles and war issues you asked me to, and my notes are in the docs attached below. Hope it's useful!

Uneventful flight back. A lot easier crossing the border into Canada than into the U.S., although I guess that's because one has to claim me and the other one doesn't. Drew says hi. Baby was kicking all the way from Savannah to Toronto.

My layover is three hours and I'm spending the time on my social media, seeing what I could see about Tom. He does have accounts, by the way—did you know that? Not thousands of followers or friends, or even hundreds, but he's out there. Maybe a publicist doing it for him? I'll continue to watch, just in case he starts posting regularly.

One other thing. While I was searching Civil War and Savannah subjects, I came across an ancestry kind of site that had some original source material that just might be related to that bird pendant you all were talking about. Can't believe that after only two days in Savannah, I'm saying 'you all' as if I'd been there forever! But I guess I still need to shorten it to y'all, right?

Anyway, there was a letter that seems to go back to the nineteenth century. I think it's from a Union soldier to his family. I copied and pasted it below.

Thanks again for your hospitality! It was a terrific break before I settle down to diapers and sleep deprivation for a while, and I really appreciate the part-time work too!
Best,
Chelan

Nevada scrolled past the battle facts material and eagerly opened the personal letter.

November 1864
My dear mother,

Hello to you and Sidney from an undisclosed location somewhere near the ocean. I cannot say too much, as you know, but perhaps you will read my excitement between the lines of this letter. I do believe that we are close to a conclusion this time. Oh, I know I have written that before, but this time there is a change coming. I feel it in the air.

We have been marching cross-country for days now. Our ranks have filled with hundreds of colored people whose days as chattel are over and who are leaving the only homes they've ever known to follow us to the sea and then north, once victory is assured and complete. I have no doubt that will be soon.

I have had news of Charles. I am saddened to report to you that he was captured and is imprisoned at a place called Camp Sumter, Georgia. Conditions are crowded and almost impossible, both for prisoners and captors. I have heard there is to be a march soon to another prison, Camp Lawton. I pray that Charles survives and that he joins me in returning home to you. I pray every day that it will be very soon.

My other piece of news is that I have accepted a commission for a young lady here, and I will soon be sending on to you a parcel of some import. She is a Southern lady, one of those magnolias made of piano wire, as Charles used to describe Emily Andrews—do you remember her, from our school days? This Southern lady, Miss Frances, lives on one of the plantations we were assigned to investigate. We commandeered some supplies, as many of our boys need food and clothing, mother, but we left behind as much as we could. It is hard to find the line.

Just as we were leaving, perhaps because we did not put spark to tinder as was done in many places, this lady brought out a family treasure and asked me to find a way to send it on to her cousin who had moved to Maine many years earlier to marry a Williams. She told me the story was that an ancestor from Coastal Georgia had sailed to England to find adventure more than a hundred years earlier and had been given a reward for saving the life of an aristocrat there. It was a piece that had been sent with Catherine of Aragon as part of her dowry when she traveled from Spain to marry the Prince of Wales in 1501, a piece of gold brought from the New World to her parents, Ferdinand and Isabella.

Miss Frances entrusted it to my care as she had no faith that her next encounter with a Union officer or soldier would go as well as hers with me. I am carrying the case on my person but as soon as I am able I will find a way to send it north, to your care, and when I am home we will search together for this cousin, Margaret Williams.

I think of you at home often, of the turning of the leaves in Maine a few months ago and of the winter coming. Do you have snow on the ground? It is still warm here and occasionally very stormy.
With fondest thoughts,
Your son,
John Webb

Nevada was so impressed with this that she had to sit down. The beach sand was getting into her shoes, but she didn't care. This was incredible! Documentary, original source material and proof of the story of the bird pendant. Nevada was thrilled, as a journalist, but she thought that Jeremy, as a movie director, would be even more excited. Not to mention his producers, executive producers, and financial backers—they would all be thrilled with this. Audiences these days loved movies about 'real people'. If you could say, legitimately, that something was a "true story", you got more attention and more respect. If you couldn't quite say that, because you'd changed important details, collapsed three real people into one powerful character, for example, you would promote it as "based on a true story". If the changes were just so abundant that all you had left from the original was a date, a setting, or a copy of the big check you'd written to obtain the rights, then you'd try to go with "inspired by a true story".

This letter would put *Too Beautiful to Burn* squarely into the category of Based on a True Story. That had to be major happy news for Jeremy and for the value of the film. Nevada also knew that the discovery of this letter would increase the value of the golden bird pendant even further. Anything with a story behind it could capture the public imagination in a way that a simple, solid object could not. She wasn't sure whether this would delight Jeremy or make him even angrier about the theft, but she did plan to tell him about it, as soon as convenient.

She spotted Roger standing near the pier, eating a po' boy sandwich, and she hurried over to tell him about the information Chelan had just sent her. He just kept on chewing and, finally, she said, "What do you think, Roger? Great addition to the story, right?"

His face showed a mixture of expressions, and she wasn't quite sure she could read it. He looked puzzled, and pained, and kind of appalled. "I don't think that letter has much to do with anything that we're doing, Nevada."

She paused for a minute to try to choose her words, carefully. "I get that this is fiction, it's a movie, not a documentary. But aren't projects based on a true story, or at least 'inspired by a true story' more powerful, more sought after these days?"

"Are you talking about a rewrite?"

His icy tone had her backing off, right away. "No, I'm not talking about . . . I don't know what—"

"You don't know what you're talking about?"

This Roger seemed to be making a signature style out of smirking. Nevada decided to meet it with amusement and try to get her balance back in the conversation. "Yeah, okay, no. I'm not talking about a rewrite, and I'm not being critical of your screenplay or the movie. I'm just saying that we now have original source material about what may be this exact pendant, and that might give the movie just that little extra bit of sizzle, in the movie-ticket-buyer's mind."

"Is that how you do your newscasts, write your news stories—always thinking about what the viewer wants? Or do you try to be accurate, honest, timely, relevant . . . maybe in spite of what a viewer wants? Maybe I want to write a story that is the story that *needs* to be told, the piece of art that has to be made. Not "the facts, just the facts". *My* version of the story, damn the facts."

She pondered this for a few seconds. "Will it cause a problem if I take this to Jeremy anyway?"

Roger shrugged. "Do what you want, it won't make any difference. I think you'll find he isn't a documentarian either."

He brushed the sandwich crumbs from his palms, then stuck his hands in his pockets and walked away. Nevada watched him go. *What just happened?*

"What just happened?" Traci was one of those assistant directors who seemed to materialize out of thin air, often in exactly the spot they were most needed.

"I think I antagonized Roger," Nevada said.

Traci shrugged. "What else is new?" She stared down at the clipboard that seemed to be almost surgically attached to her right forearm. "Hey, you haven't seen Yvonne, have you?"

Nevada scanned the pier, the sidewalk, the parking lot, and the restaurants across the road. "There she is. She's with the insurance guy."

As she watched the two cross the road, Nevada thought she picked up some sort of sign that they knew each other, somehow. They were deep in conversation, and although they weren't actually touching, the personal space between them was tight. As soon as they reached the sidewalk, Yvonne sped up and headed in the direction of her trailer. Doyle made a beeline for Nevada.

She started to walk toward craft services to get a coffee but had to stop short when Doyle stepped directly into her path. He stepped, stopped, and then said nothing. What the hell?

"Yes?" Nevada said. "Can I help you?"

Doyle was drilling eye contact at her, and saying nothing. It was very annoying. What was his game?

"Ms. Leacock, I'd like to speak with you now," he announced, and Traci took advantage of her opportunity to escape, giving Nevada a little wave and striding off toward craft services.

"Yes, Mr. O'Keefe, what is it?" Nevada crossed her arms. He hadn't used the usual Southern greeting of "Miss Nevada", and she wasn't sure what that meant. "I don't have much of a break, and Jeremy has said we don't have to speak with you, officially."

He tilted his head back and set his jaw. "This is not official. This is just a casual little chat. Off the record, I think you'd call it. I'm just going to tell you what I'm seeing here. I see a movie actor who's very overextended, financially, and I see a daughter who perhaps is closer to him than she lets on. Who perhaps has reasons of her own to be concerned about his financial capabilities. Who perhaps is on this movie set for reasons that have nothing to do with her father. I'd like to suggest that I have good cause to probe these matters much further."

And with that he stepped out of her way and walked off.

Later, when Nevada told Owen about the conversation, he snorted at that point. "Some casual little chat."

"Really." Nevada agreed.

"Classic bully," Owen commented.

"Is that why I feel so shaken up by this, Owen?" Nevada asked. "Because I do. And I'm not some newbie just starting my career. I'm the one who shakes up *other* people, not the one who gets rattled!" She started pacing around the living room.

"Because he's good at his job, Trip." Owen stood up too. "Are we going for a walk?"

"Very funny." She sat back down on the couch. Her phone buzzed, and she picked it up. "Here's Chelan again. She says there's a new tweet from Dad, and it looks like he's in Key West."

"What's it say, exactly?"

" *'Saluting the sunset at the end of the road. Florida always great but especially for relaxing and looking over new scripts.'* Sounds like he's there." Nevada was excited. Well, not excited, precisely. She was angry with him and she needed to find him, catch him, and reel him in to face his own life and get her off the hook.

"Not so fast, honey," Owen said. "We don't know for sure that he's there now, even if it is written in present tense."

"It definitely narrows the field though, don't you think?" Nevada jumped to her feet once again. "I was going to phone Lillian Howe about the bird pendant anyway. Let's go down there and see if we can round up Dad too."

She picked up her phone. "I have to let Jeremy know," she said as she tapped on his name in her contacts file. Her call went straight to voice mail. "Hey Jeremy, I'm going down to Key West for a few days. I think that's where Tom is. One other thing . . . Roger might have told you. We found a letter that proves the provenance of the pendant. An original document. I'll email it to you."

She was on her way down the hall to the closet where they kept the suitcases. As she yanked them out, Owen followed, then stepped forward to help her, still shaking his head. "Nevada, it's such a long shot, you couldn't get a bet on it in a roomful of gambling addicts with cash somebody was trying to launder. Come on. Key West is not Middle of Nowhere, Iowa. It's a big place. Biggish. Do you expect to just walk down the street or the beach and run into him?"

"Yeah, so?" She stopped her preparations. "Okay, maybe I've seen too many movies. But I do have ways of looking for him. And even if I don't find him there, I still have Chelan hunting around and Doyle O'Keefe."

"Not to mention Judith." Owen grinned, and she appreciated him finding the funny in the situation.

"Somebody will find him," Nevada said. "And even if I don't, I think it would be a good idea to visit this museum and dig into some of the info about these other two pendants, you know? Especially because one of them just got boosted, right after our movie pendant. You're the one who says there's no such thing as a coincidence—you must get that."

'You don't have to do this, Trip. You don't have a dog in this fight, as they say down here."

"Oh, but I do. They're going to blame me, if I'm not careful."

"Doyle O'Keefe wants to blame you?"

"He wants to get it solved so he can tell his bosses it's taken care of and he doesn't have to squirm anymore about letting it disappear."

"But that wouldn't bring the pendant back. Or prevent the insurance payout."

"No, but it would deflect the criticism from Doyle, and I think that's all he wants. Maybe that's all he wants . . ." She corrected herself. "I don't really know *what* he wants, but I do know how to investigate things and I'm just itching to go into this."

Owen sighed. "Ok, I'm convinced. But I can't go with you to Key West. There's just too much going on at work. You're on your own."

Her phone buzzed once more, and she looked down at the incoming email. Lillian Howe. Her response to Nevada's email, sent off while she was talking with Jeremy, Roger, and Doyle, was crisp and to-the-point, as always.

So nice to hear from you. Yes, do come visit. Name the date.

Nevada didn't know why she felt drawn to south Florida right now, but she'd had these hunches often enough and trusted them often enough, to know that it was usually worth following one. Too much coincidence, that there were two gold bird pendants known to be 'in hand' and that now both had been stolen, within days of one another. It wouldn't take long, taking a look at Key West, and it would be lovely to have a chance to catch up with her friend Lillian.

And if she happened to spot her father somewhere in the Keys, it would make the trip totally worthwhile.

CHAPTER 19

Nevada's plane touched down at the Key West airport after a very pleasant flight from Atlanta that featured a quiet, cooperative baby and a noisy, complaining businessman. Even though everyone told her she shouldn't miss the drive from Miami along the Florida Turnpike and the view from the Seven Mile Bridge, not to mention some of the other spots like Key Largo and Islamorada, she'd decided to take the overhead route.

Maybe next time she could drive. She did want to see Key Largo, eventually, but she wanted to see it with Owen. The two of them loved the Bogart and Bacall movie, and those scenes were probably the closest she'd ever come to an experience like a hurricane.

Once upon a time, maybe about thirty-five years ago now, she'd thought she wanted to shape her life around peak experiences. Not material 'stuff'. Not the newest, shiniest car, not the biggest house, not the glitziest vacations. She wanted to feel a hurricane. Climb Kilimanjaro and Everest. Run from a tidal wave, shelter from a blizzard. Chase storms. Trek through Nepal. Watch the sun rise on New Year's Day in a massive crowd of thousands of people. See a lion in the wild. Drive a car across the widest, loneliest desert on the planet. That sort of thing.

As it turned out, she'd made a lot of other choices along the way, and there wasn't one of those choices she'd undo. But she didn't forget where it was that she'd first picked up her notions of peak experiences and *Key Largo* definitely shaped the hurricane view.

The airport was only a few miles from town, and Lillian had offered to meet her. Nevada walked out into the bright Florida sunshine and past the wall with a painted mural saying something about a Conch Republic. What was that about? The air was warm and salty, with that 'we're all on permanent vacation' atmosphere, and in spite of herself, she felt her shoulders relax. Yes, she was here to try to find some answers about her missing father and, yes, she was under a cloud of suspicion in connection with a disappearance of a priceless historic artifact but, hey—it was Florida in March. It was all good.

She saw the silver-haired woman waving at her from the front seat of a Volkswagen Beetle. "Hello, Lillian! Too bad about the weather here!"

Lillian grinned. "Yes, it's paradise, especially for those of us escaping the winter rain in the Pacific Northwest. You won't need your webbed feet here!"

She popped the trunk, and Nevada slung her suitcase inside. "Are we going straight to the beach?" Lillian asked. "What would you like to do?"

"What I'd really like to do first is see the museum where the Spanish bird was."

"We're in luck," Lillian said. "They closed it for the investigation right after the robbery, and it's just reopened."

"I gather it was a major event," Nevada commented, watching the traffic flow and the people on the sidewalks.

"Oh, yes. They had the latest in technology and security, and still the thieves got in. That's what has them all buzzing, almost as much as the specific piece that was taken."

"Did they steal anything else?"

Lillian shook her head. "Not a thing. Obviously, they were just after the Spanish bird. That part doesn't surprise

GAIL HULNICK

me at all. Aside from the monetary value, it was quite exquisite."

Nevada saw the beach coming into view at the end of the street. "The monetary value part is intriguing too. I mean, where could you re-sell it? Anyone might recognize it. They wouldn't have a title document or anything to prove ownership . . ."

"Not in legitimate art and antiquities circles," Lillian said. "But there is an underworld. To some collectors, where it came from doesn't matter. They don't plan to ever re-sell the piece themselves, so they don't care about having to prove where they got it or how. They just want to have it."

She turned a corner onto Whitehead Street and slowed down. "There's the Hemingway House, where Ernest lived in the 1930s. Those cats you see in the yard are descendants of the six- and seven-toed cats he kept back then. And that's the Key West lighthouse over there."

Nevada rubbernecked and Lillian smiled. "Yes, we're all tourists from time to time, aren't we? Even the toughest of us."

"Do I seem tough to you, Lillian?" Nevada was surprised.

They rode a few more blocks in silence while Lillian considered the question. "Back in Vancouver six years ago, you certainly seemed very tough, and self-assured. But maybe I was a lot more timid and off-balance than I am now."

"Maybe I'm a bit off my game right now too," Nevada added. "I feel like a fish out of water down here a lot of the time. There's a lot that is new and strange—the climate, the accents, the customs."

"And then you've got your father in the mix." Lillian pulled the steering wheel to the right and slowed down to find a parking space. "Family can modify even the clearest of us." She tucked the Beetle in behind a brand-new Mercedes. "Let's go look at Mallory Square."

They walked along a beautiful stretch of shore with an amazing view of the Gulf of Mexico spreading out in front of them. "It's a long time till sunset, but the show starts a couple of hours before," Lillian said. "There's a sunset celebration every night, with jugglers, tightrope walkers, buskers, bagpipers, fire jugglers, and balloon artists for the kids. Best free show I've seen anywhere."

"Brings out a lot of people?"

"Pretty much every tourist in town, at least once, and a lot of the locals, all the time. My grandson Donovan is down for the weekend, and he's going to meet us for the sunset tonight."

"This could be good," Nevada said. "Big crowd, lots of people with camera phones. If Tom does turn up, there will be a lot of people besides me to notice him."

"Why do you have to be the one searching for him?" Lillian's pace was quite a bit slower than her own, and Nevada had to force herself to relax and just stroll. "Aren't there police? And what about this insurance investigator? Isn't it his job to find out what happened to the American bird?"

Nevada grinned. "Is that the official name, or is that what we're calling it?"

"Goes with Spanish bird quite nicely, don't you think?"

Nevada agreed. "It *is* his job to find the American bird, but what he seems to be most concerned with is pinning it on Tom, and if he can't get him, then me."

"What about the police?"

"There's a local sheriff and a few FBI guys. My friend Chelsea on the movie crew spotted them. She said they've been gathering physical evidence, talking to people. But nobody has approached me."

Lillian nodded thoughtfully, then rambled along beside Nevada for a few more minutes. Suddenly she recognized someone she knew. "Hello, Billy."

The elderly man was walking an odd-looking dog on a

leash in his left hand and a peacock on a leash in his right. "Hello, Miss Lillian. Welcome to the sunset."

"Thank you, Billy. This is my friend, Nevada Leacock."

Billy looked deeply into Nevada's eyes, then startled her with a wink. "Hello there."

"Billy is one of our local historians. He was here for the birth of the Conch Republic in 1982—"

"And I'm here for the Museum Hysteria of 2014," Billy finished Lillian's sentence.

"Are they hysterical?" Nevada asked. "About what?"

"This Spanish bird has them all screeching and flying around like a California condor fighting for its last meal," he said. "I read in the paper that some very senior people from Madrid are here, raising hell. Meanwhile the honchos in Tallahassee are trying to make excuses and protect the honor of the state, and the Key West cops are fighting with the FBI over who's in charge."

"And what was the Conch Republic of 1982?" Nevada asked.

Billy laughed and said to Lillian appreciatively, "She listens, doesn't she? In 1982, Key West seceded from the United States, and we celebrate its independence every April 23rd. It's not a sovereign nation, though; it's a sovereign state of mind, and its mandate is to bring more humor, warmth, and respect to the world."

"A tourism initiative?"

"Pretty much, although the history does have some serious elements to it. I'll tell you all about it some other time. Liberace here wants to continue with his walk," Billy said, indicating the peacock straining against its collar and pulling in the direction of the beach.

"You weren't kidding about the characters in Key West," Nevada said to Lillian as they watched him go. She scanned the growing crowd, wondering whether she might see Tom. Would it be that easy?

It was hard to tell the tourists from the locals,

everyone dressed as casually as possible and lifting camera phones frequently to capture a moment of the approaching sunset. You couldn't even say definitively that the ones taking selfies were the tourists since everyone did that all the time nowadays, Nevada thought. She strolled along beside Lillian, enjoying the ocean breeze and the smell of the salt air. Two men, one barely twenty-five and the second much older, approached them. The young one, a tall man in an ancient polo shirt, jeans, and flip flops, greeted Lillian with a hug.

"Nevada, this is my grandson, Donovan. He lives in Miami, but he gets down here to visit me frequently."

"Often by boat," Donovan announced as he reached out to shake hands with Nevada. "Nice to meet you. I've heard a lot about you." He turned to the older man who also had his hand extended. "This is Adam Brecklin."

"Owner of the boat?" Nevada asked.

Adam nodded. "Yes, but employer *and* friend, I hope."

"I have my own boat," Donovan said. "Doing fishing charters and day trips for the tourists. But I'm also on board with Adam, doing a special project.

"It's a deep-sea diving boat, and they're looking for sunken treasure," Lillian said with quite a bit of enthusiasm.

"Really!" Nevada was a lot more interested now. "Any treasure in particular?"

"There's a shipwreck that's just been charted about ten miles south. Thought to have gone down a lot farther east, sometime in the late fifteenth century, although the dates might be just as vague as the location," Adam said.

"A shipwreck is a story that has everything, if you ask me," Nevada said. "Coming from the west coast of B.C., we all feel that, right? Tragedy, mystery, drama. I'd love to hear more about whatever you dig up."

And I want to know more about who you are.

*

That night in her hotel room, after a visit to the Coastal Florida Museum to see the space where the other golden bird pendant had so recently been exhibited and after an hour of strolling through downtown, trying to let coincidence strike and give her path a chance to cross her father's, Nevada sat down at the desk with a thick pad of paper and a pen. The idea had been dogging her all day that the solution to this mess could rest on finding the answer to the questions: who really did take the movie production golden bird pendant? Who took the Spanish bird from the Florida museum? And could they possibly be the same person?

The first thing to do was to put herself in the shoes of this unknown thief, she thought. *When did you take it, and how, and why?* The pendant would not be an easy thing to monetize, but that had been obvious from the start. Not a matter of a simple transaction in a pawnshop, with just a little extra haggling because of its clearly unusual features. No, it would be difficult to sell it, and that would be a bright red stop sign for any reasonably cautious person.

Difficult to sell it, but not impossible.

It would not be easy to locate an antiquities expert who wouldn't immediately reach for his phone to call the police or some government or museum bureaucrat. But after some digging, the right person might surface. *Maybe* this person would be more than a little dazzled by the pendant's beauty and its implied provenance, even though there was nothing on paper to prove its origins. *Maybe* this person was prepared to entertain some creative ideas for trading on the piece's value without an outright exchange, though. A physical surfacing of the piece might bring the cultural crimes police down on all their heads. So, this diving bird needed to stay underwater. But maybe this intermediary person had an idea.

The notion was a simple one. Collateral. People used it all the time—why not on jewelry, even a museum piece, a stolen one? This piece of jewelry couldn't be worn, displayed, or bragged about. *Maybe* you could borrow against it, though, sell just a partial interest in it, while still keeping it hidden and safe, while its new suitor, the one with the lust and the extra cash, helped you figure out a way to transfer the artifact in complete secrecy and safety.

Maybe half a million was needed and half a million was promised, with an additional half million to be delivered with the bird, at the end. This was a wealthy black market. The buyer—or was there more than one?—would be willing to put forward whatever it would take to deliver the pendant. No questions were being asked. Speed was important. Speed and momentum. Any lag it took in the time to pass the thing from hand to hand could be catastrophic.

Nevada had a plot and characters going now. If there were just a few email exchanges through an encrypted port, it might become clear that the buyer was very eager to get the deal done as quickly as possible. Perhaps too eager.

Just thinking about that for a little while led to a new avenue and more traffic, so to speak. At least two more prospective purchasers would surface, Nevada thought, and now they had a bidding war on their hands.

Maybe the irony of the whole piece would that two of the buyers were the victims of the heist. One was the Coastal Florida Museum, desperate to show that although its security protocol had failed, it had the means to track down a stolen item and put it back. It had to come up with some result like that; otherwise, no other museum in the world would want to lend it any item of value, and no insurance company would cover it.

Meanwhile, over in Spain, they would be angry and determined to get what they regarded as their property back. Ironic that they'd stolen it (or at least bought it from other thieves) in the first place. But who knew? Maybe the so-called victims of the theft had it illegitimately in their possession too. Who really owns anything, anyway?

Maybe when the thieves first heard that the Spanish museum people were willing to pay to get it back, they were annoyed with themselves that they hadn't thought of holding the thing for ransom. But this bidding war idea was even better. They would play the parties off against one another, maybe even find a third or a fourth group to bid up the price. Greed grows.

Nevada's phone ringing interrupted her creative flow.

"Hey, you."

"Hey, yourself. How's Key West?"

"Just fine, cowboy, how's Savannah?"

"All good. Busy day at the hospital. Small bit of news from movie world that I thought you might like to hear."

"Yeah?"

"They've put out a reward for information about the theft of the necklace. Calling it an important piece of Civil War history and offering fifty thousand dollars for information that leads to recovering it. The news article I read quoted from the Civil War soldier's letter that Chelan found."

Nevada let out a low 'wow'. "That's a lot of money. Does it say who is offering this reward? Is it the film production company? Or the family?"

"Both. It also says that one of the stars of the movie, Tom Leacock, has made it a personal project to help track it down and anybody who helps him, or even sees him, may be in a position to share in the reward. If that's you and you think you might have some sort of connection to Tom, his search or the reward, you're asked to contact the producers or the insurance company."

"They're trying to get the whole world to turn into detectives for them," Nevada said.

"Might work," Owen said.

"Might."

CHAPTER 20

Flying north, Nevada relaxed and felt more at ease than she had in the last few days. She felt that she'd been going nonstop since the first of the month . . . and it didn't seem as though it were going to slow down any time soon.

After a short layover in Atlanta and a run from Terminal E to Terminal A, Nevada leaned back in her seat, headphones on and nose in a book. About ten minutes before they began their initial descent into Savannah, the weather turned interesting. Thunderstorm.

Nevada looked out from the airplane at the streaks of rain on the window and saw the sky brighten in the distance, thanks to the lightning. Geez. How close was that? Did the pilot see it? She must have. Everybody talked about the glamor of travel, and everybody yearned to see more of the world—thousands and thousands of places to see before you turned eighty or whatever—but no one said much about things like forks of lightning separated from your Row 12 window seat by just a few ounces of plastic.

She felt a bit wobbly as she walked through the airport but all of the other passengers seemed unconcerned, so she sucked it up and put it behind her. You get used to everything—monsoons in the northwest, blizzards in the northeast, thunder and lightning in the southeast.

She had arranged to meet Owen for dinner with Frank and Linda at one of Savannah's oldest restaurants,

Tara on the Boulevard. People were seated at outsized, round tables, new arrivals escorted to empty chairs and strangers introduced to one another. The food was served family-style, with big bowls passed from person to person. Just before everyone started eating, an older man with a look of great dignity bowed his head and said grace.

The restaurant was packed, every table and every chair taken and the servers rushed off their feet. It was not usually this popular, Frank and Linda told them, but the management had started a new program of live music, and it was really taking off. Taking off and paying off.

Nevada put down her fork, after the final mouthful of one of the finest pieces of key lime pie she'd ever tasted. Just a bit tart, not too sweet, and with a trace of the tastes of whipped cream and crumb crust lingering on her tongue. The last few seconds of flavor savor seemed to transition into the first few of auditory pleasure as the band kicked in. Not a cast of thousands—just a drummer, a piano player, and a singer—but it was all that was needed when the music flowed like that.

The group started out quietly, feeling its way into this audience. Some seventies standards, some Anita Baker, George Benson, Roberta Flack, Michael Jackson, Bonnie Raitt. Quiet, subtle, perhaps trying not to distract from the crab cake in lobster sauce or the salad with pecans and goat cheese. But, as the hours went by, they brought it up a notch or two and, by ten p.m., as the singer opened up and allowed her gift of a voice to fill the room to the rafters, a shrine to Aretha was being built in the room.

Owen was beaming, reflecting the glow that Nevada felt rising up inside her. He leaned over and whispered, "Can we dance?"

She laughed. "We'd be pretty conspicuous."

"So?" he asked, jumping to his feet.

The singer smiled and nodded at him. Nevada let herself be pulled along into the moment—what else could she do? By the time the song ended and they returned to their table, they were both smiling.

"Well, what a romantic couple," Frank said. His voice had some sort of edge to it that Nevada couldn't identify.

"You could take a few lessons, Frank," Linda said, with a smile.

Frank glared at her and Nevada felt as though she had wandered into a conflict zone. The tension between the two older people was unmistakable.

"Oh, I'm sure Frank has his own game, maybe just not on a dance floor," she said, injecting as much lightness as she could.

Frank grinned at her, and she felt she'd succeeded. "Oh yes, Miss Nevada, I take a back seat to no man on the golf course."

"There's not much romance on a golf course," Linda said.

"You reap what you sow," Frank snapped back.

Half an hour later, as they strolled from the restaurant to their car, Nevada had to find out Owen's take on the conversation. "What did you think of that little exchange?"

Owen shook his head. "I think some guys just have to be chairman of the board no matter where they are. Even if it means taking a swing at their own wife."

*

Two days later, Owen and Nevada were on their way to Jacksonville, Florida, despite Owen's fussing that he'd be away from his patients for too long. Nevada saw the smile behind his complaints, and she knew that he was happy to have her company after her time away. Jacksonville was just a couple of hours south from Savannah, and they'd been wanting to explore it since they'd arrived. But that wasn't the main reason for their drive.

Chelan had emailed Nevada that her excursions through social media land had resulted in a post from a classic car fan in Florida who insisted he'd spotted Tom

Leacock at a high-end car show, one of the biggest and best in the country, a Concours d'Elegance, on Amelia Island. And what was more, he said he had video proof.

Chelan had given them an address and a first name: Earl. He lived in the town of Fernandina Beach on Amelia Island.

The house was a copy of a Southern plantation house, faux columns and a wide porch with rocking chairs opening in a greeting to the road. They parked near the mailbox and walked hand in hand toward the open garage door. Inside, the man they assumed was Earl was bent over a table filled with greasy car parts.

"Hey, y'all, and welcome," he said, mopping at his hands with a rag and stretching his right one out in a greeting. Owen, to his credit, gripped it in a manly, friendly way—particularly impressive, given that, as a surgeon, he was somewhat particular about his hands.

"Hello, Earl, and thank you for agreeing to see us," Nevada said, looking past Earl's shoulder at the collection of motor memorabilia he had scattered throughout his garage.

He saw the direction of her gaze and laughed. "You're welcome, m'dear, and please, feel free to look around. A collection's not much fun if nobody ever sees it."

There was no actual car anywhere in the garage, just shelf after shelf of parts and models. Clearly, a knowledgeable fan could spend a lot of time here, but Nevada was baffled as to how all of this came together in any coherent way to bring about the end-result of a vehicle: a drive, a race, even something parked, to be looked at. It was like a place that was in a permanent state of becoming . . . which, if you think about it, is perhaps the definition of a road trip.

"We're here to find out more about this video you shot at the Amelia Island Concours," Owen said. Bless you, Owen, Nevada thought. Thank you for breaking the ice, for getting things going; otherwise, I might stand here forever, mesmerized by the miles of aisles of greasy things.

"You betcha, son, here it is," Earl said. He slid a DVD disk into a machine and waved a remote-control device at it.

If it were a music video or a movie, everything would be moving fast, cuts happening every few seconds, Nevada thought as she watched it. We're all used to watching quickly these days, and even the amateur video posted online reflected that increase in visual momentum. Skies usually wide and blue or low and stormy, nothing in between. Something might be flying toward our singer-heroes, in this video—perhaps daily living items like toasters, lawn chairs, a blow dryer, a razor—all symbolic of the futility and repetitiveness of ordinary human life. Our singer-heroes would be ducking the airborne missiles to a background of hip-hop music.

But instead of being a music video or a commercial video cleverly cut to look amateurish, it was footage of a car show, shot from the perspective of a gearhead. Nevada watched dozens of close-ups of grilles and headlights, dashboards and door handle styles, wondering when they might see something that would help in solving the mystery of her father's disappearance.

They didn't have to watch much longer than half an hour. Nevada was just racking her brain for a courteous way to bring this to an end, when Earl suddenly spoke. They were looking at a slow pan of a red '67 Chevy when he said, "There he is!"

And there he was. Tom was in the background of the shot, and if Nevada hadn't been squinting at this screen, intent on seeing the picture of her father that she was assured was there, she would have missed it. He was wearing jeans and a long-sleeved dark blue shirt, the collar turned up in that eighties style that he still liked. The camera angle was wide and, besides the Chevy in the foreground, there were about half a dozen other cars parked between the camera lens and Tom. Nevada watched him reach toward a woman and take a box from her. The woman looked familiar, but Nevada couldn't place her. A small bulldog sat to their left at their feet, and a '72 'Vette with Florida license plates and a Key West bumper sticker took up the parking space to their right.

"And this was on the first day of the Amelia Island Concours?" Owen asked.

Earl nodded. "Yup. Definitely him, isn't it?"

"I'm not sure. . ." Nevada reached into her bag for her reading glasses. Once perched on her nose they seemed to help a bit, but she still couldn't see the figure in the frozen video as clearly as she'd like. "Is there a way to zoom in on him?"

Earl looked annoyed. "Probably is, there's a way to do pretty much anything, technologically these days. Or somebody will invent something tomorrow. But I don't know what it is, ma'am. Just get up a little closer to the screen, maybe that'll help."

Nevada stared as hard as she could, but she still had her doubts. "I don't know, Owen, what do you think?"

Her husband crossed his arms and smiled at her. "I think it's clearly Tom. And there's something about that video that's even better. I think we have to buy Mr. Earl here a drink to thank him."

"What are you talking about?"

"Look at the woman he's with."

Nevada peered at the screen once more. "She did seem familiar to me, now that you mention it."

"Picture her with purple hair."

The woman in the video had light brown hair down to her shoulders. She might have been fifty, and she might have been ninety. Nevada relaxed, softened her gaze, and tried to open herself to an inflow of information, memory, or insight, the way she'd been taught way back in journalism school. She breathed deeply two or three times—nothing.

Then—"Cassidy Sullivan! From The Pines!"

Owen grinned. Shared triumph. "That's it, you got it, Trip."

"But I didn't know she knew my father. She never mentioned it."

"How many times did you actually talk to her? Three? Maybe four? Why would that subject have come up? If you're Tom Leacock, you think it would come up in the first five minutes, but really, it's not top-of-mind for most people when they're getting to know somebody new. 'Let's see, do you happen to be related to any famous people? Got any movie actors in your families?' "

Nevada pretended to wince. "Ouch. Yeah, okay, you're right."

"Besides maybe she doesn't know him. Maybe she only met him after she met you, or saw you, the most recent time. Or, maybe she just met him for the first time at this car show," Earl contributed. "Maybe they met online and set up a meeting at Amelia Island. Maybe that's her 'Vette and he's thinking of buying it. Maybe—"

"Thank you, Earl," Nevada cut in. "Could be a lot of things going on, but thanks to this video we now know a person we can ask."

"What do we think is in the box?" Owen asked.

Nevada wrinkled her nose, then pushed up her reading glasses to take another close look. "Could be anything. Could be car parts, could be papers, if they are doing some sort of ownership transfer . . ."

"Maybe photo albums, if there was any sort of major restoration project involved, or plaques and trophies, if she's had it winning in any shows," Earl said.

Nevada looked at the freeze-frame of the 'Vette with a little more interest. "Does it look like a Best in Show to you, Earl?"

He took another look. "Could be. Hard to tell from a still photo. I'd have to walk around it."

Nevada sighed and turned away from the screen.

"Anyway. The main thing is we know he was still in the southeast, in Florida, as recently as last weekend. And he looks good," she said, turning to Owen. "I mean, he looks healthy, normal."

"Were you worried about him?" Owen asked.

"Well, he is seventy-five, after all," she said.

"Spring chicken," Earl said cheerfully. "Still, I'm sure y'all are relieved to know he's not really disappeared or hurt or something. Now I can make you a copy of that DVD pretty quick here. I got my son-in-law to connect me another machine so I could do that, in case you wanted that."

"Could you just email it to me?" Nevada asked.

Earl looked a bit skeptical, even a little overwhelmed, and Owen stepped in. "We'll take the DVD just as it is, Earl, thank you."

Earl hesitated, then took the plunge. "Now, about that reward. Like it said on the Twitter," Earl said.

"Twitter," Nevada corrected.

"What?" Earl asked. "That's what I said."

"Never mind. What exactly did it say?"

"It was a tweet that said Tom Leacock seemed to be missing, and if anyone had any knowledge of his whereabouts, they should get in touch," Earl replied. "Now, wait a minute, maybe that was the one of the later ones. On the Twitter, there's been lots of chatter about this."

"Who was doing the tweeting, Earl?" Owen asked.

"First one was the movie company, then a lot of fans and well-wishers and such. Here, I'll show you," Earl said, pulling a smartphone from his jeans pocket. His pointer finger, as he scrolled through the tweets, looked like the front hoof of a tiny horse, pawing at the ground.

Nevada looked around Earl's garage while she waited and wondered just how much time everyone spent these days, waiting, looking at the top of someone else's head and watching their thumbs or fingers working their way through messages or websites.

"There you go!" he said, passing the phone over to her. "I was wrong, it wasn't the movie people offering the reward, it was some insurance company."

And there it was. Well.

Lots of good reasons to want Tom Leacock back among us. $100,000 reward to anyone who has info. Contact Doyle O'Keefe at Foundation-Nation Insurance Corp.

Earl squinted at Owen. "You're not Doyle?"

Owen laughed and shook his head.

Earl frowned. "I thought that was who I contacted. But I was also back and forth with a woman with a strange name. Maybe I mixed them up. But I thought I also commented to the movie people . . . no, maybe I just liked their tweet. And I did share the first one I saw, the one about him missing, I retweeted that to all my people."

On the drive back to Savannah, Nevada had very little to say to Owen. Her mind was racing with this new information. A reward! As if Tom were a fugitive from justice or a bail-jumper or something. It was one thing to offer a reward for a missing *object,* as had already been done for the heirloom pendant, but what business did Doyle O'Keefe . . . an insurance company employee! . . . have, offering a reward for information about her father?

Owen dodged a huge truck and then broke the silence in the car. "Don't you think it's a sign that they're concerned about him, that they put up such a large reward? If someone did that about me, I'd be flattered."

"No, I don't think there's anything flattering about it! Or intended to be, Owen. Doyle O'Keefe is screaming, loud and clear, on Twitter, that he thinks Tom is guilty of something and there's a reward for his capture."

"Aren't you being a bit over-dramatic? Nobody said or wrote or tweeted anything about a capture. They just said they're worried about him and will pay anybody who has information about where he is."

"Did you see how eager that little worm of a guy was

to ask us about the money, speaking of the money," Nevada said.

"Well, who isn't enthusiastic about a hundred thousand dollars?" Owen said, laughing. "Come on, Trip, I think you're focusing on the wrong part of this."

"Oh? And what is the right part, Mr. Heintzmann?"

"Tom was at the Amelia Island car show last week, in fine shape. And you have a lead. The woman, what's her name?"

"Cassidy Sullivan."

A thought struck Nevada and she pulled out her phone. She opened her web browser and typed in a question.

"Well. There you go," she said, and leaned back against the passenger seat, closing her eyes.

"Well, what? What did you look up?"

"The dates for the Amelia Island car show this year."

"And?"

"March 6 to 9."

"More than a week *before* Tom allegedly disappeared."

"Exactly."

They had taken the scenic route on Highway 17 to come back to Savannah and, for a few miles, Nevada watched the landscape roll by, the soft-focus beauty of the marshes and the creeks almost taking the edge off her bad feeling. Almost, but not quite.

"So he was at the car show just a couple of weeks ago," she said. "He met Cassidy Sullivan before I did— why did she come to our house and introduce herself, anyway?"

"Maybe she came by to see him and when you answered the door she improvised," Owen said.

Nevada reached into the purse she had resting at her feet and took out a pen and pad. "I have to write some of this down or I'll forget it. So. Dad took something from her or gave something to her at the car show. What was it? A week or so later she turns up at our rented house. Why was she there? And where is he? Why doesn't he call me or Jeremy or somebody?"

"Well, he did leave you a message," Owen said.

"That wasn't enough!" Nevada felt her stomach tying itself into a knot.

"Because you think so, or because you're letting Jeremy Walsh and Doyle O'Keefe force you into feeling responsibility for this? Into getting all stressed out over something that's beyond your control anyway? Calm down, Nevada, and think about it for a minute. Tom took off for a while, he left you a message, he said he'd be back. He wouldn't be the first guy to try to disappear in the Keys for a while. We have no reason to think there's anything more to it than that, except for the way Jeremy and Doyle are handling it."

She watched the highway signs to the Golden Isles go by, then took a deep breath.

"You're right."

"Thank you," Owen said. "Two words all husbands love to hear."

Nevada smiled, then reached down to the side pocket in the car door, where her phone lay, buzzing. She picked it up and looked at the call display.

Dad.

CHAPTER 21

She listened to the buzzing of the phone and stared at the call display. Nevada felt, rather than saw, Owen's curious glance, but she said nothing, and they rode along in silence for another few blocks. The passing billboards urged them to eat at a restaurant, shop at a furniture store, hire an aggressive lawyer. Nevada took a few deep breaths, then picked up the phone.

"Hey, Dad," she said. "Where are you?"

"That's the point of these phones nowadays, Nevada. Nobody has to know."

She heard him chuckling. "That's true, Dad, yes, and it's funny. You're pretty pleased with yourself, aren't you?"

She felt Owen turning his head and raising an eyebrow at her, trying to get a read on Tom's words and her reaction to the call. She needed to get him to pay attention to the traffic and the road, not persist in looking at her. She gave him a thumbs-up and he smiled; that was enough communication for now—she could tell him all about it later.

"I'm fine, Nevada, healthy as a horse. Where I am doesn't matter, and I won't be here long, anyway," he said.

"Everyone's concerned about you and looking for you," Nevada told him. *Well, that wasn't entirely true. But a lot of people were.*

"I need a break. And I have some personal matters to take care of."

"Dad, you should communicate with Jeremy. He's

got his shorts in a twist over your absence. He's talking about breach of contract."

"Yeah, I heard from my agent. I think we've straightened it out now, stop worrying. Look, I've got a favor to ask you. I need you to go to the storage locker where I keep my costumes collection—"

"They're also linking you to the disappearance of the bird pendant they're using in the movie."

"What do you mean, linking me?" Tom's voice was rising.

"They think you stole it!" Owen shouted in the direction of the phone. Obviously, then, he could hear Tom's side of the conversation now too.

"Who's that? Nevada, where are you?"

"It's Owen, Dad. We're in the car, driving back to Savannah," Nevada said. "We've just been on Amelia Island, and we saw some video of you at the car show being given a box by some woman."

Silence at the other end of the phone now. She could almost hear his mind working.

"Dad, I'm going to have to tell Jeremy about this. And Doyle, the insurance investigator. And whatever police are on this thing now." She waited for his reaction. "Dad, what was in the box?"

Again, silence.

Owen couldn't hold back. "Tom, Nevada is under suspicion now too. They're hinting that they think she had something to do with this mess—either protecting you or covering up that she took the pendant herself, somehow. You have to come back to work tomorrow and straighten everything out!"

Nevada listened but there was no reply. She had just about given up on Tom when he spoke.

"I'll think about it. Where are we setting up tomorrow?"

"Beaufort," Nevada said. "At that big old mansion where they did that movie with all the great music."

"I'll think about it." Another couple of seconds went by, she heard a 'beep', and the call was ended. Nevada was left with her curiosity about what the favor was that he wanted.

When they arrived back at the house, she wanted nothing more than a long bike ride, something in the fresh air and sunshine to clear her head. Owen had a dozen emails to answer, so she headed out on her own. The air was still and warm, the water in every lagoon a mirror for the white puffy clouds in the sky. About a mile from the house, she spotted two familiar figures on bikes at a stop sign.

"Lyla Jean! Austen! How ya doin' ?" she asked, as she rode up beside them.

Lyla Jean's eyes were wide. "We found eggs in an osprey nest!"

"Well, we found a nest," Austen corrected. "We don't know if there are eggs."

"Isn't that what you usually find in a nest?" As soon as she said it, Nevada kicked herself for her cynicism and need to make the smart-mouth comment. She knew that if she wanted to have young friends like these two, she needed to curb her tendency to go for the easy joke.

Nevada tried to start over. "Where was this nest?"

"Near the swimming pool," Austen reported. "In a pine tree."

"About thirty feet up!" Lyla Jean added, no offence taken at Nevada's sarcasm. "Do you want to see?"

Nevada's response was to hop on her bike and lead the way down the cart path toward the outdoor pool. Austen and Lyla Jean pedaled furiously after her; wouldn't do to let a senior citizen, as she was sure she appeared to them, outride them or beat them to what was, after all, their find. Austen overtook her just after the first block, and Lyla Jean wasn't far behind.

The lagoon at the entrance to the club was one of the prettiest in the neighborhood. Nevada watched the golfers come and go from the driving range as she rode up to the entrance, then swerved to the right and around the back, in response to Austen's one-handed directions.

The tree that was home to this nest was a magnificent live oak, hung with Spanish moss. At first, Nevada couldn't see anything but branches, but as she stared upward, following Lyla Jean's directions, she detected a clump of twigs, leaves, mud, and who-knew-what-else built onto one of the boughs high above the ground.

"Do we see any eggs or little ones in there?" she asked, shading her eyes with her hand as she tried to notice any movement.

"Not so far," Austen reported. "But we only found it yesterday. We're going to set up a schedule, watch it regularly, maybe put up a camera."

"A camera?" Nevada asked.

"They've done it other places on the island, for turtles and for eagles," Lyla Jean said. "Turtle cam, eagle cam. So, ours will be osprey cam."

"Will you have to come up with a camera yourselves?" Nevada wondered.

Austen shrugged, not taking his eyes off the nest. "Dunno."

Of course. The details didn't matter at this point, just the joy of finding the thing.

"Have you seen the birds landing on the nest?" she asked.

"Oh, yes," Lyla Jean said, eyes shining. "We saw a huge osprey circle it five times when we were here earlier today and then sit on it for a long time. We finally had to leave, to get home for lunch, and she was still sitting there."

"Or he," commented Austen.

"Or he," agreed Lyla Jean. "What's all that stuff up there, do you think?"

Nevada considered. "Lots of parts of trees and shrubs, I guess. Maybe some bits of fabric or house construction material that they've picked up on the roadsides?"

"Spanish moss," Austen added.

"It would be fun to climb up and take a look," Lyla Jean suggested.

"Fun and dangerous," Nevada said. The two kids were looking at each other in a way she didn't like. "Not even fun. Just dangerous. I'm pretty sure you can see all sorts of pictures and video all over the net. You don't have to climb up to take a look."

Again, looking at each other, then at her, then Austen winked.

"Hey!" Nevada said, laughing. "You are *not* going to climb a thirty-foot tree. You are not!"

She jumped on her bike and sped off toward the club gate. "Catch me and I'll buy you ice cream!"

They didn't have to be invited twice.

After spending half an hour with them, Nevada felt as though she'd been through some sort of spiritual car wash, everything cleaned, from the hubcaps to the gearshift console. She walked into the house and met Owen in the kitchen.

"Hello, soulmate of mine," she greeted him and then opened the refrigerator door to search for a cold drink. "How have you been? Did you get everything sorted out for your patients? How's your day going so far? Mine has taken a turn for the excellent."

Owen hugged her. "I'm glad. Not upset about your father's phone call anymore?"

Nevada shrugged. "It is what it is. He'll either turn up at work tomorrow or he won't, and then I'll adjust to whatever comes next."

"Good attitude," he said. "Try to hold onto that. Because it's about to all go downhill."

She was instantly wary. "Why?"

"In the living room," he said, taking the cold can of soda from her and replacing it with a glass of red wine.

"Here."

In the living room armchair to the right of the fireplace, her mother sat, flipping through a book about marine life.

"Hi, Mom, what's up?" Nevada glanced at the tables, looking for Judith's glass of wine, a sign that she might be ready to be mellow and sociable. "Is Owen bringing you something to drink? Have you been here long?"

"About half an hour. I didn't want anything to drink or eat, and he had some work to finish up. He didn't know I was coming here; you didn't know either. I guess I invited myself, but I have to talk to you about something."

"Certainly, Mom, let me just go change, quickly," Nevada said. "I've been bike riding, and I don't want to sit down in these."

"You look fine, Nevada, you don't need to change."

"It's not about the way I look, Mom," Nevada said, trying to maintain her autonomy and remind herself that she was not eight years old anymore. "I want to change into something more comfortable and that I haven't been sweating in for ninety minutes."

"Nevada, please don't be coarse," Judith said. "Sit down over there on the couch. I won't keep you long."

"No? Mom, you know you're more than welcome to stay for dinner," Nevada said. "Then we could discuss whatever it is you have on your mind with as much time as you need."

"No, thanks, Nevada," Judith said. "I have dinner plans already, with one of the other guests at the hotel. I came back from a walk in Forsyth Park, met her in the lobby, and we found out we both have an interest in the Bonaventure Cemetery and colonial history."

"I've never known you to have an interest in colonial history," Nevada said.

"Well, Emily has a way of making it absolutely compelling, and I do now," Judith said. "Her people came over from England in the eighteenth century and were among the founding families in Savannah."

A-ha.

"How much of it do they own, Mom?" Nevada hadn't been able to get to her bedroom to change clothes but she was still standing, not sitting on the couch as ordered, and she counted that a small victory.

"Very funny, Nevada, I have no idea. Why are you always so sarcastic and cynical?"

Because you're always so transparent and mercenary.

"I'm sorry, Mom, let's start over. How long are you staying, and what can I do for you?"

"You can help me get your father to see reason. He *has* to increase my alimony. I'm in over my head, and the tax department letters are coming every week now. The accountant says I can hang on for about six months, but I have to do something now to fix things."

"Why is this any problem of his? Or anybody else's? How can he be on the hook for your spending a decade after your divorce?"

"If we hadn't divorced, I would have no financial problems, Nevada."

"Then maybe you should have figured out what to do to make him happy to stay," Owen called out.

Judith looked ready to explode, and Nevada almost laughed. "No help needed from the peanut gallery!" she called back.

"Nevada, don't be fresh," Judith said. "I've come to you for help with my money problems, and you reply with just rude, juvenile comments and behavior."

"I have money problems of my own, Mom. I can't help you."

Judith was suspicious. "You have plenty of money, Nevada, anybody can see that."

"Nobody can ever tell anything about anybody's financial situation just from external appearances."

"Well, maybe so, but I'm talking dire circumstances here. I can't pay my phone bill for the next month."

"You want me to pay your phone bill?" Nevada asked.

"Your father was taking care of that and now he's not," Judith said. "I have to have a phone. How can I build my business or try to find a job if I don't have phone service?"

"I don't know, Mom, but I also don't know how that's up to me," Nevada said. "You're a grown woman, you have to sort out your own income and expenses."

"Hear, hear!" Owen joined the discussion, calling out from his desk in the next room.

Judith wasn't ready to surrender. "In some families, they are close. Everyone rises or falls together."

Owen appeared at the living room doorway. "You may or may not be close, Judith, I don't know. But what I do know is that the heart is one thing and the wallet is another. You can't take advantage of everybody just because of connections on a birth certificate," Owen said. He walked to the couch and stood over Judith. "Didn't you say you had a better offer for dinner somewhere?"

Judith rose. "Alright, I'll go. Nevada, please let me know if your father gets in touch with you. And if you are in touch with him now, tell him I need help." She picked up her bag from the coffee table. "And that this is not what he promised me, back when we started, in the sixties."

She stomped toward the front door; Owen held it open for her and closed it behind her. After she was gone, Nevada felt worn out.

"Let's recap, shall we?" Owen suggested. "Your boss thinks you should be able to protect his film production and keep your father under control. Your mother thinks you should protect her from having to make a living. Your father thinks you should protect him from your boss and your mother." He guided her toward the couch. "No wonder you're exhausted."

"Let's not forget the insurance investigator thinks I

stole a priceless piece of antique jewelry."

"Has he actually said that? Was anybody else around when he did?" Owen asked.

"So far, just hints and innuendo. The kind of crap it's hard to defend against."

Owen nodded. "I know what you mean. Things are much better when people are direct."

"And only speak when they have proof of whatever."

"You'd think an insurance investigator would be much more cautious." Owen dropped onto the couch beside her. "Wouldn't you think he'd be more like a cop and less like the average person who can get away with unfounded allegations and outrageous speculation because no one is going to act on anything they say anyway?"

"I think he's under a lot of pressure to solve the thing." Nevada closed her eyes. He was right, she was close to exhausted. "The insurance company bosses, but also Jeremy, the movie producers, the cast and crew who feel unsafe because of the feeling that thieves are somewhere around them . . ."

Owen pulled her feet up onto his lap and started to rub them. "Just relax. Even insurance investigators under pressure have to conform to some sort of code of ethics. He can hint around all he wants; if he doesn't have any proof you had anything to do with the theft, then he can't accuse you. Or Tom."

"I hope you're right."

"I know I'm right," he said. "Let's talk about something else. When are you going to introduce me to these bird-watching kids you met?"

"Come bike riding with me on the weekend, after I get back from Beaufort, and I'm sure we'll bump into them."

He looked at her closely. "Are you feeling better about Savannah, Trip? Are you starting to feel a bit more comfortable here?"

What she was really feeling was a bit more depressed

here, more and more like just hiding under the covers or on a couch, staring at a television every day. But she smiled comfortingly because she knew that was what he wanted her to do. "I feel comfortable, darling. I don't really belong here, but I can stay a while."

Next morning, Nevada drove to Beaufort, South Carolina under a sky so blue she wished she knew how to paint. A photograph would have to do, and she pulled over after crossing the bridge over the Savannah River to park and get her shot. The bridge was named after an historical figure who had some association with political turmoil and racism, and there had been several attempts to get it renamed. The South and the North were still dealing with the aftermath of the Civil War, despite Martin Luther King, Jr.'s dream that character would mean more than skin color. It was very sad, and the pain inflicted on all sides was evident and intense. Nevada wished she knew what the solution was, but she was as far from it as anyone else, and had far less legitimacy, as a newcomer, to be suggesting anything. But she could wish them all well and hope that the next hundred fifty years would show the way to a reconciliation. The U.S. Civil War was a war that had never really ended; even now, in 2014, the vanquished were still fighting some of the battles, and the liberated were still experiencing some of the emotions of those in chains.

Beaufort was a small South Carolina city forty-two miles from Savannah and tidily positioned to serve as a location for any film shoot requiring old mansions, waterfront, Gullah culture, or quaint historic downtown streets. It was the sort of place where cars and trucks looked out of place, as if they'd rolled through a time warp and ended up in this place by cosmic accident. Nevada followed the signs and parked in the school lot that had been set up for the movie people. She'd barely stepped out of her car and grabbed her clipboard when Doyle O'Keefe showed up at her elbow.

"Miss Nevada! Any word from your father?"

Nevada looked around desperately for an escape excuse and found one in the purple hair and bright yellow pantsuit of a woman walking between the vehicles just a few rows over. "Ms. Sullivan! Hello!" she called in Cassidy's direction.

She watched Cassidy stop, look her up and down for a moment, then make the decision to walk in Nevada and Doyle's direction.

"Hello, Miss Nevada. Nice to see y'all."

"How does Beaufort end up on your agenda this morning?" Nevada asked.

"I'm an extra," Cassidy said brightly.

"You are?! Whatever for?" Nevada would rather drive the same two-mile strip of highway seventy-five times in a row than work even one day as an extra. Long boring hours being herded from one holding pen to another, a few short minutes of doing something or other, on the AD's cue, all for the kind of pay that left people raiding dumpsters. Oh yes, the glamor of Hollywood.

"Life is nothing but a series of experiences, Miss Nevada, don't you think?" Cassidy was dog-less today, but her accessories included a bag big enough to carry a table lamp and a folding camp chair.

What did she mean? Did she include the experience of stealing a priceless cultural artifact? And why was she at a car show, meeting with Nevada's father a month ago? Nevada knew she would have to find a few spare minutes for an interview today with Miss Cassidy.

Nevada and Doyle watched her march off in the direction of the extras' gathering spot, then he turned back to Nevada. "You know that I could get the police to bring him in for questioning, just like that."

"Why don't you just do that, Mr. O'Keefe?" Suddenly, she was just sick of him. Sick of the entire scene and the hassle that looking after her father had turned out to be.

Doyle stared at her, his eyes hooded like a snake's. "Why would you say that, Miss Nevada? You don't mean that."

Her cell phone buzzed. "I have to take this," she said, without looking at the screen, and walked off toward the back of the set.

Chelan's name was on the call display. "Hey. How are you?"

"I'm just fine," her friend replied. "Soaking wet, all day every day here in Vancouver, but otherwise, just fine."

"Yeah, we may have gun violence and racial tension and economic gaps and a drug crisis down here, but we've got the good climate." That sounded pretty sarcastic. Nevada hoped she wasn't coming across to Chelan as sneering. "What's up?"

"So I came across something on a photo-sharing site that I think could be a lead," Chelan said. "It's fuzzy and the caption is very vague, but I think it could be your bird pendant."

"That's fantastic! What's the URL?" Nevada asked, fumbling in her bag for a pen.

"I'll text it to you."

"Thank you! Chelan, this is just great. You've been great. I really appreciate you sticking with this."

"I'm starting to be as focused about it as you are," she said. "Besides, it really gives me a way to keep on using my skills, a way to distract myself from the feeling that I'm nothing more than a big wagon, hauling around this baby."

Nevada didn't know what to say; this was unfamiliar territory for her.

"Sorry, I didn't mean to start spilling," Chelan said with a laugh. "It's just that it's easy to forget you have a career and a purpose in life when you're so dominated by pregnancy. At least it is for me. Truly, I really appreciating this quest for your father's whereabouts and this ancient piece of bling as a way of reminding myself I'm still a reporter. Thank you."

"You're welcome." What else was there to say? "I'll take a look at this site and see where we might go from there."

The social media site was not one of the half dozen most popular ones. It was easy to navigate, though, and seemed, like most of them, to be populated by hundreds of thousands of people who had no qualms about sharing pictures and thoughts on every conceivable subject. Chelan was right, the photo of the pendant was quite indistinct, but the caption could certainly be read as relevant: *never before available. 15thC. DM for more info.*

Nevada was just thinking over the pros and cons of setting up a user account to interact with the poster of the photograph when her phone buzzed again with an incoming text from Chelan. Did she want Chelan to continue the research, set up a screen name, try to get an online conversation going with the person offering the pendant for . . . for what? Sale? Did fine art thieves find their clients in this way?

Maybe it was possible that the thief had stolen it on commission but now was trying to raise the value of it by presenting it online?

The appeal of having Chelan take this over was compelling, but what if she inadvertently said the wrong thing, gave too much away, used a phrase that spooked somebody? Nevada gave herself a shake. Why did she have so much difficulty trusting other people? Chelan could probably handle this better than she could herself.

She texted back *go for it* then crossed her arms and started scanning in each direction as far as she could, looking for Tom. She wished she'd brought some binoculars, although it occurred to her that if he did show up on set here today, he would probably seek her out.

"Hey, Nevada, how are you?"

The voice was warm and musical, and when she turned to see its source the Southern belle costume that Yvonne Lee was wearing added the perfect echo to the faint accent she'd heard. *Young* was the word that leaped to mind. "Hi, Yvonne. You look lovely."

"Thanks. They really dressed the part in those days, didn't they? Princesses through and through." She smoothed the shimmering green silk of the voluminous skirt down from the tight black waistband. "It's comfortable today, but I have to wonder how they survived in July when the temperature was into three digits!"

"I think they all went north to escape the heat," Nevada said. "The ones who could afford dresses like that, anyway. How's work going?"

Yvonne smiled. "It's fine. Next set up is still an hour away, and I got bored in my trailer so I thought I'd take a bit of a walk, till they call me."

"Are you enjoying this one?"

"Yeah, it's good. They're all good, really," she said, grinning. "I'm a middle child in a family of seven, and everybody was talkin' all the time. Anywhere I get to put on a pretty dress and say a thing or two without someone interruptin' me is a good place."

"I always wondered about what it would be like to grow up in a big family," Nevada said.

"And I always wondered what it would be like to grow up with a father who was an actor," Yvonne added. "Rather than a politician."

"Politician?"

"Old time, long time. Family business." Yvonne undid the lemon-yellow ribbon tied under her chin and took off her broad-brimmed straw hat. "Makes for an interestin' childhood, but you gotta watch your step every minute. Can't let anybody down, ever, and God forbid you ever do anything to embarrass them."

"God forbids a lot of things down here, it seems to me," Nevada joked.

Yvonne got it, but didn't take offense. "That's the truth. But He is great and He is with you every step of the way, if you let Him."

"Has it been difficult for you, being an actress in Hollywood, coming from a conservative Southern family?"

Yvonne shrugged. "They think I'm the odd one. But you know, it's tough in some way or other for everybody who goes to L.A. "

"And for you it was the Southern background?"

"No, I'd say it was more than that, it's that there's so much pressure to put out, all the time."

Nevada just looked at Yvonne for a long moment. She could feel a sort of heaviness around her, a combination of beige, gray, and black that didn't jibe with the sunny, spring-like colors of her dress and hat. "Is it that bad, still?"

Yvonne rolled her eyes slightly and made a face. "Do you know the word some of them use to describe the actress they want for a part?"

"Yeah, I think I do."

"Yeah. Well." Yvonne put her hat back on and started to tie it into place. "So far I haven't had to go ahead and make that my method of getting cast. I'm proud of that. But the pressure is all around, all the time, and there is just so much competition for roles."

Nevada nodded sympathetically. "I'm sure it isn't easy."

"It's not. But I'm a survivor, and I'll bet you're one too." She smiled her friendly smile. "I think I'd better get back to my trailer, in case they're lookin' for me."

As she watched her go, Nevada pondered the various things she'd said. Why did they all seem slightly weird, even ominous? Was it just Yvonne's actor's way of speaking rather slowly and seriously? Or was Nevada being paranoid?

CHAPTER 22

Lillian gripped the seat cushions on the tiny boat as casually as she could manage. She was not an experienced sailor and even the water on a small lake when she could see the far shore gave her an uneasy feeling. The endless ocean was so intimidating she could barely take it in.

But Donovan, her cherished grandson, had asked her to come along on this little day trip, and she couldn't say no this time. The Florida sunshine was warm and golden, and she had to admit the view of Key West from this side was charming. Donovan had invited her out on his boat many times and she'd always found some excuse. When she was kidding herself, she said that this time she had run out of excuses. When she was being honest, she admitted that adding Adam Brecklin to join the group increased the appeal of the outing.

The boat seemed tiny to her, compared to the infinity of the ocean, but in reality, Donovan told her, it was a respectable forty-two feet. She could tell he was very proud of it and she gave herself a moment to feel proud of him, proud of his determination to own his own boat and be self-employed. Donovan insisted with a smile that the boat was as much hers as it was his, thanks to her financial support, and so she should spend at least as much time on it as he did. She'd joked back that it was more the bank's than either of theirs and maybe they should leave it parked, nice and safe, at the marina just down the road, on dry land like the bank. Docked, Grandma, not parked, Donovan said, and then they each stuck their tongues out at one another. She was enjoying being a grandma more each day.

They weren't fishing, just out for a sight-seeing cruise this morning. "It's just a little recreation before we get down to serious work on Adam's boat at the dive site," Donovan said. "Exploring the shipwreck."

Exploring a shipwreck. Only three words and yet Lillian couldn't be more entranced than if she were listening to a pitch from one of the most persuasive salesmen in the world.

Adam took over. "As you probably know, the Florida coast has dozens of ships lost in storms lying on the ocean floor. Divers explore the accessible ones all the time, and a lot of them have been mapped and combed over completely. The expedition we're on is different."

"Is this the one you mentioned the other day?" Lillian asked.

Adam nodded. "The location of this ship has been hard to pinpoint, all these years, and if we find it—when we find it—we'll be the first to find out whether the stories are true."

Donovan looked like an eight-year-old on Christmas Eve, his eyes huge. Lillian found herself barely able to breathe. "What are the stories?"

"That it was a Spanish galleon that went down in a hurricane in 1490-something, carrying tons of gold. Over the years, there have been a few efforts to go after it, but every expedition plan failed, usually for lack of money. I'm going to capitalize it properly—I already have. I really think I've got all the right people on board too."

Donovan beamed. "I'm all in."

Adam beamed back. "Yes, you are. Good man! It will be terrific experience for you and a story you can tell your grandchildren, the day we start to bring up the—"

"Treasure," Lillian filled in.

Donovan brought out a cooler and passed around beers. As Lillian sipped hers, she stared at the shore and tried to imagine a voyage hundreds of years ago, a ship laden with booty fighting hurricane winds and eventually going down. She almost envied Donovan his chance to be part of such an exciting project. A lively wave tossed the boat upward, and she grabbed for the rail at the side of the bench. *Almost* envied; she wouldn't actually sign on for the job he was going to do for a million dollars.

*

Nevada was looking at water that day, too, but from the much more stable footing of a boardwalk beside a lovely marsh. Beaufort, South Carolina had invested in its downtown and waterfront areas and showed the pride of place that was typical of many small Southern towns that aspired to bring in the tourists. She was sitting on a bench only a short walk from the production trucks and mobile dressing rooms—just a few hundred steps, but far enough to let her clear her head.

"Hello, Nevada! How nice to bump into you down here!"

She turned her head to see Frank Leonard standing at her elbow and smiling at her in a jolly way. He was carrying a shopping bag, and his eyes were hidden behind aviator shades. In his polo shirt, khakis, and deck shoes, he would look like everyone else at The Pines, but here he looked rather unusual, particularly given that there weren't too many other men she'd seen this morning who stood about six foot five.

"Hello, Frank! How are you?"

"Just fine, thank you. Linda's over at the café having lunch with a friend, and I'm passing the time shopping and trying to come up with the right gift for a teenage nephew. Do you follow these things? What would a thirteen-year-old boy want for a birthday gift these days?"

"No idea," Nevada said, laughing.

"Me neither. But I try. May I join you for a while?"

He politely waited for her nod, then sank down onto the bench. "Aah, good. I was getting a little warm, I don't mind telling you."

"Just wait till July," Nevada said. "I'm told the heat is unbelievable."

"I've been here in July, and yes, it is. But there's air conditioning everywhere, so who cares?" Frank reached into his shopping bag and pulled out a video game box of some kind. "What do you think?"

"Like I said, no idea." Nevada smiled warmly to take the edge off her words. Just beneath the box, she could see a newspaper and, when Frank picked up his new toy to look it over, she could read the headline. *Priceless Antique Stolen from Movie Set*. Crap.

Frank noticed the direction of her gaze. "Yeah, that's really something, isn't it? What are you hearing on set, Nevada? In my experience, movie crews gossip nonstop. They usually know everything that's going on. What's the buzz? Any clues? Ransom demands? Or has it just disappeared? Any speculation about who done it?"

Nevada felt frozen by the barrage of questions. What was she supposed to do, tell the truth to this man who was so important to her husband's situation at the hospital? That her father, the has-been movie actor, might have taken the necklace, and even if he hadn't, the suspicion swirling around him was going to be enough to sink what little career he had left?

"I haven't heard much, Frank," she said. "But the theory seems to be leaning toward something like insurance fraud or maybe a desperation grab by an extra presented with an opportunity. They're checking everybody out pretty thoroughly."

"Are you helping? I would guess that someone with your journalism experience could be very useful."

Nevada laughed. "Not really. There's a lot of difference between a police investigation and a reporter nosing around. I don't think there's much I could offer."

"Don't sell yourself short, my dear," Frank said. "I know most people don't have much use for the media, but I've never been in that camp. You underestimate the media at your peril, I always told my staff."

"What would be your guess, Frank?" Nevada asked. "You mentioned something a moment ago about ransom—how would that work?"

"I guess I was thinking with my old movie producer hat on, with that one," Frank replied. "If the family that owns the piece of jewelry, or the museum, wants it back badly enough, maybe they'll be asked for some significant money for its return. Or offering. I guess that would be a reward, more than a ransom, but it's the same idea, essentially."

"What about a theft on behalf of some rabid private collector who just wants to have the thing to look at, in the privacy of his own home? We know it would be really difficult for anyone to fence something that unusual and, now with all this press, so well known. But if there's somebody who doesn't care about the re-sale value . . ."

"I think we've seen that movie," Frank said. "That's a Hollywood notion, or a plot. Not anything you might see happening in real life."

Nevada stared at the hotel across the river, willing herself almost into a semi-trance so that she could slow down the velocity of her thoughts and perhaps make room for a flash of inspiration. "What else could it be? What about a crime that has nothing to do with the value of the pendant itself but has something to do with a vendetta against the owner or anger at the movie production, for some reason?"

Frank nodded. "That has to be worrying our friend Jeremy Walsh right about now. The last thing he needs is some looney tune lurking around trying to find a way to sabotage his set and his film."

"Are you going to drop in to see him today? We're filming just around the corner at the Tidalholm mansion."

"Not today. Linda wants me to take her out to Hilton Head this afternoon. I have to meet her in about two minutes." He stood up and took his plastic shopping bag. "Nice to see you, Nevada."

She smiled and nodded, then watched him set off toward the residential part of town. Were there any cafés over there? She wondered if he knew he was going in the wrong direction. She almost called out, then decided to just let it go. Not her job, to make sure Frank got to his destination.

When Nevada arrived back on set, she was surprised to see Cassidy Sullivan strolling along near the trailers. Usually, extras had very specific boundaries, around what might almost be described as a holding pen, and they weren't allowed anywhere near the stars' or directors' hangouts. This was twice now, in a very short period of time.

She saw Cassidy before Cassidy saw her, and she had a few seconds to marvel, yet again, at the very intense shades of the woman's hair, turned back from brown to purple, her yellow pants, and her red sweater. She shook her head, and she must have been smiling in what Cassidy took as a friendly way because, seconds later, she was the recipient of a warm hug.

"Nevada! Nice to see you!"

Clearly, Cassidy wasn't flying under the radar here. "Nice to you see you again too, Cassidy. What are you doing over here?"

"Jeremy asked me to meet him for a quick chat about Spanish gold and Civil War heirlooms and such."

"You?" As soon as she said it Nevada was aware of how rude it sounded. She'd been on vacation too long— her filters were going.

Luckily, Cassidy laughed. "Yes, me. Believe it or not, Nevada, I do more than haunt estate sales looking for Confederate coins or old pocket watches."

Something about the way she said it and a slightly

different tilt of her head stopped Nevada and made her take a good look at Cassidy. "Why are you telling me this now?"

"Good question." Cassidy nodded approvingly. "I looked you up online. And I figured a major-market newsroom director might be more interested in my other side than the Southern belles I've mostly known around here."

Despite her preoccupation with her father's troubles, her mother's complaints, and her own growing sense of concern, Nevada decided she should focus on this woman and really listen to what she was saying.

"I study twelfth-century civilizations centered on what are now the North American and Central American continents," Cassidy continued. "Mostly from the anthropology and archaeology perspectives, although I also have a PhD in art history. That's how I started out, actually, but then I became entranced with the role of art creation in the communication and culture-sustaining activities of some of these ancient societies. Then I wanted to know more about the language and traditions they passed down—that was the anthropology degree—and then I wanted to be there, right on the scene and in the moment, when they dug up some of these ancient treasures and masterpieces, so I had to do the archaeology PhD too."

"I'm impressed," Nevada said, smiling and thinking, *I'll have to revise my opinions on purple hair.*

"Just following my nose," Cassidy said.

"But what are you doing working for minimum wage as an extra on a movie set, then? With all of that education, why aren't you at some university, rolling in the big bucks?"

"Too independent, I guess. I like Savannah, and there's nothing I want to do here, employed by anybody. So, I pick up a contract here, a contract there, and my time is my own, to plan and use as I please." Cassidy struck a little pose. "I've always been curious about movie-making, and I love to dress up, as you can see. So here I am."

"I get it. I've sometimes thought that if I didn't have to make a living or get along with the love of my life, I would go volunteer on a rock-and-roll festival tour. Or maybe run away and join the circus."

"I don't think that's a thing anymore," Cassidy said. "The concert idea sounds better. Anyway, I just told the AD I was going to the restroom, so I'd better get back to the holding area."

"I don't think there's any restroom near here."

"I think you're right—I'll have to search farther afield. Nice running into you, Nevada," Cassidy said. "Maybe we can grab a drink or something back at The Pines."

"Love to," Nevada said, then watched Cassidy head off toward an area down the road where lights were being set up around a vacant lot.

Just past that corner, in the distance, Nevada saw a figure that looked familiar. Very tall, wearing golf clothes—was that Frank again? On set? Or *was* that part of the set? Maybe not. She watched him walk farther away and almost took out her phone to try to zoom in with the camera and see him up close, but then remembered the prohibition against anyone using their camera on set. Even if she had no intention of using it to get surreptitious fan-photos of movie stars or marketable behind-the-scenes shots, she wouldn't want to have to convince anybody.

She stood there for a few minutes, willing Frank, if it was him, to walk toward her rather than away, but it didn't happen.

Lingering over her lunch, Nevada couldn't shake her curiosity about Cassidy. She was still pondering when Jeremy approached her, wanting to discuss yet another unusual request. Really, the man made a career of them.

"Nevada, I've just had a run-in with Roger, and I need your help," Jeremy said.

"Hah! No way," Nevada commented, tucking into her Caesar salad and grinning at him.

"You can't say no—you work for me."

"Hah, again. I've never been able to get away with that with any of the people who work for me, so why should you?"

"Because I'm Hollywood, and you're just TV news," Jeremy said, reaching over and filching one of her croutons. She rapped his knuckles with her fork. Best to keep this as light and friendly as she could, since he seemed to be willing to lighten up on blaming her for every one of Tom's comings and goings.

"Alright, what's up?" she asked.

"I want to incorporate some of the 'Savannah is a very old, very haunted place' tone into this movie. I don't think it's wrong—the original town goes back a hundred and thirty-some years before the setting for this movie. But Roger seems to feel it's not authentic or necessary and is refusing to write anything." Jeremy took off his ball cap and wiped his forehead with the back of his sleeve. "I don't know, maybe he's just lazy or maybe it really is a professional point, but I need some new ammo to take to him, something more specific to ask him to fold in. We do have that soldier's letter that you and your colleague turned up, but I'm leaning another way, maybe even another sequence. Could you do a little more research for me?"

"Yes, of course, Jeremy. I know what you want," Nevada agreed. "By the way, any sign of Tom today?" Jeremy couldn't see, but she had two fingers crossed for good luck and the right answer behind her back.

"No, nothing at all."

"Are you sticking to your ultimatum?"

Jeremy sighed. "Not really. What can I do? I don't want to recast, at this point, although that's not out of the question. But he's not done yet. Let him know that, would you, if you hear from him?"

"I haven't," Nevada assured him.

"I know you haven't. I know you would have told me," Jeremy said. "But let's just hope he shows up tomorrow and that he realizes he's getting another chance."

Later that evening, as Nevada drove home from Beaufort, she dropped the self-confident face she'd adopted with Jeremy and pondered what she'd do next with this assignment. She'd start with an online search, of course, but she knew that there was a lot of material in Savannah, real and up close, that she could take a look at. Cemeteries, for example. There seemed to be one on almost every second corner. And there were history buffs who led tours all over the downtown district where the colonial and then antebellum events took place so long ago.

She was just in the midst of contemplating a midnight exploration of some of the allegedly haunted buildings in the historic district, and planning her approach to Owen to get him to accompany her, when she noticed a vehicle looming in her rearview mirror. She checked her speedometer—had she slowed down too much while being so absorbed in her thoughts? No, she was okay, but just to be cooperative she accelerated a little.

He was still there, headlights glaring in her rear-view mirror.

Nevada frowned. What was his problem? The fast lane was wide open, why didn't he just pull out and pass her?

She touched her brakes lightly and then let her car slow down. She wasn't going to go the next thirty miles along the highway with this guy on her bumper, pushing her to drive faster than she wanted to.

He was still there. Nevada put on her signal and pulled over to the fast lane. Maybe he liked the right-hand lane, this guy, and just wanted her out of it?

He pulled out right behind her. Now there were only about two feet between her bumper and his fender, and he was hanging on right behind her as if they were attached. This was getting creepy.

Nevada pulled back into the slow lane, and the vehicle was right behind her again. From the height of the headlights, it looked like it could be an SUV, maybe a pickup truck. She fumbled through her bag on the passenger seat beside her and pulled out her phone. She knew she wasn't supposed to use it while driving but if she needed to call 911 and get the cops here, she would.

She felt a light tap on her bumper. Then the SUV dropped back, pulled out into the fast lane and then even with her, keeping pace no matter what she did. All of the windows were tinted to the point of zero light transmission and she couldn't see the driver or even whether there was more than one person in the SUV. Keeping her eyes on the road, Nevada reached for her phone and tapped the emergency numbers.

When the state police patrol appeared five minutes later, Nevada's harasser pulled off at the next exit. The trooper seemed inclined not to take it too seriously.

"I'd say 'nothing personal', ma'am," the officer said. "More likely just a bit of mild road rage. Guy didn't like something you did back a few dozen miles—maybe you cut him off or something? Then he decided to teach y'all a little lesson, maybe scare you a little bit. You aren't scared, are you?" The personable young officer smiled at her, and she had to admit she did feel safer and a little embarrassed. Maybe she had jumped to conclusions?

"No, not at all, thank you," Nevada said, returning his farewell nod. She got back behind the wheel of her car and drove off. For the next ten miles she tensed up every time another vehicle was anywhere near her. Get a grip, Nevada, she thought. You won't be able to walk around every day and enjoy your life if you let yourself get so jumpy about a little bit of aggressive driving. Shake it off.

By the time she passed the gate into The Pines and pulled up to her driveway, she was calm again. Just as she climbed the front steps to the door, her phone buzzed with a text.

Going to drive with u again soon
 NOT SO NICE NEXT TIME
Time to leave Savannah

CHAPTER 23

Nevada was so shaken that it took her a moment to realize that the door had opened and Owen was there, his arms held out to her. Not his usual style—what was going on? Could he possibly already know about the jerk following her on the highway?

"Hey, what's up?"

"I have something to tell you," he said as he gave her a hug. "Come inside."

The living room coffee table had been set with wine glasses filled with a ruby wine, a small plate of sushi, and four lit candles.

"My, my," Nevada said, deciding that the tale of her encounter on the drive home could wait a while. "Have I forgotten an anniversary of something?"

Owen grinned, then picked up a glass of wine and held it out to her. "A toast."

She took it, touched her glass to his, then took a long pull on it. Man, that tasted good. After the day she'd had, no surprise here. "What are we toasting?"

"A new job opportunity. A glorious job opportunity." He looked into her face with the expression of a little boy who just couldn't wait to let out a secret. "I had a call from Vancouver General. Pediatrics. They want to offer me a dual appointment with the Cancer Institute."

It was his dream job, the job he would design for himself if anyone would let him. Nevada was thrilled for him for about half a second and then felt a tide of resistance rise within her.

He read her face instantly. "What is it?"

She didn't—couldn't—answer right away because she didn't know what it was that was blocking her. She'd thought she wanted to leave Savannah and get back to Vancouver. She knew that if she stayed away too long, it would be very difficult to get herself back up to speed, trying to run a newsroom in Vancouver. There were so few jobs left in journalism that there was a lineup of qualified, talented people waiting to pour into any opening, like water into the hole after you pull your hand out of a pail. She had thought she really didn't know what she wanted to do or where she wanted to be, and now, here was a gift of a solution. So why didn't she feel at all excited about the news that Owen was giving her?

"Is it a short-term contract?"

Owen looked at her intently. "A year. What is it, Trip? This isn't sitting well with you, I can tell."

"I'm not sure," she said carefully. "I thought I would be delighted at the prospect of getting back to Vancouver—"

"I thought you would be too," he interrupted.

"But for some reason I'm not," she finished. He waited, but she had nothing more to add.

"Well, alright then." He blinked hard a few times as if he were trying to clear his vision.

"Really? It's alright?"

"Yes, of course, Nevada," he said. "Everything we do, we do together. We only came here to the Deep South because we both agreed it would be an interesting adventure. We won't go back to Vancouver unless we both agree it's the right time to do that."

"But what about the job, the chance to pursue both your specialties?"

"There will be other opportunities coming up. And if they really want me, maybe they'll wait." He reached for the wine bottle and poured them each another glass. "So, it's decided then? I still have a lot of work to do here. We'll go back to Canada when the time is right."

*

The waves offshore at Key West were surging today even though it wasn't the time of year for what Lillian liked to think of as "interesting weather". June to November, those were the prime hurricane watch and warning months; this bit of April squall was pure entertainment, not danger, and nothing to worry about. She pulled her sweater belt a little tighter around her middle, then pushed her sunglasses up a little higher on the bridge of her nose. It was a strange day, with the sun bright and warm but the wind contradicting it.

Ordinarily, on a day like today, she would have been tucked in cozily at her favorite coffee shop, or perhaps the library or the museum, glancing at the palm trees swaying in the strong wind, then giving most of her attention to a good book or her computer tablet. But Donovan had called last night to tell her that he was going to be in town and wanted to get together.

Lillian thought it was wonderful to have a twenty-something grandson who wanted to share the details of his life and some of his experiences, vicariously, with an old lady like herself. No, not an old lady—an *advanced* person. Hadn't she heard from many another grandparent who lamented that their young family members pretty much disappeared unless there was money or a holiday meal being handed out? She was grateful for him, for sure. But he seemed sometimes to think she was seventy-something going on twenty-one, and his expectations were pretty high.

Today, for example. He had called her and asked her to meet him at the main dock. Told her to wear deck shoes and be ready to spend a few hours out on the water. He wanted to show her the dive zone that had been staked out for exploration over the coming weeks. She'd jokingly suggested he just take some photos and email them to her.

Nobody uses email anymore, Grandma, he'd said.

Lillian checked her watch and saw that she had just five minutes. She picked up her pace along the marina seawall and scanned the horizon for a powerboat named *The Francis Drake.* "What color should I be looking for?" she'd asked Donovan, and it had given him a good laugh, as she intended.

"Grandma, you're so nautical," he'd said. "You know it's white, virtually all boats are white."

"Why is that, anyway?" she'd asked. She could picture him shrugging.

"Who cares," he'd answered. "Do you want to come along? You've been on my boat, but I don't know if you've ever had a ride on a powerboat like this one of Adam's. Plus, he wants you to go, and I'm supposed to call him back and let him know."

Ah. So, there was more to this invitation than just a grandson enjoying the company of his grandmother. Again, Lillian was grateful; at least this information had arrived last night when there was still time to make sure the clothes she wanted to wear were clean and available. The alarm clock had been set for the extra time she needed to do her makeup properly. She'd even given an extra half hour to her hair, straightening it and taking out every last bit of frizz. Now this annoying wind had come up, and her hair looked like she'd spent six hours riding backwards in a convertible. Well, she'd done the best she could and, if Mr. Brecklin could be put off by a little bit of messy hair, then he was more trouble than he was worth. Lillian chuckled to herself.

She spotted Donovan on the deck of a massive white whale of a boat tied at the very end of the dock. It looked as though it might be the only spot big enough for it. He waved to her and she waved back, then realized that Adam Brecklin stood beside Donovan, waving his own greeting to her. Very enthusiastically. Oh my.

Both men jumped from the boat to the dock to greet

her. Donovan took her hand and arm, holding her just above the elbow in what seemed like a rather possessive way. Adam leaped back to the boat and reached out his hands to receive her. She had planned to get herself aboard under her own steam, but as the boat pitched and rolled with the water action, she found herself leaning on Donovan and then gripping Adam's hands tightly so that she wouldn't fall. Adam led her toward the stern and settled her into a well-upholstered deck chair.

"There!" she said brightly. "Thank you both so much."

"Grandma, I'm so glad you were able to come along." Donovan stepped behind the wheel and turned the key, sending the boat's engine into a low-pitched idle. She could tell he was showing off, just a little.

"Lillian, may we offer you something to drink?" Adam beamed at her, then looked over her head. "Oh, and I should be making introductions."

Lillian turned in her seat to take a look. A roundish man in a tight-fitting suit appeared from the bow, walking carefully and holding on to the edges of the cabin.

"This is Doyle O'Keefe, a friend of mine from Savannah," Adam said. "I invited him to go out with us today because he has an interest in shipwrecks."

Doyle snorted. "In a manner of speaking, I suppose I do. How do you do, Miss Lillian," he said, greeting her with a rather formal nod. Lillian couldn't remember her name being mentioned, but there were a lot of things she didn't remember nowadays and if she spent her time trying to recall she'd never have a new thought.

"How do you do, Mr. O'Keefe," she replied. "Have you gone along to look at a shipwreck dive expedition on other occasions?"

"Mr. Adam is making a bit of a joke because of my profession as an insurance investigator," Doyle replied. "Missing or destroyed valuables of any kind are my specialty. I suppose you could just as easily say I have an interest in hurricanes or fires or earthquakes. I'm not actually here about this shipwreck though."

"And what is everyone expecting to find on this one?" Lillian asked as she moved over to make room for Doyle to sit down.

The men looked at one another, and no one spoke.

"Treasure," Adam finally said. "I don't think anybody ever needs to get any more specific than that."

His cell phone rang, and Lillian thought she recognized the ring tone as a bit of the tune "Rock Around the Clock". He glanced at the call display, then stood up from his deck chair.

"I'm sorry, Lillian, but I have to take this call."

She nodded, gave him a smile, and decided to overlook his phone addiction. Donovan concentrated on steering, edging the big boat out of the marina. She was impressed at her grandson's skill in maneuvering this glistening white craft past all the other yachts that seemed to be docked just inches from one another. The breeze was soft, and the water a shade of blue that ought to be captured in a painting or a very special dress. Lillian felt blissfully happy.

The sound of shouting cut through her enjoyment of the day. Was that Adam? She could hear a man's voice, a few curse words, and then almost a sort of hissing, as if someone were trying to pull back or hold back any more angry words. She looked toward the bow and there he was, phone to his ear. Even though he had his back to them, she could hear every word, now that her attention was focused in that direction. Sound travels very clearly across the water.

"Look, how many more ways do I need to say it! I'll do my best, but I can't promise anything. You have to give me some time."

He paused to listen for a few moments, then repeated, "You just have to give me more time. Alright? Are we done here? You have to let me go or I won't be able to get anything done, and you won't get any of them. Ever."

Lillian sensed he was on his way back toward the seating area of the boat, and she quickly turned her attention to a beautiful sloop they were gliding past.

"I am sorry to take off like that," Adam announced as he rejoined them. "How is everyone doing? Does anyone need another drink? Lillian? Doyle? Donovan, I won't ask you 'cause we have to at least have the captain fully sober!" He chuckled as he went around collecting their glasses. Lillian thought it was quite amazing that he could switch moods so quickly. She briefly considered asking him about the call since everyone had heard his side of it, and he knew that everyone had heard, but she decided to go for the diplomatic side.

Doyle had less grace. "What in the Sam Hill was that all about?"

Adam made a face. "Client of mine. Looking for some assistance that he thinks is too slow in coming."

"What's he want?" Doyle asked.

"Oh, he thinks I should be putting my attention toward a project that was already in progress and has just gone off the rails a little bit. Rather than toward a new initiative," Adam explained.

Lillian thought that sounded perfectly clear and had about as much detail as it was polite to expect. She was about to change the subject when Doyle spoke again.

"Why wouldn't it be possible to use your resources for both?" he asked. A reasonable, relatively intelligent question, Lillian thought.

For some reason, though, it seemed to irritate Adam. She was beginning to realize that he was a bit of a volatile character. The air between Adam and Doyle seemed charged, somehow. Lillian glanced at Donovan to see whether he was picking up any of this, or might be ready to take a part in the conversation; but he had his back to them all, his hands on the wheel and his attention on the marina and the open water that lay just beyond the channel markers.

"That should be up to me," Adam said. "We've just got a client here who is pushing at the boundaries a bit too hard, and somebody needs to get him back to the right place."

Doyle looked over their heads, out toward the water and the other boats. "What if he doesn't like that?"

Adam seemed frozen for just a moment, and then he laughed. "Come on, Doyle, you've seen me in action often enough. I'll make sure he's a happy camper, and it won't be hard to do. And in the meantime," he said, waving an arm to include Donovan, Lillian, and the whole rest of the marina, "everyone else can just carry on, having fun with us looking for this sunken ship and all its treasures!"

Donovan turned back from the wheel briefly, to grin at them all. Adam put his right hand into a fist, held it toward Lillian, and she returned the bump, as she'd seen the American president doing on TV. When it was Doyle's turn to return the friendly salute, though, the insurance man's face looked anything but collegial.

*

Nevada called Chelan as soon as she thought the sun would be up on the west coast.

"Hey, I need a sounding board," she said, pulling her chair up to the window to look out at the lagoon.

"I'm down," Chelan said. "Does it have to do with your decision about staying in Savannah?"

"Not really. I go hot and cold on that . . . and right now, it's on the cold side. The latest is, I had a guy try to drive me off the road."

"You're kidding! What for? Road rage?"

"Don't know. Unlikely it was random since he knows my phone number, somehow. Sent me a threatening text."

"Geez, Nevada. What's going on?"

"I don't know. It might be connected to the movie production. Roger Ridley, the screenwriter, seems deeply annoyed with me, pretty much all the time. He didn't like it when we turned up that authentic letter from our Civil War soldier . . . maybe he feels like he should have been the one to find it. That I'm showing him up, somehow."

"But you told me he was hostile even before then," Chelan commented.

"Yeah, and he doesn't seem like the type to try to run a woman off a road."

"Plus, it would be a bit of an overreaction for anybody," Chelan said. "Can you hang on a minute? Drew's just going out to work and I want to say good-bye."

When Chelan returned, she came back with another theory. "Is it connected to the theft of the bird pendant, do you think?"

"Well, if he took it and isn't too good at absorbing guilt and stress, that *might* be showing up as aggression."

"Or if he thinks he's a suspect, that might do it, too," Chelan said. "*Is* he a suspect?"

"I wouldn't have thought so," Nevada replied. "But we haven't really heard anything official about suspects being identified."

"If you were guessing, who would you say?"

Nevada gave it some thought. "An international gang of art treasure thieves. A rival film director trying to make sure *Too Beautiful to Burn* isn't finished and distributed in time for next year's awards."

"Be serious."

"Alright. Could be Tom . . . he's said he needs money."

"On that motivation," Chelan said, "it could be your mother, couldn't it? Wasn't it kind of weird how she turned up here in Savannah? Hasn't she made friends with Jeremy Walsh?"

"Yeah, it was," Nevada said. "But I can't imagine her having the nerve to go through with it."

"We're just talking about motive right now. And

means and opportunity. And who might be a suspect."

"Okay, also Clio, Dad's new girlfriend."

"Okay, maybe. Who else?"

Nevada sighed. "I've run out of ideas. I do know some people seem to be ready to accuse me, but stealing is the last thing I would ever do."

"I get that, Nevada. How about Jeremy? Or the assistant director? Or the props key? Or any of the other actors?"

"It's a long list, I know."

"Let's just hope the cops and the investigators have more information than we do, a clue or two to help narrow things down."

"By the way, have you come across anything more online about that photo of a bird pendant you saw? Did anybody respond to your post?"

"Not a thing," Chelan said. "I put up an invitation to communicate on a private message and the next day the photo and the post were taken down."

Another dead end. Nevada wondered how much more time they'd have before the trail was totally cold.

CHAPTER 24

The day had turned very warm. Back home in Vancouver, this would qualify as the height of summer, one of the hottest days of the year. Here in Savannah in April, it was only the leading edge of the hot months; by July and August, the temperatures would zoom skyward into the triple digits. Nevada appreciated the shade of the pine trees lining either side of the path leading to the village grocery store. She heard a golf cart approaching from behind and pulled off the path to let it go by. It seemed to be advancing on her at a sensible speed, one more thing to appreciate, as that wasn't always the case. Some golfers seemed to zip along on these paths at the same speed they'd drive their sports cars on the road.

"Nevada. Hello."

She took a closer look at the driver and recognized Frank Leonard. He pulled up beside her and stopped.

"Hey, Frank, how are you?"

"Having a great day, thank you. Just shot a seventy-two, and I'm on my way back to the clubhouse to celebrate a little bit. How are you? How's life on the movie set?"

Nevada smiled. "It's good."

"Maybe not all that good, though?" Frank asked. "I heard they haven't been able to recover the heirloom that was stolen."

"Yes, that's true," Nevada said. "But I don't think it will be long before they sort that out. They seem to have quite a few leads on who might have taken it and why."

"Oh? What's the buzz?"

"That it was an inside job. That it hasn't been taken far and is still in Savannah, somewhere."

"Interesting. What's your source for all this?"

The silence between them went on just a few beats too long for a normal pause. Nevada tried to grin at Frank. "Come on, now, you know I'd never answer that question."

Frank laughed, then leaned forward to start up his golf cart. "Yes, I know. Shouldn't have asked."

She wasn't sure why she felt like holding back on him. Maybe it was the eager way he was asking her these questions.

"There's been another theft of a similar pendant," he said. "In Florida. Key West, I think it was, although it might have been Boca. From a museum where they had an exhibit of Spanish historical artifacts."

"Yes, I know," Nevada said. "Some of the movie people think there's a connection."

"And what do you think?"

"Certainly a lot of similarities between the two events," Nevada commented. "I'd be looking into it, if I were investigating."

"Oh, yeah, me too," Frank agreed. "I'll have to keep an eye on the news, see if anything more turns up. Got lots of time for that, these days. It's a funny thing, when you're retired. You looked forward to having all that free time, back in the day when you were constantly running late, never taking a vacation, working 24/7. Then once you have it, it's too much." He stared full into Nevada's eyes, then laughed. "I can see I'm not convincing you."

Nevada laughed back. "Not really, Frank. I'm one of those still thinking that retirement looks pretty glamorous. If you have enough money."

"If you have enough money," Frank agreed.

Nevada considered her next words for a minute.

What the hell.

"I think it's the money aspect that has them suspecting me, on set."

"What do you mean, Nevada? Why on earth would they even consider suspecting you?" He was just as concerned and easy to talk to as she'd anticipated.

"There's no reason they should—I'm not a thief and never could be. Neither is my father. But they seem to be suspecting him, too."

"That's ridiculous. Both of you have dozens of other resources, if you have a financial challenge." He stared her in the eye, hard. "You don't really, do you? Have a financial challenge, I mean. Because I'd like to help, if there's anything I can do."

Nevada shook her head with as much clarity as she could convey. "I'm not telling you this because I'm looking for money, Frank. Owen and I are just fine. No, I was just talking about the pendant disappearing from the movie set and some of the theories that are flying around."

Frank was still concerned. "Is there someone in particular who seems to be targeting you? I can't believe that Jeremy suspects you."

"No, he doesn't. At least, he hasn't said anything directly to me. No, it's just the insurance people, and the cops, a little bit. But they're probably making the conversations with everybody just as uncomfortable."

"I think so," Frank said. "That's what they're trained to do."

Several moments went by as they both gazed out toward the marsh, deep in thought. Frank didn't seem to have anything more to add but Nevada had a sense that he was looking at her very closely.

"Well, I'm off to the clubhouse now," Frank suddenly said. She watched him disappear under a live oak and then spent a few seconds pondering the conversation before she turned her attention back to her bike and the scenery around her. Man, what a day! She couldn't remember when she'd ever taken so many moments to just enjoy her surroundings—was she getting old? Or soft? Hah. She leaned her bottom against the bike seat and pushed off with her right foot. In seconds she was cruising along the path again. Overhead, egrets were soaring in a flying wedge, leaving their overnight perches, heading off to wherever it was they went during the day. A squirrel zipped across the path in front of her, and she braked gently.

Just a few hundred yards ahead, she saw Austen and Lyla Jean parked at the edge of the lagoon beside the library.

"Hey you two, how ya doin'?"

"Just fine, Miss Nevada. How're you?" Austen seemed intent on watching the water's surface. Was he trying to spot an alligator?

"Well, I'm fine, Austen. What's new?"

"We've been watching our baby birds every day!" Lyla Jean was eager to report.

"They're not baby birds yet, they're eggs," Austen corrected. "The nest is getting bigger and bigger, and the birds bring new stuff to add to it every day."

"Excuse me," a familiar voice said from behind them, and Nevada realized that it was Frank again, coming back from the other way. They pulled their bikes as far over to the right as they could, under the trees, and Frank edged his golf cart past them. He waved as he passed but didn't stop.

"Well, you let me know once they hatch, would you?" Nevada said. "I'd like to come see them."

On her way home, just past the rookery, Nevada felt the buzzing of her cell phone in her jeans pocket and hopped off her bike to take the call.

"Hello?"

"Nevada, hi. Jeremy Walsh here. Although I guess you know that."

"Hi, Jeremy. What's up?" The last time they'd spoken,

even though his words were mild, his eyes were guarded.

"Thank you for the research you did for me the other day. I have a short assignment for you, if you're up for it. Doyle O'Keefe was telling us this morning about the downtown bed and breakfast he's staying in—*Southern Song*, I think it was called— and there are some great ghost stories."

"The whole town has ghost stories," Nevada commented.

"I'm thinking we'll just weave in something as a trait for one of the characters," Jeremy continued. "Maybe as one more source of fear for the sergeant sidekick or a boundary for the mentor character—I'm still working on that. But in the meantime, I'd like to have half a dozen true stories to base this on. Well, semi-true, you know what I mean." Jeremy stopped to catch his breath. "Doyle said he thought you'd be the perfect choice to get this done."

"What does Roger think of revisions to his script, at this late date?" Nevada asked.

"It's not a Roger Ridley film, it's a Jeremy Walsh film." She could hear his irritation at her question. "Besides, he's whining about it being inauthentic and not relevant to the main plot. Whatever. What do you say, can you do that for me?"

"Sure," she said. "Have you heard anything from Tom, by the way?"

"Not a thing. Hey, Traci, are we almost ready?"

Nevada could hear others talking to him in the background and knew that the call was almost done. "Alright, Jeremy, I'll get on it. For tomorrow?"

"I need it yesterday."

"While I've got you, can I ask you something? About Roger?"

"Shoot."

"Why is Roger so hostile to me?"

"He's like that with everybody."

"Nah, you're dodging the question. He's abrasive,

sure, but to me he is unusually antagonistic."

Jeremy sighed. "Well, he might have got the idea that you'd be an acceptable replacement, if he screws up."

"Where he get that idea?" Nevada asked. Jeremy's silence answered. "From you?!"

"He's been a pain in the ass, Nevada, and I might have suggested to him that nobody is indispensable."

"Is this the way you manage people?"

"Look, is there anything else? That's all the time I have for that ego on steroids, Roger."

"Just one other thing, Jeremy. Is there any news about the pendant?"

"Cops say they've got a clue or two. Lotsa follow-up going on. They've got a pipeline, information's coming in."

"What do you mean, a pipeline? You mean, like a mole?!"

"You watch too many movies," Jeremy said. "Gotta go." And the call was ended.

Nevada turned the bike around and pointed it toward the house. She felt energized. Nothing like a research question and a good dive into a book or a website to get her mind off the things she couldn't change and the things that led to gloom and doom speculation.

When Owen called to say he was working late, she was so caught up in reading about Georgia's haunted history that she gave only five minutes to wondering whether he actually was avoiding her company because he'd had second thoughts about not being able to accept the new job in Vancouver instantly. Through the evening at her desk and into the late hours, falling asleep reading in bed, she gobbled up stories about murdered plantation owners, desperate widows, and dying soldiers. Years ago, this sort of exploration would have taken half a dozen trips to a library and hundreds of books consulted or checked out. These days of the internet were truly miraculous.

She didn't hear Owen come in, and in the morning when she carried her computer tablet out to the deck to read while she had her coffee, he was still asleep. The weather had taken a turn, and this morning there was fog on the lagoon. Nevada watched the white mist drift in and out among the pines, while darker gray air hung in the sky right above their canopies. It was the sort of view you could imagine using as the backdrop to a scene from a movie about zombies or ghosts, maybe vampires.

Savannah's connection to the 'other side' was often reported, and in some quarters, it was referred to as 'the most haunted city in America'. Nevada didn't think that extended to the golf course communities twenty miles away, but you never knew. You also never knew, until you started to research, how much a phrase like 'the most haunted city in America' was based on fact and how much on tourism promotion.

She sipped her coffee and watched as a group of egrets dipped over the water, their powerful wings thrusting them through the air and up on the wind currents. What would you call a group of egrets, she wondered idly, reaching for her computer tablet and typing in the search. A congregation or a wedge. Hmmm. One question led to the next, and Nevada searched for the names for other groups of birds: A cotillion of terns, a stand or flamboyance of flamingos, a wake of buzzards, and a banditry of chickadees. She smiled and got up to refill her coffee cup. Okay, so here was her time-waster for the morning. She sat back down in her favorite chair and followed the link to the flamingos page.

The cell phone ringing disrupted her virtual stroll. If it were incoming email or even a text message, she'd be able to ignore it, but there was still something about a ringing phone. Even one with a Bruce Springsteen ringtone.

Or maybe, especially.

"Nevada? This is Yvonne Lee."

Well. Why was the star of *Too Beautiful to Burn* calling her?

"Jeremy gave me your number. He told me y'all's researching Savannah's history, about ghosts and cemeteries and such, and since I'm doing some of that too, we might want to get together."

"Hi, Yvonne. Sure. I could do that. What are you thinking?"

"Let's take one of those tours. I'll get my assistant to set it up so that it's private—let me know if you've come across anything particular we should make sure to see. I'm going to invite Sandra, too. You know her, from the crew? Maybe some other people. Does tomorrow night work for you?"

In less than five minutes, the cell phone rang again, with Yvonne's assistant telling the details. No flies on you, Nevada thought, as she added the date and location to her calendar. 11 p.m. tomorrow night, Wednesday. Haunted Savannah tour. Graveyard.

*

They met at an old warehouse in the Starland District. Yvonne and Sandra seemed almost giggly with anticipation; probably nervous, Nevada thought. She checked her own feelings but couldn't find any anxiety. She was quite blasé about the whole event—ghosts weren't her thing. She'd spent the early part of the day doing more online research, and she'd learned enough to be even more skeptical about the outcome of this evening's excursion. Savannah had its share of sad and painful stories of violent deaths and lives full of suffering. Many of them had popped up in the history books and, when lined up with mysterious or unexpected experiences such as a sudden blast of wind, an unusual smell, or a hazy vision of what might be a person or a person's clothing, the result was a ghost story. Of course, it grew in the telling over the years and eventually was a detailed, often gruesome account. The storyteller either believed in it earnestly and without logic or privately laughed at it while collecting revenue from a willing dupe. At least, that's the way Nevada looked at it.

A brand-new limo with fully tinted windows and elaborately equipped interior had been booked to carry them around. Two large men with serious faces came with the car, sitting in the driver's and the front passenger seats. It wasn't unheard of for late-night forays around Savannah to result in stumbling into a situation where there were people with guns; the movie producers had no intention of letting one of their stars be mugged, or even mildly frightened. They'd lost control over Tom Leacock, and they were still furious over that one. Jeremy had been ordered to be absolutely sure that Yvonne Lee and the other lead actors were present and accounted for each and every day of shooting.

"Hey, ladies, look at the supplies!" Yvonne had found the compartment with the crystal decanters and glasses.

Nevada smiled and held out a hand. Yvonne played bartender, pouring her a white wine.

"Sandra, do you want a drink?" Yvonne asked. She got no response.

Nevada thought Sandra might be a little intimidated about socializing with the movie star. Nevada, by contrast, was feeling relaxed. She sipped her white wine and made eye contact with Yvonne. She was old enough to be Yvonne's mother, after all, and even though she had no experience with parenting, she did have some with mentoring, and one twenty-eight-year-old was pretty much like another, right?

"So how are things going on set, Yvonne?"

"One hundred percent," the actress said, giving back the gaze in that way that actors have been taught to fix right on you. "It's such a good part, and I think it's going to be my breakthrough."

Nevada wished she had a dime for every actress who probably believed that. She'd watched so many of them start out with energy and ambition, becoming the "It Girl", as they called it in the early twentieth century when movies began and one of the "Top 10 Sexiest Stars" in some magazine or website list in the twenty-first. Look them up on IMDb fifteen years later, and their careers had glided to a stop, like a sports car running on fumes. Inevitably? Nevada wasn't sure she was quite cynical enough to draw that conclusion.

She smiled at Yvonne. No comment was needed and would have been wrong; ambition was a good thing, and besides, who knew? Maybe this one would be the exception.

"Ladies!" Yvonne lifted her wine glass. "A toast!"

Nevada was game. She raised her glass upward too. "But, Yvonne, help me out here. Are we still allowed to say 'ladies'? I'm trying to keep up."

"We are," Yvonne declared. "If it's 'ladies' who are saying it, in a sort of winky way to one another. Old or middle-aged men aren't."

"How about old or middle-aged women?"

"Sure, why not?" Yvonne tapped Nevada's glass then took a big gulp.

"Good, because I just can't get my mouth around 'bitches'," Nevada said, winking.

"Me neither," Yvonne laughed. "Except when I'm around my grandmother, when she's not expecting me to clap back."

Sandra had been silent for too long, and Nevada decided to try to draw her into the conversation. "Hey, Sandra, we might see something tonight that will give you a new idea for props on this movie. Maybe a bloody amputated hand, or a headless horseman, or a gravestone that sinks into the dirt by itself."

"Ooh, yeah, or a violin that starts playing all by itself, or chains that rattle, or an old portrait that moans and shrieks." Yvonne was getting into it.

Sandra, who was looking through the window at the darkened street, seemed preoccupied—maybe stressed right into the 'frozen with fear' zone? Nevada took a closer look at her, then moderated her tone. "Is this bothering you, Sandra? Really, let's not take it all so seriously. It's just for fun that we're doing this, just for a little real-life context for this make-believe stuff we're going to be doing for a movie."

Reaching out her hand for a glass, Sandra didn't take her eyes off the street through the car window. "I've read that Savannah is one of the most haunted places in America. The whole city is built on a graveyard, they say."

"You could probably say that about most places, if you think about it," Nevada commented. "I mean, it was first settled in the 1730s, people died over the years, they were buried, cemeteries were established. Lots of dead bodies in almost three hundred years."

Sandra looked a bit thoughtful, but still unconvinced. "I guess so. But what do you think we're going to see tonight?"

"We have an appointment with a local medium!" Yvonne was practically bouncing in her seat. "Doyle O'Keefe found her for us. She's a senior leader in one of the churches apparently, but she also has a connection with the psychic world that goes back generations in her family." She looked intently at Nevada. "Doyle thought you might find all this kind of disturbing."

"What does that mean, a connection with the psychic world?" Sandra asked.

"Apparitions, visitations, communication with the other side," Yvonne whispered. "She's also an expert in Savannah history and is just a goldmine of stories about the past here."

"Sounds like she's exactly what we need," Nevada said, trying to add enough approval to make up for Sandra's complete lack of enthusiasm. The woman almost looked as though she was ready to open the door and jump out.

"That's what I told Jeremy and Roger," Yvonne said.

"Roger too?" Nevada asked. "So he knows about this

now. I heard he didn't want this haunted subplot added to the script at this point—maybe no subplot at all?"

Yvonne tossed her head in what Nevada imagined was the style of Southern belles back in the nineteenth century. "He's only the writer, Nevada. Jeremy wants this added, says friends of his in town are saying you can't do a Savannah story without touching on this dimension." She grinned at Nevada. "So to speak."

"So to speak." Nevada grinned back. "Alright! Sandra, are we ready? Let's meet this psychic."

The route took them along darkened streets and, as they got closer to the riverfront, around the edges of historic squares. Nighttime light pollution isn't Savannah's thing anyway, Nevada thought, but with these huge live oak trees and all the dripping Spanish moss, this was probably about as dark as she'd ever seen it, anywhere. She recognized Forsyth Park as they passed it and saw a street sign for Abercorn, then was disoriented as they made a few turns. They glided up to the cemetery on the West Oglethorpe Avenue side, and as the driver parked the car, Yvonne already had her hand on the door handle. She was the first one out of the car, after their driver and his helper. Nevada wasn't far behind her, but Sandra was definitely hanging back.

"It looks closed," Sandra said. "I think I read online that they close it at five, except for tours. Would we count as a tour? I don't know, guys, I think we'd see much more in daylight, don't you? Be able to read the headstones and stuff?"

Yvonne shook her head and headed off along a path, calling over her shoulder. "How long has this been here?"

"Since 1750," Nevada called back through the car's open door, wondering how many residents in the neighborhood they were disturbing. Hah, maybe their shouting would be heard and cited as proof that ghosts were moving around the graveyard. "Sandra, we're all leaving the car, and we'll be walking about a half a mile away from it," Nevada said. "Do you really want to sit here by yourself, at midnight, beside a cemetery?"

She got out and went through the archway at the entrance, then stopped, not sure what to do next. A few yards ahead, she saw a round light bouncing along and, in a few seconds, realized that it wasn't some sort of indication of haunting. It was a flashlight, carried by a large woman wearing a full-length skirt, a raincoat, and a beret.

"Miss Yvonne?" she asked.

"The flashlight was a great idea," Yvonne replied. "Yes, I'm Yvonne Lee. Are you Latrelle?"

"I am." The woman stopped within a few inches of them and seemed to be looking over their group, taking the measure of each one. "I'm told I am to be your guide tonight through this place of burial."

"Told by whom?" Nevada asked. She wasn't sure whether she was joking, investigating, or just running off at the mouth from apprehension. The word that crossed her mind about this new person was 'otherworldly'.

"We're researching for a movie set in Savannah," Yvonne said. "It's the story of a Confederate woman who is taking whatever steps she must to survive."

"It's also the story of a priceless gold pendant that gets stolen during the Civil War," Sandra announced, obviously having changed her mind about waiting in the car.

"Given as a gift," Yvonne corrected her.

"Lost somehow," Nevada peace-made.

Latrelle didn't seem to be listening to them. Her face was a mask of intensity and concentration. She turned a full 180 degrees and set off toward the center of the cemetery at a pace that Nevada would not have a believed a woman her size could achieve had she not seen it for herself. In minutes, she was so far ahead of the three others that Nevada couldn't see even her dark outline— only the bouncing light from her flashlight, illuminating the path ahead of her, among the graves. Nevada noted that their burly bodyguards had chosen to remain at the edge of the cemetery near the limo.

"Wow, she can really move," Yvonne panted.

"Sssshhh," Sandra spat out at her. Yvonne's head snapped to the left to look at the props woman. This wasn't the usual way she was addressed when they were on set. This 'leading lady', like all of them, was probably expecting a lot more deference. She seemed to decide to shake it off, however. After all, when you're in a graveyard at midnight, following a strange woman deeper and deeper into it, maybe safety in numbers becomes a more important concept to you than stardom.

Latrelle had stopped beside an immense gravestone that towered about eight feet into the air. "This sacred place was the final ground for people right back to colonial times," she said. "For about a hundred years. Yellow fever. Duels. Not during what you call the Civil War. But in those years, also, much pain, much pain on this ground. Like everywhere in the city. Soldiers camping, taking. Geechee trying to survive."

"Were your people from around here?" Yvonne asked. "The city or from the islands?"

"Long ago, the rice plantations on the islands," Latrelle said. "Before that, Angola."

Much pain, indeed.

Latrelle's eyes closed, she hugged herself and swayed as she hummed some song. Actually, hummed wasn't really the right word. It was more like what Nevada imagined keening sounded like. No words but incredible emotion expressed in the sound.

Suddenly, there was a whoosh of a sound and a flock of small birds flew in. They landed on tombstones and on the ground, and in minutes there were too many of them to count. Latrelle smiled what might have been a self-satisfied smile—at least, that's what Nevada thought she saw, but it was so dark that she realized she was probably interpreting body language rather than seeing a facial expression.

"What's going on?" Yvonne whispered.

"She's calling spirits!" Sandra hissed. "Dead people!"

"Cool!" Yvonne said, using that all-purpose word. "Do you think we'll be allowed to talk to them?"

"Dear God!" Sandra seemed so distraught, it was amazing that she was able to converse even in this minimal way.

Nevada was watching Latrelle as carefully as she could, in the dark, hoping for some sort of clue about what their behavior and their role was supposed to be. The woman seemed to have forgotten their presence completely. She held her arms upward, swayed, and muttered. Nevada couldn't take her eyes off her.

Which was probably why she missed the first sight of the second bobbing white light. Sandra suddenly clutched Nevada's arm. No sound came from her, but she was pointing, insistently, toward a headstone to Latrelle's left.

A bit of gray mist, in the vague shape of a circle (or perhaps an oval), hung about two feet above the granite marker. Nevada scanned the entire area and, once Sandra let go of her, did a full, 360-degree turn, looking for something that might be the source of the light. Another person, back in the darkness, holding a flashlight? The driver or the guard, perhaps? A battery-operated, ground-level footlight, maybe even dozens of feet away, projected toward the space above this tombstone? Maybe a light coming from some building, off in the distance?

She saw nothing. Nothing that would provide a rational explanation for this very real . . . *something* . . . she had seen and felt.

And then she smelled something.

What was that? Burning toast? Why would there be a smell of burning toast in a graveyard? Maybe it was more like the overheated smell of a piece of electrical cord, or a space heater? Again, why here?

Nevada heard Sandra whimper. The woman wasn't

waiting to see anything more, and she took off in the direction of the cemetery entrance, at first at a walk, then breaking into a jog. This was a good idea—Nevada shook off her shock and started to stride after her. She wasn't going to lose her dignity completely by running, but she was on her way out of there. Big time.

She heard Yvonne calling from behind them. "Ladies!"

When Nevada got to the limo, she found Sandra already inside, tucked as far into the back seat corner as she could get. The driver and bodyguard were already in their seats, and the engine was running. Five minutes passed, Nevada leaning from one foot to another, looking anxiously down the path, trying to get a glimpse of Yvonne. Finally, she spotted the actress walking rapidly toward the car. She looked like a woman who wasn't lingering, but she didn't look terrified.

"What happened?"

"Get in the car, and I'll tell you while we're leaving," Yvonne said.

Once they were inside and driving away, replenished glasses in every woman's hand, Nevada exhaled and asked again. "What happened?"

"Latrelle kept on making those noises for a few more seconds, then she seemed to run out of steam. As soon as it was quiet, I asked her, 'What was that white light we saw? That misty shape? Was that a ghost?' She just looked at me like I was a fool and said, 'What do you think?' And I said, 'I don't know what I think, that's why I'm asking you'. She just looked off into the distance for a long time, then she said 'Maybe'."

Yvonne took a long swallow. " 'Maybe', that's all she said. I could figure *that* out for myself. We stood there for another few minutes and nothing was happening, so I decide to go. She wasn't happy about that, I think."

"Why do you say that?" Nevada asked.

"I could hear her behind me, and she said, 'All of you

should go!' and all of a sudden she was shouting. 'You should go! All of you should go! They don't want you here, especially the ones of you who try to tell their stories. You get it wrong, all wrong, and you should go. No one can rest'."

As the car carried them through the Historic District, none of the three of them spoke, each deep in her own thoughts. Just before dropping Nevada off at her car, Yvonne said, "Well, that was extreme, I have to say. What do you think, Nevada? Pretty terrifying, am I right? Doesn't it just make you want to get outa here, get back to civilization, back to L.A. and Vancouver?"

Nevada smiled. "I don't quite see it that way. L.A. has its own ghosts. And no, nothing like that would scare me into making decisions, really."

But when she told Owen later at home about the events in the cemetery, she was a lot more cranked up. His reaction was calm and detached. "So, what do you think, Nevada?"

She was pacing the living room. "Man, I never thought I'd be flustered by something like that, but I was. You know I think all of that stuff is just hokum, but I know what I saw, and there *was* something there!" She sat down on a couch with a thump and wrapped her arms around herself. "I wish you'd been there with me."

"You don't have to convince me, Trip. I believe you."

"You do?"

Owen sat down beside her. "You know I see a lot of death, in my job. I know that there are a lot of things going on that we don't understand and aren't usually aware of. It doesn't scare me."

Nevada just looked at him. She wanted him to keep talking.

"It surprises me that it scares you," he said, leaning to put his arm across the back of the couch and then around her shoulders, tugging her back into the curve of his body. "Come on, relax. You're here, not out there in the dark.

Whatever you saw lives there, not here."

"What do you think she meant, 'you get it wrong, all wrong, and if you try to tell our stories, you'll have to go'?"

"With all due respect to the journalist in the room, she didn't say, 'if you try to tell our stories, you'll have to go'. At least that's not what you told me, the first time through. You said she said, 'you get it wrong, all wrong, and you should go'."

"What's the difference?" Nevada snapped, but she smiled, a little bit. She knew he'd caught her in a misquote, and she knew he knew getting every little word absolutely correct mattered to her. Mattered, period.

"I think, like anybody, she . . . they . . . have their preferred account of whatever, their point of view, and they want that version told. Just like I do, just like you do, just like anybody."

Nevada pondered this for a while, then put to him the question that was burning.

"Do you think it's time to go? Maybe in some weird coincidence of timing this is proof that I should have been more . . . cooperative . . . last week when you were talking to me about going back to Canada. Maybe we'd already be on our way there, and I wouldn't have had to meet Miss Latrelle and whoever or whatever else that was."

Owen shrugged. "Maybe, maybe not. We make our best decisions in the moment with the best information we have at the time. That's the way it always is."

"So, last week we decided not to go back north. What about now? Do you still want to go? Would the job offer still be open?"

"I don't want to go if what we're doing is running away from something." Owen fumbled in his jacket pocket and pulled out his phone. "How about some music?"

He pulled up the Leon Russell album that was one of her favorites, and for a few minutes they listened to the brilliant, jagged piano playing fill the room. "Seriously, Nevada, would you say that you really were frightened?

Enough to actually leave a city that you like otherwise?"

"No."

"Would you say that you have work to do here, helping Jeremy with the script and helping your father and mother face their challenges?"

"Yes."

"So, there's the decision."

"But what about your job offer? About you wanting to go back up north?"

"I don't, anymore. I have a lot to do, here. The back-to-Vancouver idea is history."

Nevada sat up and looked him full in the face, asking a wordless question.

"Really," Owen said. " 'The past is history. The future's a mystery. Today is a gift'. That's why they call it the present."

She half punched, half hugged him. "You're too corny."

"And you love it."

And she did.

CHAPTER 25

The water gleamed in the early morning sun, and Lillian was sure she had seen a few dolphins leaping and playing off in the distance to the south. Without thinking about it, she'd taken her morning walk out to the end of the pier, and she found herself scanning the horizon, looking for a boat that she might recognize.

Donovan had called her last night to say he'd had the call from Adam and they were to cast off at dawn from Key West, heading about ninety miles south to a secret spot, to anchor and dive the place they had calculated that the Spanish ship had gone down.

Lillian was appalled by all this. That close to Cuba? Didn't they have to get a permit of some sort? Would there be Cuban government boats out there that might spot them and take exception to their presence? Donovan assured her that Adam had thought of everything they needed, but Lillian had her doubts. The man had certainly seemed as though he had it together when it came to socializing, but Lillian just couldn't picture him master-minding a complex operation like this diving expedition.

But what did she know about it, really? Maybe it was just her grandmotherly worry at work. She'd expressed all this to a younger, childless friend once and the woman had asked her, in exasperation, did she want him to stay at home, under the covers, in bed, and never venture forth, never have an experience, never take a risk? What kind of life would that be?

Her friend was right, of course. Lillian was proud that Donovan had snapped up this job and could head out into the ocean on an adventure like this. She put a hand up to her forehead, shading her eyes against the powerful sun that made its presence known despite her Jackie O sunglasses. She didn't know anything about binoculars or telescopes and didn't own any, but she wondered if she had such a thing, would she be able to see all the way to Cuba from here? Probably not. Probably like every woman or child who'd ever stood on a shore trying to catch sight of a boat that carried a loved one, she could do no more than wait there and yearn.

That night as she pulled her small casserole dish from the oven, the penne pesto bubbling cheerfully under the cheese-and-French-breadcrumbs topping, her phone rang.

"Hello?"

"Hi, Grandma!"

"Donovan! Hello, dear. How was your day?"

"Fantastic, Grandma. Adam said I should call you right away, that you'd be worrying."

"Knows women, that man," Lillian commented. "Did everything with the dive go well?"

"It did! Grandma, you would have been fascinated. I've never been involved in anything like that. I mean, fishing, crewing, it's all been fun, but this was a whole other level. We had these amazing maps and charts, and we had to drop anchor in a very precise spot. Then the divers went down. Their tanks were calibrated for exactly a certain depth and a certain length of time, and we had to hold the boat just so . . . oh, and the technology, Grandma. We had these scopes and screens and mechanical arms— it's a very exact process."

"It sounds intriguing, Donovan," Lillian said. "And what about the treasures? Did you find anything?"

"I can't say much, Grandma," Donovan replied. "Adam says he'll make me sorry—ow, hey, alright! I'll stop!" Donovan was laughing so hard he could barely speak. "He's right here, you can probably tell. I'm not supposed to say anything at all. What about a photo, can I send her a photo? Where else would it go, Adam? Just one photo, to her email account. She uses email, not texting."

Lillian waited for Donovan to finish his conversation with Adam. She could hear a lot of off-phone chatter.

"Okay, Grandma, I'm going to send you a photo of the cargo they brought up. It's amazing—this is stuff that's been at the bottom of the drink for hundreds of years."

"Isn't it all eroded, or corroded, or something?" Lillian asked.

"Yeah, a lot of it, but some of it still looks like just what it is. There's a fork and a spoon, some plates from the galley, and some leather pieces that might be a book, some coins and some buttons . . ."

"Did you dive, Donovan?"

"No, Adam says this is no place for a newbie. Grandma, I gotta go. One of our divers has major ear pain, and we're heading back now."

"Oh, good, I was wondering how long you'd be staying there. Thank you for calling me, you're the best." Lillian's feeling of relief flowed out of her in waves toward the horizon.

"No, you're the best," he answered in their usual way. "I'll buy you dinner one night next week."

*

Nevada stretched out on the couch and took her computer from the coffee table, flipping it open and starting her email program. Lillian was reaching out from Key West and in seconds the email current between them was flowing fast and strong, as Nevada updated her friend on the hunt for Tom and then Lillian updated her about the hunt for sunken treasure that Donovan and Adam had underway. It took no more than a few exchanges before Nevada picked up on the vibe that Lillian had news to tell. She asked, and in seconds Lillian emailed her the photo Donovan had been allowed to share with her. It showed a jumble of artifacts, the way they might look if a wave of water had carried them from a sinking vessel to shore, rather than dropped them on the ocean floor. Most were covered and encrusted with the layers of many hundreds of years of ocean dirt—it took a good imagination to see that this one was a spoon, that one was a comb or a pocket watch.

She picked up her phone and punched in Cassidy's number.

"Take a look at this photo I'm going to send you, okay?"

"Sure, what is it?"

"Not sure," Nevada said. "It's a photo from a shipwreck. Old galley utensils, tools, and so on. Anything that water wouldn't destroy."

"Okay. What's the date?"

"It's a Spanish ship that went down about 1495 AD. Off the northern coast of Cuba."

"Sweet. Send it to me, and I'll get right back to you."

Nevada barely had time to pull a cold drink from the refrigerator before her phone was ringing.

"Nevada!" Cassidy's voice was excited.

"What is it?"

"You said these are items from the fifteenth century?"

"That's what I've been told." The careful reporter.

"What would you say if I told you there is one piece in there that is not from the fifteenth century, not even close."

Nevada sighed. She was disappointed for Lillian. And for her grandson. "I was concerned that it might be a big hoax, full of fakes. What do you see?"

"Not a hoax, although I guess you could say it's a mystery. What is this piece of jewelry—gold jewelry—doing in this shipwreck? It looks to me like this piece was made in the eleventh century . . . maybe even the tenth! Maybe in a year that had three digits, not four. 950 or 975 or so . . . did you hear me, Nevada, the tenth century! Where did it come from?" She could tell that Cassidy was giving a lot of significance to this find. "Was it there by accident, from an earlier storm at sea? Or did somebody bring an ancient treasure onboard, try to carry it across the Atlantic?"

"It's quite a story. I'll tell you the whole thing over a meal, I'm starving," Nevada said. "Can you meet me?"

"Half an hour," Cassidy said. "Come over to the Blue Heron Club. My treat."

*

The club had recently been redecorated in an up-to-date contemporary style, a change that wasn't sitting well with the members who preferred the nineteenth-century look. Nevada heard a few negative comments in the restroom when she stopped in on her way to the dining room to meet Cassidy, and she just had to shake her head. Well, you just can't please all of the people all of the time.

The room was packed with golfers who'd just come in from a round and real estate agents showing prospective buyers details of the few properties that were available. It was quite the gathering place too for all the retired people who needed a place to see and be seen, a place to show up and hang out, now that their days in the neighborhoods where they'd raised their children and the cities where they'd built their careers were past. She spotted Louise, Joan, and Blair, women she'd met on the tennis court; Frank from Owen's hospital board having an 'it's five o'clock somewhere' cocktail with Parker, the lawyer who'd handled their rental lease; and then Cassidy, sitting at a high table for two near the bar. The hair was still purple and today she was wearing a full-length skirt in a yellow floral print with a moss-green low-cut top. Nevada went over to join her, and within minutes, they'd ordered their sweet teas, decided to split the grouper special, and logged in to the email account on Nevada's tablet to look at the dive expedition photos.

"There, right there, see that?" Cassidy's intensity was contagious. "That's not a fifteenth century style, it goes back much farther."

Nevada peered at the chain of tiny links and the bird that appeared to be dangling from it. This was unbelievable, she thought—it looked just like a picture of the bird pendant that was the center of the Savannah movie story. "I really have no idea what I'm looking at . . . or for," she said. "Tell me."

"Alright." Cassidy settled in with the animated manner of a teacher happy to have the opportunity to answer a question. "Almost everything else here is Spanish, circa 1495, standard sort of equipment on seafaring vessels of the day. There's even a few pieces of jewelry, maybe stuff the 'conquistadors' picked up, or traded for. It's all about five hundred years old, right? Now, look at this chain, look at the curves in the links, the planes of it . . ."

Cassidy leaned over the image with a magnifying glass. A magnifying glass! In these days of insta-zoom, really? Apparently, so. Nevada leaned in, too, and studied the ancient necklace. The more she gazed at it, the more she thought she could see the distinctions that Cassidy was pointing out: a certain heaviness in the shape of the oval that made up one link; an angularity in the shape of the link that connected the bird pendant to the chain; something primal about the bird's wings, its head, its breast.

"It's so similar to the ones that have disappeared," Nevada almost spoke to herself.

"I thought so, too," Cassidy said.

"Have you read anything new about the investigation of the Florida Museum theft?"

"The most popular theory seems to be the sophisticated gang of art thieves with a high level of tech knowledge," Cassidy replied.

Nevada stared at the pendant. "They all look just the same, I'm thinking," she said. "But I'm no expert. Unless I saw all three side by side, I doubt that I'd be able to tell."

Cassidy smiled. "That's a trio of ancient bling, right there. Any museum, anywhere in the world, would be tickled pink to have all three to display, together."

Nevada shook her head. "I just can't get my head around why anybody would steal something like that. There's no market, is there? And if they can verify that this shipwrecked one is more than a thousand years old, and that the others are a match to it, won't that make them absolutely impossible to sell?"

"Not to certain types of collectors. And not to the people who supply them, the people who understand the way the mind works. Do you know what I mean, Nevada? Do you collect anything? I've got my little sideline with junk jewelry, I think you told me your husband does clocks, your father does costumes—"

"Shoes and boots, actually," Nevada said. "And I like old movie posters."

Cassidy reached for another biscuit. "Yes, some of those are just works of art, aren't they? Now imagine you knew of a place where you could get your hands on an original, one-of-a-kind, the very first one made, ever. But you'd have to take it, no-questions-asked. And let's suppose it's one you've been hunting for decades, a lifetime, even. And you have a lot of money, and you're used to having anything you want, but you find out that you don't quite have enough for this piece. It's a stretch, and you can't quite make it. Or maybe you *do* have enough money but whoever owns it won't sell it. So, you steal it."

Cassidy read Nevada's face. "I haven't convinced you, have I?"

Nevada laughed. "No, but good try. Really, I do get it, Cassidy, and I can imagine the thinking behind a theft like that, but action is different than thinking."

Cassidy nodded. "Well, yeah. But not to collectors like that."

Nevada looked at Cassidy thoughtfully for a few

moments. Had the time come to confront her? She decided that it had.

"Cassidy, could I ask you about something that has been bugging me? I heard the other day that you and my father were both at the Amelia Island car show recently, and that you met."

Cassidy nodded but said nothing.

Nevada forged on. "So . . . what was that about? I also heard that he gave you a box, something in a box."

"How would you know if there were something in the box?"

"I don't know, exactly, but it's a reasonable conclusion to draw," Nevada said. "*Was* there something in the box?"

Cassidy gazed at her for a long moment, then sighed. "There really is no privacy or anonymity left in the world, is there? Do you remember when it used to be that a person had the right to protect their own image, to require that anybody wanting to take their picture ask permission? Now we've got everybody saying that anywhere in public or at some event that *might* be news is an acceptable place to take any photos you want. Do you remember when something had to be 'in the public interest' before it would be reported or photographed? And that used to mean 'for the public good'? Now all it means is 'interest' in the sense that if somebody—anybody!—is interested or curious, that means it's 'in the public interest', and we can snap and chat away all day long!"

Nevada contemplated Cassidy as she ranted on. What was this about, really? Cassidy suddenly stopped talking, seeming to run out of steam. Nevada waited, until it was clear that Cassidy wasn't going to say any more.

"My father is under suspicion of having stolen a priceless museum-quality artifact," she said. "He's disappeared now and we're all worried. Sort of. Then we see you—or at least, *photos* of you, taken at a public car show—receiving a box of something from him. What was in the box?"

"A pair of Paul Newman's boots, the ones he used to wear when he was racing. Your father had picked them up at a costume auction years ago, and he'd advertised them online. My husband is a car nut, and the boots are going to be the best birthday present he ever got."

Nevada was mystified. "Why would Tom do that? Sell them, I mean. I know why he had them—he had a lot of things, costumes, famous props. He collects."

"And sometimes collectors sell, to free up cash for something new they want to buy. Simple as that, Nevada. He wasn't selling me a priceless piece of jewelry that he'd stolen from the set. He was selling me an old pair of boots."

Nevada thought it over. Plausible? Maybe. Raising cash by selling off a piece or two from his collection, that sounded like her father. The box had certainly looked big enough to contain boots. Far too big for the pendant's case, but that might have been a cover-up, she'd thought when she first saw the photo.

"Why was he selling them to you? How did you even find out about them?"

"He put them into an online auction," Cassidy said. "I was searching and his name came up."

Nevada thought this one over. "I thought it might have had something to do with you suspecting him of the theft."

"Or maybe even that he had a necklace in the box and was selling it to me?" Cassidy shook her head.

It was strange but Nevada felt as though the woman across the table from her was changing, with each twist in the conversation. When they'd first started lunch she was Cassidy 1.0. Then, when the magnifying glass came out and the academic researcher face went on, she seemed a different woman, a Cassidy 2.0. Nevada considered her carefully. Was there a Cassidy 3.0?

"Another thing I've been meaning to ask you."

"Go for it."

"When you showed up at my house that day with the package delivered to your house by mistake—was that a mistake or was that on purpose?"

Cassidy smiled. "I wanted to meet you."

"Why?"

Right before her eyes, Cassidy seemed to change again, putting on a tougher, older, more experienced expression. She sat straighter, raised her chin, and suddenly seemed to wear her flowery, ultra-feminine outfit like a uniform. The woman must be an actress, Nevada thought.

"Why?" Nevada repeated.

Cassidy looked around the room; she seemed to be making sure they were alone and unobserved. "Alright. Nevada." She made a decision to speak. "Just like you, I wear a few different hats, have a few different skill sets. One of them is law enforcement."

"You're a cop?"

Cassidy nodded. "Undercover. I'm assigned to this stolen pendant case."

Well, blow me down. About a hundred questions roared into Nevada's mind.

"Are you close to solving it?"

Cassidy shrugged.

"Are there any actual physical clues?"

"I can't tell you much, but I can say that there is one piece of evidence that points to a local vacation rental."

Nevada managed to speak that one question that blazed. "Am I a suspect?"

"Then. Not anymore. And neither is your father."

"Do you know who *did* take it?"

Cassidy shook her head. "We have theories, of course. We do think it's connected to the theft of the one from the Florida museum, even though the way that one was taken was so different than the method used in Savannah. That one was obviously the work of a sophisticated team of expert thieves. The robbery on the movie set was much less professional. But it's my guess that these two pendants are on their way into the hands of the same person, if they aren't there already. I don't know how this third one, the one in the photo you just showed me, fits in—"

"But you'll find out," Nevada finished.

CHAPTER 26

The rest of the world had just as much interest in the shipwreck dive expedition as Lillian had. Other people on the crew besides Donovan took it upon themselves to share just one or two photos and in less time than it takes to bake a cake, the news and photographic evidence of the discovery had reached every edge of every continent. After that, it didn't take the international press long to uncover the Cuban bird pendant story. That's what they were calling it, the Cuban bird pendant. Not the Spanish bird, not the Florida bird. Lillian completely agreed with them now. The ancient artifact belonged with its indigenous creators. Donovan disagreed.

"Grandma, you're being really one-sided in your opinion about this," Donovan pronounced over their slices of key lime pie.

"If I'm being rigid, Donovan, it's because it's an issue with only one argument that can be made," Lillian said. "It was stolen hundreds of years ago from the village where it was made, and it should be returned there. To a Cuban museum, anyway, if the exact village can't be determined."

"Adam says there are dozens of examples of events in war time, or during exploration, or because of turmoil of any kind where the original ownership of something becomes murky and a new beginning point in history is established," Donovan said. Rather pompously, Lillian thought.

"Well, Adam is a revisionist, then," Lillian said with a

laugh. "That's just an excuse, and a very convenient one that could be used by almost anybody. 'Oh, excuse me, officer, there was a big thunder-and-lightning storm that messed up the electrics in the alarm system of that big house and so the front door just opened, I don't quite know how that happened, but it did. And nobody was there, and that Charles Dickens first edition just kind of fell into my bag. Somebody had to protect it, the windows were broken and it was raining really hard, and I didn't want it to get wet. So, I took it and then I gave it to my son and he gave it to his son and on to his son and so on and so on and now nobody, really can say who it belongs to, right?' "

He was laughing. "I had no idea you could be so sarcastic, Grandma!"

"I'm not being sarcastic! That's essentially the argument your Mr. Brecklin is making . . . and he isn't the first."

As Lillian finished the last delicious mouthful of her dessert, a familiar figure caught her attention as she scanned the storefronts across the street. Key West was not a big place, and it wasn't unheard of to run into acquaintances here and there, but when Lillian spotted Doyle O'Keefe, the man she'd met on Adam's boat, in front of the bookstore, she had a moment of doubt over the coincidence. And if he truly was browsing through the books, he did it differently than anyone else she had ever seen. He spent twice as much time with his back to the outdoor racks, staring across the street toward the café where she and Donovan were enjoying the afternoon, as he did actually picking up a book and looking at its cover.

It occurred to Lillian that he wanted to be noticed and, sure enough, when she raised a hand to wave, he instantly waved back, set the book down, and headed across the street.

"Hello, Miss Lillian! Donovan, hey there," he said, reaching out to shake hands. "Nice to bump into you.

Mind if I join you?" And in seconds, he was seated to her left, with a menu conveniently offered by the server and accepted.

"Hello, Doyle," Lillian said. "Still in Key West, I see."

"Doing some company work with one of our hotel clients here," he said, giving the menu the attention a lawyer gives the fine print. "What looks good? What are y'all having?"

After he'd surveyed all his options and settled on a po' boy sandwich with a side of hush puppies, Doyle leaned back for a chat. "So, quite the haul you and the boys made at that dive site, Donovan. Who knew that old wreck would give up so much?"

"Yeah, those divers are talented," Donovan commented.

"Any idea where they took everything?" Doyle asked. "Where they're storing the stuff?"

Donovan shook his head. "Oh ... but he might know. Hey, Adam," he said, as the older man walked over to their table.

Well, this was just turning into quite a crowd. Lillian wondered whether Donovan had anything to do with setting up this 'accidental' meeting with Adam and decided that his surprise seemed as genuine as her own.

"Hello, how's everyone doing?" Adam asked. His smile and the friendly eye contact he directed at Lillian lasted only a moment, interrupted by the ringing of his cell phone. The man certainly seemed to be in much demand, every minute. Lillian couldn't imagine even a trauma doctor on call, getting this many phone calls.

"Adam Brecklin," he said. "Yes, I understand. Yes, we're working on it. Yes, working on it." He listened for a few moments to what sounded to Lillian like a tirade pouring from the phone. Adam's face began to look almost harsh, the planes of his cheekbones sharpening and his eyebrows drawing together. "There's no need to speak that way. We'll take care of it." He listened for a few more seconds, but it appeared that his caller was gone.

Doyle was watching him. "Angry client?" he asked in what Lillian imagined was intended to be a sympathetic tone.

"Angry investor," Adam said. "Of a sort."

The three others waited to see whether he wanted to discuss it any further.

"Angry investor who feels he isn't being kept well enough informed about this dive expedition," Adam went on. "He's been involved in several projects like this lately, and he's on some sort of quest for a complete set."

"Complete set of what?" Donovan asked.

Adam shook his head. "Beats me. His words, not mine. I think there might be some kind of Big Five for diving expeditions—maybe doing all the oceans or certain depths or something. Anyway, he's pissed—excuse me, Lillian, he's angry about what's going on down here."

"Any chance he might make a visit?" Doyle asked.

"Don't know. Maybe," Adam replied. "Is that a problem?"

Lillian looked back and forth between the two of them. Suddenly, it felt as though there was a very tense conversation going on.

Just as suddenly, Doyle stood up. "I'm very sorry, y'all, but I'll have to leave you now."

"But your lunch!" Lillian protested.

Doyle pulled out his wallet and laid a couple of twenties on the table. "That should take care of it."

"No, I meant, you haven't eaten and the food should be coming any minute."

"I really can't stay, Miss Lillian." With a brief, but very courteous bow he was gone.

*

Owen attacked his dinner as though he hadn't seen food in a week. Nevada watched him for a few minutes, realized he must have had a horrendous day, and thought about what she might say to make it better. He noticed her examining him.

"What is it, Trip?"

"You only eat like that when you've had an awful day," she said. "It's like you're smothering whatever's bugging you by piling food on top of it."

"Pass the biscuits," he said.

She smiled and handed them over. "You listened to me vent about Cassidy Sullivan and about Tom's latest, now it's my turn to listen for you. Then let's go out for a bike ride, do some bird watching or something."

"Okay, sounds nice," Owen said. "Today I had this very strange appointment with a new patient. Referred by a primary care guy named Washington, but when I called his office, they insisted they hadn't sent anybody over. Anyway, this guy came in looking like he hadn't slept for a week, in a lot of pain, you could tell. Tall, skinny guy. Wearing a very good suit. Name was Tremblay, Tremé , something like that. We got started on his history, and he starts telling me how wealthy he is and that he's looking for a private physician who can be on call for him 24/7. He says he's been diagnosed with stage 2 prostate cancer, can afford to fight it big time, and quotes an annual salary for me that is astronomical. The hitch is that he lives in Toronto and wants me there full-time."

"How astronomical?" Nevada asked.

Owen grinned. "Cutting right to the chase, as usual. Four fifty a year."

"For one patient? Wow. What did you say?"

"Well, I tried to be diplomatic but I really don't want to work for just one patient, like some kind of personal employee. I told him I had too many commitments in Savannah to agree to a plan like that, but that I knew quite a few very well-qualified physicians in Toronto and I could give him an excellent referral. He got mad as hell in about half a second, just blew up. Said I was being unprofessional and unethical, said I was discriminating against him, said he wouldn't take no for an answer. He started pacing around the examining room, and then it got really weird. He was shouting by then, and yelled that 'we know where you live' and 'you don't get it, Dr. Heintzmann, this is not a request.' Finally, Angie, the clinic manager, knocked at the door and opened it. She said she'd called the police, and the guy put his pants and shirt on and took off."

"No wonder you're wolfing down the mac and cheese and the crab cakes!" Nevada was joking because she didn't know what else to do. "Seriously, Owen, this is a bit scary, don't you think? Do you have any idea what the guy's story was?"

Owen shook his head. "Man, I know it's the South and their ways are different here, but that's a bit too strange, even for here." He chewed in silence for a few minutes, then sighed. "I just don't know what to make of it. Is there anything for dessert?"

*

Nevada had become very adept at spotting newcomers on set. Her job carried no responsibility for security matters, but her natural alertness and powers of observation just pointed her in the direction of taking notice and paying attention.

Even in a busy, downtown location like the one they'd descended on today, with dozens of tourists and shoppers passing by or standing on the fringes trying to see something interesting, a stranger would stand out. A movie crew is like a big family at a wedding dinner; you may not remember the name of that cousin with the eighties haircut and the blue sweater but you know, generally, who he is. Anybody not related stands out as unfamiliar and you have to ask: 'who is that?' Then someone tells you it's your cousin Stacey's plus one or the groom's college roommate.

Same thing on set, except that the security people consider it a personal failure if anyone has to ask 'who is that?' The good ones, anyway. Everyone visiting the set had to have clearance and have their name on the list. No exceptions. The major movie stars had extensive security requirements, and no production company wanted to be turned down or blackballed over security concerns.

That day at Reynolds Square downtown, she noticed the tall, skinny man right away. He was hovering near the craft services table and, at first, she thought he might be a new employee there. But he was consuming, rather than supplying, his red hair falling over his forehead as he leaned forward to look over the selection of biscuits, then add three to his plate.

Chelsea walked by, her hands full of bags of brand-label cosmetics.

"Hey, Chelce, who is that?"

Chelsea stopped in her tracks and took a long look, wrinkling her nose as she thought. "I'm not sure . . . oh, yeah, I know. It's Yvonne Lee's new manager. They sent around an email about him. He'll be here today and tomorrow."

"Thanks," Nevada said, still staring at the man. Something about him was familiar; she was sure she knew him in some other context. Not worth pouring too much mental effort into it, there were a dozen different places she might know him from—friend of her father's? Former TV face now working behind the scenes? L.A. party-goer? Vancouver party-goer?

These minor memory lapses of hers were more frequent now. She mourned a few losses from her twenty-something days and this was one of them: her old Alfa Romeo, her need for only four hours' sleep a night, and her memory for all names and faces. Relax, you, she thought. Relax and it'll show up.

Once Jeremy wrapped for the day, Nevada drove home on automatic pilot. She was tired, which surprised her, because she really didn't think that she was working all that hard, just hanging around the set most of the day. Waiting could be hard work, too, she supposed. Once she got home, she fixed a sweet tea, wandered out to the patio, and sat down on the lounge chair, her laptop computer propped up on her knees. She opened her email program and saw the emails from Chelan and Lillian right away. Chelan was still hot on Tom's trail through the social media websites. He was tweeting and posting several times a day, apparently. So far, it was only text, but Chelan was checking every post, watching for photos that might give some clue to his whereabouts. She wondered if he knew he was off the 'list of suspects'. He (or someone working for him) was astute enough to turn off the location information on his posts, but eventually something would show up, Chelan was sure of it.

Lillian had written another email (which she persisted in calling a 'letter'—Nevada could relate). What did Nevada think of the photo she'd sent from Donovan's treasure hunt? Was there any more news about her father? Any chance she wanted to make another trip down to Key West? Would she "please find attached" a photo of Donovan's boat and another photo from the shipwreck dive expedition.

Sounded quite appealing, Nevada thought. Maybe there was work like Donovan's for her down there. Maybe, if she knew anything about diving. Or boats. Floating around on the turquoise water, staying warm, soaking up the sun, finished with the day's work every day when you put in to shore, nothing to stew about or dwell on once you were off the clock.

These days, Nevada's thoughts seemed flooded with a regular river of ideas about her next move. She knew she was less enthusiastic about returning to the Vancouver newsroom with each passing week in Savannah, but she didn't know why, exactly. Was she just burned out and would this leave of absence, once it had run its full course, leave her refreshed and ready to continue her career? Perhaps, though, she was at a crossroads and maybe that was the reason she felt so lethargic?

Should I stay or should I go?

She clicked on the first attachment. Nice boat. The white hull gleamed in the brassy Florida sunshine. Donovan stood proudly at the wheel.

The second photo showed Donovan on the dock, posing in front of a much larger craft, with crew members here and there, one cleaning something, one bent over lines at the stern, one mid-jump from the deck to the marina dock. Nevada stopped scanning and focused on that third man, then enlarged the image as much as she could on her screen. That man looked *really* familiar— where had she seen him before? She stared for what felt like half an hour, willing herself to relax and let the answer flow into brain cells as receptive as she could make them.

And then she had it. The stranger on the *Too Beautiful to Burn* set that she had seen just this morning. The tall man that Chelsea had said was Yvonne Lee's manager.

What was he doing on Donovan's shipwreck expedition out of Key West, Florida? And, as she said to Owen later, how and why did he arrive in Savannah so fast?

CHAPTER 27

J udith was dressed in the latest Southern style, her flowered dress light and filmy, a blue denim jacket layered over top. She sat on a high bar stool at one of the patio tables, the one with the best view of the river. Nevada squared her shoulders and walked over to her.

"Hello, Mother," she said, then climbed up to the seat across from her.

"Hello, Nevada. You're right on time. It's just going to be a quick drink . . . I have a flight to catch in about three hours."

Nevada signaled the server, who was at her side in about five seconds. "I'll have an Arnold Palmer," she said.

"Oh, don't be a spoilsport, Nevada," Judith said. "Have a drink with some alcohol in it."

"No, thanks, not today," Nevada said. "What's up? Where are you going?"

"Back to L.A. I've been here long enough, nobody seems to want to spend time with me, and my new friend—the one whose family owns the Oak Tree stores?—wants to see the west coast, so we're going together."

Bingo. Nevada hadn't heard such good news in . . . well, she didn't know how long.

"That's awesome, Mom. It sounds like a very nice time."

"Oh, it will be," Judith said, putting lips on her straw and taking a long pull on her drink. "We'll see the sights,

250

I'll introduce her to some people."

"Sounds like everything has settled down for you then, everything turned out alright."

Judith's face took on a rebellious look. "I won't say it turned out alright . . . your father never did come around to seeing things my way. But I know when a scene is done and this one is. I'm not saying the whole movie is over, but it's time for the next part."

"So, you're moving on." Finally, Nevada thought.

"I'm not saying that. I'm not 'moving on'. Horrible phrase. I'm just saying it's time to go back to L.A."

As Nevada picked up the tab and air-kissed her mother good-bye, she couldn't help but feel relieved. One less complication . . . a complication that really had no reason to arise in the first place. Judith belonged in L.A. and it was a good thing that she was going back there. She'd had no good reason to come to Savannah and no hope of a satisfactory outcome. She would have to find some other way to try to address her financial challenge.

*

The osprey nest was high in the oak tree tops, but Nevada and Owen could see it easily. It was as large as an adult human, and the birds had probably been working on it, returning to it and adding to it, for decades. She stared at it, then took out her phone and snapped a few pictures.

It hadn't been difficult to persuade Owen to get up from his desk and come for a bike ride. They both needed the fresh air.

"I don't see any babies, but that doesn't mean they aren't there," Nevada said.

"I don't see any either. Or any eggs." Owen was looking around for some other vantage point from which to look it over. There was a slight rise in the landscape just behind the stand of trees beside the cart path. Nevada led him over to it, and they came upon the two kids, lying in the grass beside their bikes.

"Sshhh," Austen said. He was lying on his stomach,

braced on his elbows, and peering through a set of binoculars large enough to cover most of his face.

"They've got something up there, something shiny," Lyla Jean whispered. "We saw it yesterday, and we came back today with Austen's daddy's glasses."

"I've been looking at it for hours," Austen announced. "I think it might be jewelry."

Nevada stiffened and held herself as quietly as she could, reaching a hand toward Austen. "May I?"

He handed over the binoculars, and she squinted through them, scanning the nest from back to front, front to back.

And then, she saw it. Something shiny, gold and shaped like a bird, a chain dangling partway down from the assortment of twigs, leaves, and Spanish moss on the tree branches.

"That's it," she murmured as she handed the binoculars over to Owen.

"That's what?"

"The bird pendant."

"You're kidding me!"

"I am not."

"Come on, Nevada. I can see that it's a necklace and that it's a pendant shaped like a bird but it could be just something that looks like the missing one—"

"It's the one."

"I'm going to go and get it," Austen announced and before she could stop him, he was halfway up the tree trunk. Heads tilted back, they all watched him climb toward the nest, hand over hand with complete confidence.

"What's going on?"

The voice came from a golf cart that had stopped on the path near them. Owen was the first one to react.

"Oh, hello, Frank," he said. "This is Austen, and he's just demonstrating his tree-climbing skills for us."

"Is that safe?" Frank asked.

"Oh, I'm sure he'll be fine—he's very athletic," Nevada answered.

Austen came down with the chain of the pendant between his teeth. He jumped the last few feet to the ground, then held it out for them all to see.

"I'll take that." Frank's voice was firm, with the authority of the senior executive he once was, and his right hand was outstretched, palm up, to receive the golden bird.

"What?" Owen asked.

"I said, I'll take that," Frank answered, staring at the exquisite piece of jewelry resting in Austen's hand. "It's priceless and we have to handle it very carefully."

"You're absolutely right," Nevada said. "I know just the person we have to bring it to."

"Cassidy Sullivan?" Owen asked.

Nevada nodded.

"Who?" Frank said the word but both kids seemed to have the same question in mind.

"Cassidy Sullivan," Nevada repeated. "She's a resident here at The Pines who is an—"

"Expert in tenth and eleventh century fine art," Owen filled in. He was ahead of Nevada but she got his train of thought almost immediately. If cop Cassidy wanted to stay undercover, Nevada didn't want to be the one to make her angry by revealing her identity.

Austen looked back and forth between the two of them, then made up his mind. "Alright. Let's take this to Miss Cassidy."

"But then who will watch the osprey nest? What if something hatches?" The voice made them all jump. Two men had walked up behind them. Nevada turned to see Doyle standing next to a lanky, red-headed man. Who *was* that? She stared and then the pieces snapped into place.

"That's the stranger I saw on set," she whispered to Owen. "Yvonne Lee's manager, who also works for Adam in Key West."

It was Owen's turn to stare. "That's the man who came in to my office to talk to me about being my patient," he said. "Bernard Tremblay, wasn't that the name? He was talking about putting me on salary, on an exclusive basis. Far away from here."

"Why would Yvonne Lee's manager want you for a doctor?"

"Why would my potential patient want to work for an actress?"

"And why were you in Florida?" Nevada addressed Tremblay directly.

For the past few minutes, Austen had been edging toward the bike he'd left lying on the ground near the tree. He almost made it, but Doyle spotted him.

"You! Stop right there!" He whirled on the boy and made a grab for him.

Lyla Jean leaped at her bike at the same moment and in seconds she was speeding away. Doyle clutched at Austen with even more determination. He got hold of his T-shirt and it almost seemed like game over—then Austen jerked backward and tossed the necklace toward Nevada. She and Doyle both reached for it, and Austen made use of his opportunity to get free of Doyle and make another lunge for his bike. Nevada caught the necklace just as Austen zoomed away down the street.

"Go, Austen! Get help!" Owen shouted.

Doyle looked ready to grab one of the golf clubs from Frank's cart and start swinging.

"What now?" Tremblay asked.

"Let me think," Doyle muttered.

"Well, that's going to help us all," Frank said.

Nevada stared at him. Which "us" was he referring to? She would have thought he was including himself with Owen and herself, but the tone of sarcasm signaled something else.

"We still have them," Doyle said to Frank. "And the pendant, we've got that back now."

"She's got that," Frank said. "Do you have a plan for getting it from her or are you going to let her keep it a while, now that the osprey's had its turn?"

"It won't be hard to get it from her," Tremblay said, and she didn't doubt it, coming from him. Owen moved closer to her and closed a hand over the one she was using to clutch the priceless treasure.

"It will be a lot easier now," Frank, stepping forward, his left hand swinging up from his side. He was pointing a gun. He shook it a bit as he saw them all stare at it.

"I always keep one of these handy," he said. "When you're my age, you need a little extra authority."

What was he talking about, was he nuts? For a brief moment she thought she might have misunderstood.

"Frank, are you on their side or on our side?" she asked.

"Not our side," Owen said.

"My own side, nobody else's," Frank said. He waved the gun again, for emphasis.

Nevada turned to look around for any other people who might be watching them and might bring help.

"Stand still. And hand that pendant over, I said." Frank was looking around the silent street, too.

"What pendant is it, Frank?" she asked, playing for time.

"It's the one from the movie, of course," Frank said. "This idiot managed to drop it somewhere after he boosted it from the props room. I guess these birds must have picked it up."

"Who could have predicted those bird-watching kids would spot it?" Nevada said.

Frank shrugged. "Whatever. I've got it back now. I've got all of them."

"You have the one from the Florida museum?" Nevada asked.

"Yeah, I had a professional get that one. Should have

done the same thing here, not wasted my time with these bozos."

"But you don't have them all," Owen said. "The one from the shipwreck, the one that's been down there for hundreds of years—"

"That's my expedition," Frank said. "I hired the team, I paid for it, it's my project and it's my haul. So I'm three for three."

In the periphery of her vision, Nevada saw the Pines security men coming from the far side of the lagoon, staying low and taking cover behind trees and bushes. Three of them and a woman. Was that Cassidy?

Nevada knew she had to give Frank a push. "

"No, I don't think so," she said. "I have a friend in Key West who is wired into that dive expedition and she knows where the Cuban pendant is. You don't have it, you're just blowing smoke."

The security guards crept up behind Frank while he talked. "You don't know anything," he said. "But the whole project did almost tank early on, thanks to your refusal to take the hint and go home to the frozen north. Nosy media, it's the main goddam thing wrong with this country—"

The guards were watching for their opportunity. A man with arms almost the size of the nearby tree trunks lunged forward and tackled Frank, smashing his massive hand down on Frank's forearm in the same motion. The two others went for Doyle and Tremblay.

Frank dropped the gun.

Cassidy stepped forward and put the handcuffs on each of them, one by one.

"I've had an arrangement with Pines security for weeks," she said in answer to Nevada's unspoken question. "As soon as they got the call from those two kids, they brought us in."

Nevada looked around and saw half a dozen other agents arriving from all points of the compass to the base of this tree. She uncurled her fingers and held the bird pendant out to Cassidy.

"Will you look at that," Cassidy said, as she carefully took it, then wrapped it in a velvet cloth and handed it over to one of her colleagues.

A few moments later, Austen and Lyla Jean rode up on their bikes. Nevada and Owen swarmed the kids as tactfully as they could, making sure they were alright. Austen waved them off.

"I'm fine," he said, then walked over a couple of steps to confront Frank. "Why would you do things like this? Just for some old jewelry?" He seemed upset yet determined to try to get an answer.

Frank ignored him. "You know you have no case against me," he said to Cassidy.

"Everybody here heard you confess," Nevada pointed out.

"It was coerced. Made up, false. They can't even get me on a gun complaint. It's registered, I have a permit."

"They can't even say it was concealed," Doyle said.

"Shut up." Frank said.

"And there's no evidence of any kind," Doyle continued.

Cassidy spoke to Doyle but she didn't take her gaze off Frank. "What we do have, Mr. O'Keefe, is a piece of notepaper from your bed and breakfast inn, the *Southern Song*. It was on the floor in the props room where they were keeping the pendant. And we have video from the night of the theft of a man in a seersucker jacket just like one of yours."

Frank looked Doyle up and down, then laughed. "I guess they've got you, you idiot."

Doyle snapped. "They've got you too, Mr. Frank. I'll tell you anything you want to know," he said to Cassidy.

"Did you take it?" she asked.

Doyle nodded. "I did. Then I dropped it in the parking lot by accident and this huge, crazy bird swooped down and grabbed it." He wiped a hand across his sweaty forehead. "Mr. Frank hired me."

They all stared at Frank. His shoulders slumped. "No honor among thieves, I guess."

"None," Cassidy said. "Now I come back to the young man's question. Why did you start all this?"

Frank shook his head, as if to clear it. "I don't know— didn't you ever collect things? Did you ever want something really, really bad?" He watched Austen nod his head slowly. "That's why."

Nevada had a few questions of her own. "When did you get started on all this?"

"Months ago," Frank replied. "Moved into this neighborhood when I heard the movie was set up here and the bird pendant would be here. Didn't know you'd be here, or that Tom Leacock would be such a problem."

Nevada stared at him as if she'd never seen him before—and in a way, of course, she never had.

"Sent Doyle over to break into your hotel room, tried to scare you off. No dice. Then we tried to dazzle your husband with a new position, at a more prestigious hospital, back in your hometown. Figured you'd plan to follow him, like you're supposed to. That didn't work out." Frank was becoming quite worked up. "I needed some time and space for Doyle to locate the pendant he was stupid enough to lose, on me, and for Adam to find the one that had gone down in the shipwreck off Cuba hundreds of years ago."

Nevada was still processing the information. "So . . . were you the one who tried to run me off the highway and scared the crap out of me?"

"That was Doyle," Frank said. "Mostly his idea. You were making him pretty jumpy, you know, with your questions. The day you were asking him if he'd ever heard of burglars-for-hire on the internet I thought he was gonna jump right out of his skin. He was scouring both our laptops, trying to wipe out any search history or email trail about that French bunch we hired for the Florida job."

Did you put up a photo online of the Florida museum pendant to try to smoke out whoever was holding the other one?" Nevada asked.

"That was us," Cassidy said. "Same motive."

"We thought we'd try to scare you off again with the haunted stuff, " Frank went on. "Yvonne was the one who cranked up the ghost baloney in the graveyard, by the way. And we had Dewey, her manager, down to the marina to help us out with the dive expedition. He owed me a favor . . . and so did she."

"All for you to try to possess a few pieces of old jewelry," Nevada said.

"Come on, that's not what it's about," Frank said. "You get it, I know you do. It's about collecting, it's about *having* rather than just seeing or even touching. Having something rare, that nobody else has."

"Competition," Owen said, his face sad, with an expression of weariness that Nevada had never before seen him reveal.

After she watched Frank driven off in the back of a car, Nevada patiently answered all of the questions from the various law enforcement people. Despite their efforts to hang on to their professional manner, she picked up on an undertone of surprise. It wasn't often that something like this happened in a neighborhood like The Pines.

Like never.

CHAPTER 28

You spend a lifetime building up a reputation and it turns out that no matter what you do, people always believe the worst. Some people, anyway. The suspicious people, the ones who don't have enough going on in their own lives, the—what do the kids call them? The haters. Yeah, the haters.

They suspected you despite the fact that there really was no evidence, certainly no proof, circumstantial or otherwise, of anything.

They suspected you and they refused to cut you a little slack or grant you a little sympathy, even when your house got ransacked and you had every reason to be terrified. Every reason to need protection and extra attention.

You set up the situation, created the perfect event, hiring those local bogus burglars to toss your place. And still the powers-that-be weren't seeing it your way.

You won't ever work with Jeremy Walsh again, that's for sure.

Every last bit of personal gear boxed up and moved out of here. You look over the shelves and through the drawers like they asked, and then you check out your look in the mirror one last time. Close the trailer door, and that's a wrap.

The last day is always a chore. Pretend like you'll miss it, pretend like you'll miss them. Hand out a few little gifts, shake some hands, pose for some pictures. Come on, come on, let's get going. It's just a job and it's over, let's get going.

You pick your way through the cables, past the lighting trucks, the makeup trailer, the food trucks. The girls are packing up at the costume trailer, dozens of trunks and boxes. You know you should just pass by, but that slender, dark brown box with the cream velvet lining that the props assistant is closing practically screams your name. Oh my, but that's a pretty thing in there.

Yeah, you already have five of those, silver, gleaming, handles curved and inviting a grip, with edges sharp enough to cut off a hand. Five, maybe even six.

But you know those are different ones, not this one. This one is one of a kind. You step confidently over to the box and open it. Act like you're doing something you're supposed to and most people will let you. A closer look—and it's even more spectacular than you thought. Not quite a full-on sword and maybe not quite so old as some you have. But definitely worth adding to the collection.

Could you get them to make it a gift?

CHAPTER 29

Nevada had a prime spot from which to watch this final setup for the Savannah movie. Over two months, they'd been all the way north as far as Charleston, west to Atlanta, and south to Jacksonville, and now it was all wrapping up in Savannah, in front of the historic house that had once been a general's headquarters. The early spring weather had budded into the hot, sunny pattern that would blossom as the deep, humid weeks of summer, and eventually reach a peak, start to dry out and shrivel into the days of change that are November. But many months before all that happened this year, the people from this film crew would be long-gone, back to their homes on the west coast. Or perhaps on their way to another temporary world, filled with momentary relationships and brief enthusiasms.

Her father would soon be en route to another one of those temporary worlds. This time, she hoped it would be with much less stress and commotion. Tom had been cleared of all involvement in the disappearance of the pendant, and after the police had rechecked the security video from the movie set, they apologized to him for the mix up over the time and date stamp on the recording. Yes, he had been there, he'd circled around it that day and had done some daydreaming about snatching it, but he hadn't taken it, and the proof was there: everyone saw the pendant used in the dailies of the scenes filmed *after* Tom had shown up in the security video.

Doyle's attempt to frame Tom had backfired; everyone remembered how enthusiastic he'd been about the video and how certain he was that Nevada and her father were involved in some way. Frank had already caved anyway and nothing Doyle could say could stuff the genie back in the bottle. Careful questioning from an experienced police detective pushed Doyle to add the details Frank had left out—specifically the location of the Spanish bird from the Florida museum and the Cuban bird recovered during the dive expedition. His confession implicated Adam Brecklin, Yvonne Lee, her manager, and the professional thieves who'd gotten past the sophisticated security system in the museum. It also lifted any suspicion hovering over Donovan Howe.

Nevada was very surprised to hear about Yvonne's participation. She'd heard from Lillian that Donovan was stunned by the news that his mentor was a crook—and Lillian was a bit shaken up herself. She was a lot more familiar with deception than was her grandson, but that didn't make it any easier.

Judith had phoned to say she'd arrived back home in L.A. No info on whether she had found a new means of escaping her money crunch, and Nevada really didn't want to know. Tom had signed on to a new role in a film to begin shooting next week in Croatia. Nevada didn't envy him the fast turnaround or the exotic location; sometimes she just didn't know how or why he kept up with it, especially given his age. She was looking forward to nothing more strenuous than a weekend on her Savannah patio with a good book and an even better husband.

*

Lillian was about to seat herself when she saw Donovan's hands reach around her to grip the chair back and pull it out. He must have seen that done in one of the old forties movies that he loved. She gracefully allowed him, then slipped into the chair and turned to thank him.

"It should be me thanking you, Grandma," he said as

263

he took his seat across from her. "Nothing but excitement when you're around."

"Oh, I think you can take all of the credit for that, Donovan," Lillian said. "You were the one who introduced Adam to me, remember, not the other way around."

"I'm sorry he turned out to be such an asshole," Donovan said. "Oh . . . maybe I should have said 'jerk'."

"You can say asshole in front of me—I'm not your mother," Lillian said, smiling. "Jerk is good too. But we really have Nevada Leacock to thank."

"Let's drink a toast to her," Donovan said as he looked over the wine list. "I'll have a beer, how about you?"

"Sure, I'll do that," Lillian said.

They gave their order to the server, then Donovan leaned back in his chair and looked around the room. Despite everything that had happened, he still looked so relaxed.

"Grandma, how are you doing? Are you very disappointed about the guy?"

"Well, Donovan, I've been around a long time, as you know," she said, winking at him. "It takes all kinds of people to make a world. It would have been nice if he'd turned out to be a special friend, but I wasn't counting on it."

"I've been thinking about something, Grandma. Since we're living so close to each other, would it make sense for you to move to Miami? We could get a two-bedroom apartment or a house. I could help you, getting to appointments or lifting heavy stuff . . ." Now it was his turn to wink. "Seriously, I think it could work out really well."

Lillian was suspicious. "Did your mother suggest this?"

"What? No. No, she didn't. You think this is about her wanting to supervise you, long-distance? No,

Grandma, it's not that."

Lillian sipped at her beer and pondered. "Is it . . . how do I say this? I don't mean to offend you, Donovan, but is it that you want me to supervise you?" He frowned, and she rushed to explain her thought. "I mean, is it that you want somebody there to say hello at the end of the day? Or the end of the trip, if you're off working on a boat somewhere?"

"Yeah, sure. That kind of thing. I just think we'd be good roomies," he said with a grin.

She grinned back. "We would, but I don't think it's a good idea, dear. Too easy. You need to live your life, meet friends, put down your roots in Miami if that's your choice of place. If you live with me, that will just delay all that, and one day you'll wake up and you'll be forty or something and you'll realize you've been hiding for ten years."

He didn't comment, but she could see from his face that he understood what she was saying.

"And for me, it would be too easy too. Plus, if it *is* that easy, it's more likely I'll be turning into a needy case, don't you think?" She laughed and shook her head. "I'm old, but not *that* old. I still have a lot of living to do and a lot of looking around, to find out what it's all about. I want to do it my way, not your way, charming as you are."

She could see he was looking at her doubtfully, as if he weren't quite sure which to believe: that she didn't want to share daily life with him because she wanted him to be independent and self-sufficient or because she wanted herself to be. She gave his shoulder an affectionate push. "Come on, I might take it into my head to move back into my car, like I did six years ago," she said, recalling the stage she'd gone through in Vancouver.

"That's exactly it, Grandma! I can't let you do something like that."

"I was joking, Donovan, but you know . . . you can't stop me. None of us can stop anybody else from doing anything they really want to. And we shouldn't try. My life is mine and yours is yours."

"What would you do if I moved into my boat, full-time? Or my car? You wouldn't like it."

"I might wish more comfort for you. I'd probably bring you cookies and blankets," Lillian said. "But I'd respect your right to decide. Just like you're respecting mine."

He stared at her for a few more seconds, then smiled. "I would have thought a person would know, once you get to the . . ." He stopped and seemed to fumble.

Lillian laughed. "The age I am? The old age I am? You can say it—it's okay. Despite what our culture wants to say about the glory of being young and the horror of getting older."

"You hear people say stuff like 'old age is not for the faint of heart'."

"Yeah, I know. And for kids, saying 'he's old' is like saying 'he's a waste of space'. But the way I look at it is, that's their loss. Being older is better than being younger."

Donovan grinned. "Not sure I'm convinced, Grandma, but it does give me something to go forward to, rather than feel like the best is all gone, already."

"Exactly. Have you ever seen a boat that looks graceful, or inspiring, going backward? The best is always forward."

Donovan held his hands up, palms forward to her in surrender. "Alright, alright! You're piling on, enough! But . . . let me know if you do find out what it's all for."

Lillian smiled back. "And you let me know when you do."

CHAPTER 30

The door to the director's trailer slammed open, and Jeremy stomped out, down the steps, followed by Roger, carrying a sheaf of papers that he waved around while he screamed.

"Jeremy, it's not too late! Come on, it's never too late until after the wrap party—and even then, you can fix things in editing, or do reshoots! Come on, we have to add this scene!"

Jeremy stopped at the bottom of the stairs and faced the agitated screenwriter. "No, Roger. Read my lips . . . Gawd, I hate that saying." Jeremy set off at a fast pace across the square and toward Broughton Street, Roger jogging to keep up. "Look, the movie's in the can. We don't need anything more."

"But this is brilliant, just listen! The pendant necklace never does turn up in the cousin's will, in Margaret's hope chest, and never is kept for a hundred fifty years, treasured and passed down within the family. It disappears when the soldier dies, and it's never recovered. Isn't that better? Not a Hollywood ending, not a happy ending—"

"No." Jeremy stopped in front of Nevada and Owen, who were soaking up the April sunshine from a bench under a live oak tree. "Am I right, Nevada, do you agree? We don't need an alternate ending for this film. It's done."

"Got no comment, Jeremy, sorry." Her cell phone rang and gave her a graceful escape. She read Chelan's name on the call display.

"Hey, Chelan, what's up? . . . Yeah, you too. We're heading up to Vancouver in a few weeks, tie up some loose ends . . . No, not staying on here. Going to go a bit west and a bit north, but not quite so far . . . Nashville, actually."

Jeremy touched a finger to his ball cap and headed off, maybe in the direction of the ice cream store. Nevada nodded at him, her mind still on her conversation with Chelan. "Yeah, Nashville. Owen has been invited to teach there for six months, and I'm taking some time for myself." She paused to listen, then ". . . I know, I did say that, and I did send out some applications, but I didn't get a single response. Not one. Then Matthew Dixon found out I'd been looking for a new opportunity . . . 'behind his back', as he called it. 'Disloyal' was another thing he called it . . . No, I'm not upset. He wasn't exactly the dream boss, anyway, was he? It was time for a change, and I'm all good with it. I'm a little surprised I didn't get any other offers though."

She felt Owen squeeze her shoulder, and she turned to smile at him, to show she wasn't saying this in bitterness. The reassuring smile and the communication to him went first, but a split second later she realized that she really did feel it. She *was* up a rung on the lesson ladder. She didn't feel disappointment, and she didn't want any of those jobs anymore. They weren't what she was here for.

Nevada's chin went up, and she looked out over the square, full of ancient trees and monuments to the past. She really didn't care, and she didn't want to run a newsroom anymore. She didn't want to repeat herself or be stuck doing the same year of experience, fifteen more times.

Knowing what she *did* want was tougher, but that would come, eventually.

". . . Yeah, so we are in the same boat. Sort of. Except you're busy cooking the next generation, aren't you? Isn't that enough? Oh, sorry, no, of course it's not." Nevada pulled a face at Owen, and he started to laugh out loud at her. "I think they go to trial some time before the end of the year . . . Frank, yes, Doyle and Adam too . . . not sure about Yvonne, but it's going to interfere with her movie career, yeah, for sure . . . The pendant that was on the movie set is back—Sandra is holding it in both of her hands, in front of her where everyone can see it, every minute, pretty much all day every day. The one that was on loan from Spain to the Florida museum is back in Madrid now. And the one that was lost for five hundred years is in the hands of the Cuban government. I heard some muttering that they might be trying to repatriate the other two as well."

Nevada looked up and across the square. *Was that Tom, coming toward them?* "Well, of course, Chelan, if there's anything I can do to help, I will. Give my name to anybody you want, and I'll give you a terrific reference."

Nevada ended the call and looked up to see her father standing in front of her, hand in hand with a teenager. No, maybe not actually a teenager, but a very young woman wearing a short navy-blue skirt.

"Hello, Dad. This must be Clio?"

"It is," Tom said. "Clio, my daughter, Nevada, and her husband, Owen."

After that, an awkward silence settled in as the four of them looked at one another. Nevada cleared her throat. "Well, Dad, I was happy to hear you're completely in the clear now."

Tom made a face. "I still think it's appalling that I was ever suspected in the first place."

"So do I, Tommy," Clio said, linking her arm through his. "Don't suppose there is any option for us to sue, maybe the production company? Maybe Frank Leonard?"

"What for?" Nevada asked. She hadn't meant to be aggressive, but she could see Clio cringe a bit.

"I don't know . . . harassment maybe? Causing stress and anxiety? Maybe . . . ruining his reputation?" Clio was fumbling.

Nevada laughed. "I think his reputation is probably just fine. Where are you two off to next?"

"We're going to go and take a look at the bird pendant before it's locked away for the next fifty years or so," Tom said.

"The American one?"

"Yes, the family came to Savannah yesterday to take it back, the minute Jeremy is done with it. They want to meet Tom, too, so we have an invitation to lunch," Clio said.

"Want to come with?" her father asked.

Nevada smiled. It was the sort of invitation she'd have donated a kidney to get, in years gone by.

"No, thanks. Owen and I have plans. Y'all have a good one."

THE END

ABOUT THE AUTHOR

Gail Hulnick is the author of mystery novels *The Lion's Share of the Air Time, Resorting to Murder, and Resorting to Larceny,* and travel memoir *Rumble Strip Canada 150.*

She lives in Savannah, Georgia with her husband.

A SNEAK PEEK AT BOOK THREE OF THE MEDIA MYSTERIES

Sleeping Dogs Lie

Chapter 1

There was nothing so golden as an October morning, with the entire park to herself. Just silence, empty spaces, and solitude.

She wasn't completely alone. Carl was there, of course. The chocolate Labrador retriever walked over toward a palm tree and seemed to stop to examine something in the shrub beside it. Lillian watched while he strolled toward it, backed up a few steps, and then turned to look at her.

She didn't react, even though she could sense that he was trying to entice her to come over to his side. She had things of her own on her mind, and exploring trees wasn't a high priority.

Carl abandoned his silent call to Lillian, then put his head down to sniff. Lillian couldn't see anything unusual about the tree from this distance, but her eyesight wasn't what it once was. Carl certainly seemed intent on investigating.

She turned her head to the west, toward the shore about half a mile away, where she could see the waters of the Gulf of Mexico shimmering in the moonshine. She could hear the waves if she concentrated, and one more time, she appreciated that she didn't have to have a conversation with Carl. He expected nothing more than the opportunity to get out in the fresh air, and once he was in the park, he entertained himself, silently and energetically, giving no impression that he had any sense of time passing. He was always 'in the moment'.

Time with a good dog is just as wonderful as time by yourself, Lillian thought. *And so much better than time with another person whose company or conversation you didn't care for.*

For a few minutes, she watched her chocolate Lab dash back and forth from the base of the palm tree to the sidewalk. Then, across the lawn, she saw an ocean-gray luxury car pull slowly through the parking lot. This tiny island in southwest Florida was packed with expensive cars; you couldn't drive three blocks without seeing half a dozen Bentleys, Rolls Royces, and Jaguars.

Most of them had out-of-state license plates but very few were driven all the way south from Michigan, Wisconsin or New York. Every year about this time, huge tractor-trailer trucks started to show up on the streets of this little beach town, as the winter residents had their vehicles shipped down. Some people warehoused their cars in Tampa or Fort Myers while they were up north for the summer, but some wouldn't be separated from them, even for a few months, and so they sent them back and forth, like a box of favorite clothes or books that you wanted with you, no matter where you were.

Lillian squinted to get a good look at the car, then walked slowly toward it. As it moved under the streetlight near the entrance, she could see the plate. Orange and black, New York. A Bentley. It would not be unusual to see that car here on Alamos Island, but at six a.m. it was unusual to see anything or anyone at the park. That was why Lillian did Carl's morning walk at that time every day.

"Carl!" she called in her no-nonsense voice. Something made her feel that she wanted him, his sixty pounds, and his protective nature beside her.

The dog instantly ran to her and dropped into a sit. Then, as they both stared across the park at the car, its headlights came on.

Lillian felt blinded and frozen for a moment, but it did not startle Carl. She heard him give a low growl that escalated into excited barking and before she had a chance to snap his leash back on, he was off at a run toward the Bentley.

"Carl!"

But it was no use. He'd taken over, and to his doggie mind, those bright lights were a challenge to be met.

Now what? The car swung to the right and was heading for the parking lot entrance. Was the dog going to try to catch it, run it down? Retrieve it? It was a lot bigger than a duck. Herd it somewhere? Not usual Labrador behavior. Jump up on it? Lillian could just imagine an angry Bentley owner berating her about a scratch on his paint job.

"Carl! Come!"

It was no use. He was ignoring her. She jogged along as quickly as she could, but her seventy-one-year-old legs hadn't been given much recent running practice. Carl was barking like a crazy thing; they'd probably wake up the whole neighborhood.

The big car stopped, then the headlights swung around again in Lillian's direction. Dear God, were they coming at her? Was he driving up onto the lawn, cutting across the grass toward her? Why? If he wanted to talk to her about her dog's behavior, why wouldn't he park the car and walk over to her?

It amazed Lillian that she was thinking so much, so early in the morning and in such a situation. What did it matter *why* this car was coming at her and why the driver was sending it that way? It was happening!

Carl seemed to be surprised by the direction change of the car, too, and Lillian took advantage of the moment to snap the leash onto his collar. She pulled his head toward her and re-asserted her authority.

She waved. "Hey! Stop your car! My dog is under control," she called. Maybe his window was down and the driver could hear her?

If he did, he gave no sign. The car seemed to pick up speed; it was heading straight toward them.

Lillian looked around. Where could they go? This was a wide, open area of the park; a vehicle would have no trouble chasing her, if that's what the driver wanted to do. Speed would be on the machine's side. What did she have on hers?

Surprise. And a bad attitude. She was darned if she was going to let some irresponsible, weird stranger in a public park disrupt her and Carl's morning walk.

Lillian reached down and unsnapped Carl's leash. "Get him, Carl!"

The dog didn't need any second invitation. He went back into full voice and stormed toward the car.

CHAPTER 2

Lillian had no idea Carl could move that quickly. In seconds, he was dashing into the Bentley's path, then swerving to confront the driver's door. He stopped short of actually scraping his nails and paws along the door, but he seemed to be on springs, repeatedly jumping up to bark ferociously at the driver, with just a pane of glass separating their faces, before falling back down.

He was so intent on declaring his hostility that Lillian wondered whether he recognized the driver or the car. Maybe it was just that, somehow, he felt the Bentley had invaded his territory or threatened his pack.

Lillian was about thirty feet from the car when it suddenly stopped moving in their direction. The headlights were almost blinding her, but she thought she could see two figures in the front seat. The driver put it in reverse, got it back to the parking lot, and headed for the entrance to the street.

"Ma'am? Are you okay?"

Lillian heard a voice coming from behind her and turned to see an older man wearing pajamas with a robe, and carrying a flashlight.

"Yes, I'm fine," she said.

"It looked like that car was about to drive right at

you," the man said.

Lillian nodded. Now that Carl had stopped barking and things had settled down, she realized she was shaking like a palm frond in a named storm. Even so, she had the presence of mind to snap Carl's leash back on his collar.

"Do you know whether he was trying to run you down?"

Maybe if she pretended she didn't have a voice, he would go away.

Lillian shook her head.

"We should find a bench and you should sit down. You don't look good."

Lillian shook her head again.

The man stuck out his hand. "My name is Arlo Serranno. My wife and I live in that house over there, right beside the park." He used the same hand to point out his home, which saved them both embarrassment if she delayed any longer in shaking his hand.

Lillian felt Carl pull toward the bush he'd been inspecting when the Bentley had arrived.

"I'm over here most days pretty early, walking my dog, Digger. Today she was a bit slow waking up, and I was just in the kitchen, making coffee. I looked out the window and saw that giant car driving up onto the grass and I couldn't figure out what was going on. I thought he was all alone in the park, then I saw you and your dog and, I don't know, something told me I should get over there and just add myself to the picture, you know? I had no idea what was going on, but if that driver of that car thought you were all by yourself there in the park, you know, I thought I should show him different.

"Being all by yourself is a bad idea, most of the time,

if you ask me. Especially for older people, you know? Not that you don't look like you're barely old enough to vote, but you know, people our age, we shouldn't be all alone. Nobody should, really. Not at any age. You want to be with other people, be with family, do things together. And *do* things, am I right? Not just keep busy, but do important things, help people, make things.

"My brother is always going on and on about retirement, but I think it's a bad idea. Just hang around and watch TV, count your money to make sure it lasts long enough, sleep all the time. There's enough time for sleep and being alone after you're dead, you know what I mean?"

If Arlo had noticed that Lillian didn't want to chat with him, he would not let on.

Lillian let him ramble on while she kept an eye on Carl, who was acting absolutely frantic and crazy. He was running back and forth, as far as the leash would allow, from the bush by the palm tree to Lillian's side and away again.

Then, on a dime, he stopped, just inches away from the palm's trunk. Lillian stood very still. She'd worn capris, a short-sleeved blouse, and flip-flops for her walk on this balmy morning, but she suddenly shivered as if an icy wind had blown through.

Carl whined and as Lillian approached him, she could see what looked like a pile of something under the bush. What should she do? What was her responsibility in this situation? At the very least, maybe they should call 911, get some professional help.

But if it was nothing more than a pile of leaves or garbage somebody had dumped? She'd look like an idiot. Carl raised the ante, from whining to barking. He was almost hysterical, a mood she'd never seen him in. Lillian pulled her phone from her pocket and bent her head to look at the screen while she tapped in the numbers.

"Who are you phoning?" Arlo asked.

"I'm calling 911."

"Good idea."

Arlo didn't seem inclined to wait for the cavalry, though. He followed Carl to the edge of the bushes, then got down on his hands and knees.

"It looks like a pile of garden stuff," he said. "Maybe the landscaping crew was just putting it out of sight till they could come back to clean it up. They made it nice and tidy, putting that tarp on top."

Suddenly, Lillian felt the leash pulled almost out of her hands as Carl lunged toward the pile, grabbed the piece of canvas at the top of it in his teeth, and pulled.

A beautiful dog lay there, its head at an odd angle and its two back legs strapped together with what looked like a person's belt.

This story continues in Book Three of the Media Mysteries:
Sleeping Dogs Lie

You can stay in touch with Gail by joining her VIP Reader Group at www.gailhulnick.com or
www.windwordgroup.com

Thanks!